Praise for the Inconstant Moon Trilogy

HUMAN RESOURCE

"A very smoothly done puzzle story."

—Thomas Easton, *Analog*

"Unfolds with dark undertones and hidden agendas all around. The lunar environment is richly detailed. I look forward to the upcoming sequels." —*SFRevu*

"Adventure and hard science combine in this fast-paced thriller." —*Library Journal*

"Terrific." —*The Best Reviews*

FALL GIRL

"Action, adventure, and intrigue." —*The Best Reviews*

EXIT STRATEGY

PIERCE ASKEGREN

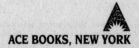

ACE BOOKS, NEW YORK

THE BERKLEY PUBLISHING GROUP
Published by the Penguin Group
Penguin Group (USA) Inc.
375 Hudson Street, New York, New York 10014, USA
Penguin Group (Canada), 90 Eglinton Avenue East, Suite 700, Toronto, Ontario M4P 2Y3, Canada
(a division of Pearson Penguin Canada Inc.)
Penguin Books Ltd., 80 Strand, London WC2R 0RL, England
Penguin Books Ireland, 25 St. Stephen's Green, Dublin 2, Ireland (a division of Penguin Books Ltd.)
Penguin Group (Australia), 250 Camberwell Road, Camberwell, Victoria 3124, Australia
(a division of Pearson Australia Group Pty. Ltd.)
Penguin Books India Pvt. Ltd., 11 Community Centre, Panchsheel Park, New Delhi—110 017, India
Penguin Group (NZ), Cnr. Airborne and Rosedale Roads, Albany, Auckland 1310, New Zealand
(a division of Pearson New Zealand Ltd.)
Penguin Books (South Africa) (Pty.) Ltd., 24 Sturdee Avenue, Rosebank, Johannesburg 2196,
South Africa

Penguin Books Ltd., Registered Offices: 80 Strand, London WC2R 0RL, England

This is a work of fiction. Names, characters, places, and incidents either are the product of the author's
imagination or are used fictitiously, and any resemblance to actual persons, living or dead, business
establishments, events, or locales is entirely coincidental. The publisher does not have any control over
and does not assume any responsibility for author or third-party websites or their content.

EXIT STRATEGY

An Ace Book / published by arrangement with Albe-Shiloh, Inc.

PRINTING HISTORY
Ace mass market edition / March 2006

Copyright © 2006 by Pierce Askegren.
Cover art by Larry Rostant.
Cover design by Annette Fiore.
Interior text design by Kristin del Rosario.

ISBN: 0-441-01356-2

ACE
Ace Books are published by The Berkley Publishing Group,
a division of Penguin Group (USA) Inc.,
375 Hudson Street, New York, New York 10014.
ACE and the "A" design are trademarks belonging to Penguin Group (USA) Inc.

PRINTED IN THE UNITED STATES OF AMERICA

10 9 8 7 6 5 4 3 2 1

For Brenda Clough, Roger McBride Allen,
and Mindy Klasky, in that sequence;
they know why.

Special thanks and profuse apologies
to editor Ginjer Buchanan and agent Jennifer Jackson;
they know why, too.

PROLOGUE

THE ship slid silently through space, in a low, fast orbit around the Moon that made the bleached-bone world seem to race past. Beaneath it, arbitrarily speaking, was a dead world, an array of mountain rings and shadowed craters, of meteoric rubble and gray lava plains. Above it was the endless emptiness of deep space, blackness that stretched on forever.

The scattered stars, stark and unblinking, were too many and too distant to provide easy reference for the eye. Instead, they merely accentuated the emptiness that yawned between.

Trine Hartung trudged along the hull of the ship's third habitat module and paid the stars scarcely any attention. She focused instead on the pools of light cast by her helmet lamps or the steel plates they illuminated. Surrounding those pools was darkness, black and absolute; the habitat module lay between Trine and the Sun, and the shadow it cast was deep enough to make her surroundings invisible.

The wand of the manual diagnostic array she carried swept in and out of the lit area as she swung it slowly from side to side.

Trine's suit was standard issue, reliable and utilitarian, but it didn't fit her stocky body particularly well. It bit into places that Trine didn't like having bitten, and its interior was slightly smelly and more than slightly noisy. Her suit hissed and gurgled and hummed as it kept her alive, and the vacuum of space sealed the noises inside with her. Even louder were the dull thuds that she felt more than heard as she walked. They were the metallic thumps that her smart-boots made as they found steel, clung to it, and then re-leased. Nothing that she could do, or the suit could do, could eliminate the background clatter, but low-volume au-dio feeds helped blunt it.

"—the new Bazuki Brothers, on tour from Earth," a syn-thesized voice whispered in her left ear. "Performing this week in the Party Sector. In-person admission is still avail-able. Contact Zonix and dance through the night."

Trine liked the announcer's voice and synthesized per-sonality, but she didn't mind when the words faded and music replaced them. Complex chants interwove and over-lapped, accompanied by drumbeats and the lilt of gourd flutes. Long months of listening to such feeds in the solitude of her work had trained Trine's ears. She was certain that the musical instruments, at least, were no more "real" than any other computer-generated signal, but the voices seemed flawed enough to have originated in genuine human throats.

The singers were good. Trine smiled. She had two stan-dard weeks of earned downtime to her credit, two weeks that she had to use or forfeit. Perhaps a visit to the Party Sector was in order, if she could arrange some time in the gym first.

The other earphone issued a steady flow of instrument readings, gleaned from her suit's Gummi-Brain and from the ship's systems. She had set her right ear to audit the survey channel, a work habit that had prompted more than one disapproving comment from her supervisors. Mismatched feeds could cause vertigo and disorientation, they had said. Listen to the Mesh or, better, listen to the world around you. Don't listen to both, not at the same time, her trainers had told her, but Trine had always favored personal experience over professional recommendations. Variety, even constant variety, was a good antidote to boredom.

She was making good time in her transit of the hull. Ahead, rising above the cylindrical habitat hull's horizon, was Earth, some 400,000 kilometers distant. Most of the world of her birth lay in shadow, but a sizable crescent was lit by the Sun as the Earth moved past it. The frosted blue-green was familiar and welcome enough to make her pause in her trek.

She had worked Ship Site for five years and had seen the double dawn countless times, but the vista never failed to impress. She could have viewed it from her own quarters, of course, real time or prerecorded, but reality had a grandeur all its own. There was a quality to it that she could recognize, if not articulate, and she had argued the point countless times with friends, to no avail. Apparently, she could see something that most others could not.

When she paused, the rumbling mutter in her right ear slowed to a crawl. The scanners had moved to idle mode, and the suit's processors had consumed the information on hand. While they waited for more, the suit feed had reverted to Mesh-only. The ship's Gummi-Brains fed her time checks, radiation counts, temperature values, diagnostic numbers, and system alerts in monotonous sequence. Trine listened long enough for boredom to set in again and then moved forward. Immediately, the technical feed became more complex as her suit's Gummis told her eagerly of the diagnostic wand's findings.

She was more than halfway around the hull now. Pitch shadows made way for the Sun's harsh rays, and Trine no longer needed her helmet lamps. They clicked off automatically, and the crystal structure of her helmet visor realigned itself to protect her vision. Even so, Trine blinked as her eyes adjusted. When they cleared, she paused again.

Someone was on the hull with her, ten meters straight ahead. That was a surprise. She should have known about the presence in advance. She had checked the schedules before embarking and checked them again several times since. No one should have been on this part of this hull except for Trine.

"Feeds off," Trine said in her command voice. As her earpieces fell silent, she continued. "Proximity whois."

"Unknown," her suit replied, in a flat mechanical tone that reflected its limited capabilities. "No recognition signal received."

That was a surprise, too. Trine had never before encountered anyone without a live identification beacon in his or her suit.

To judge by stance and suit proportions, the stranger was a man, and the spacesuit he wore was an EnTek Ultima. It was sleeker and more stylish than her own, and more expensive by far. More than once, sealed inside her cheap, work-issue suit with the sweat and stink of her own body, Trine had wished for the creature comforts of an Ultima.

The expensive suit marked the man as a likely VIP. Dignitaries wore Ultimas when on official tours or at media events. That made the situation even more puzzling. Trine could never have expected anyone who merited an Ultima to forego its most basic safety measure, much less wander alone and unattended on Ship Site. Even in its current late stages of construction, the ship was a raw and unfinished place. Major ship components, the habitats and engines and cargo holds, hung in a jumbled cluster, linked by a network of cables and girders, awaiting final integration. Trine could negotiate the mechanical territory with the casual ease of long familiarity, but not a stranger.

He stood with his hands at his sides and his boots broadly placed, helmet swiveled back a bit as he seemed to consider the Earth and Sun above.

Her first thought was that some authority figure had decided to run a surprise inspection, but there were other possibilities, and more ominous ones. Three times in the preceding five weeks, Ship-Site management had initiated major security scrambles; three times, Trine's work squad had been called upon to account for its activities and work product. That had to mean that someone expected trouble, and expected it soon.

The man in the Ultima suit might be trouble.

She opened the appropriate suit-to-suit Mesh channel and hailed the stranger. "Hello, sir. Can I be of service?"

The Ultima's helmet turned in her direction. *"Thank you,"* came the reply. It was a masculine voice, calm and neutral. It was scarcely less warm that the voice of her suit systems. *"I'm fine. You're Trine Hartung, right? Your suit thinks you are."*

He had read Trine's whois. Everyone on Ship Site knew who everyone else was, or could find out easily. Nearly everyone, at least.

"Yes, sir," she said. The honorific came easily. Trine's mother had raised her to be polite to strangers, and her supervisor had reinforced the lesson.

"Environmental systems engineer," he continued. *"Five years working Ship Site. You qualified for the crew candidate*

pool after fourteen standard months and achieved Duck-worth company bones status six months after that."

His words in her earphones were calm and casual, even detached, but Trine didn't like hearing them. This wasn't information that would be particularly hard to find, but it wasn't anything that could be read from her suit's whois signal.

"Bones status was mostly a formality by then," she said, playing along warily. The Allied Lunar Combine would never qualify an individual for the crew candidate pool without planning to offer full employment. "You've done your research," she continued.

"Not really. I'm doing it now," the man said. He sounded faintly amused, or at least pleased with himself. *"Interesting."* He paused. *"The Africans are good, aren't they?"*

The comment made Trine nervous again and a bit defensive. Ship Site people worked and lived closely together. It was part of the job and part of crew training. Personal privacy boundaries were mostly quaint affectations, but only mostly. Limits remained. It was one thing if a VIP accessed Trine's employment files, and quite another if he was monitoring her suit systems and ambient Mesh feeds. That, and the man's light tone, irritated her.

"Who are you?" she asked bluntly.

"You're not scheduled to work this shift," the man continued, without answering. *"You should be belowdecks, recreating and refreshing. Why are* you *here?"*

"Who are you?" Trine asked again. She mimicked his question. "Why are *you* here?"

The first response came from her suit brainware. *"Proximity whois response: Hector Kowalski. ALC Over-Management. Primary title, director of Security Operations."*

Trine blinked. No wonder the man had access to her

employment files. With a title like that, he likely had access to everything about everyone. It explained the Ultima suit, too.

"I'm checking seals, sir," she said. "Ship systems report incremental pressure loss, and I wanted to see what I could find."

"Automated systems can do that better," Kowalski replied. His tones were still cool and polite, but Trine had a feeling he didn't like seeing her prowling the hull on her own time.

"Automated systems can miss things. I wanted to do it myself," Trine said. "I don't like the suit, but I like being outside. How about you?"

Kowalski laughed, a dry chuckle that sounded as remote as contract language. *"It's impressive,"* he said.

"There are tours," Trine said. "If you're going to be here long, you could—"

"I leave for Villanueva in seven hours," Kowalski said, interrupting. Villanueva Base was the ALC's primary lunar installation, a self-contained habitat dug deep into the Moon's crust, home to thousands.

"Short visit," Trine commented.

Kowalski laughed again. *"I've been Ship Site six weeks,"* he told her. *"I spent most of it on the outside, but that was with escorts or running with security teams. I wanted to see if things looked any different when I saw them by myself."* He paused. *"They do. More impressive."*

That didn't make sense. "I would have noticed you," Trine said. "You're wearing an Ultima—"

He interrupted again. *"I'm wearing an Ultima now,"* he said. He emphasized the final word.

The puzzle's last piece fell into place. Kowalski, for whatever reason, had been working undercover, or at least angling not to draw attention. That was why he had forgone the comfort of the Ultima suit. His presence also explained the recent security drills.

"How'd we do, sir?" she asked. This time, the honorific was deliberate.

"I can't talk about that," Kowalski said. *"But you can tell me what you've found."*

He wanted a verbal report, Trine realized. The data that the ship and suit systems gathered were his for the asking. For whatever reason, he wanted *her* thoughts.

"Nothing out of the ordinary," she said slowly. Speaking with more assurance as he listened without comment, she told him about the three minor pressure leaks she had found, flagged, and temporarily patched. None had seemed of suspicious origin; at worst, they indicated sloppy workmanship. No matter on how grand a scale the ship's construction was, and no matter how advanced the tools and processes used to accomplish it, this was a project like any other. It relied on human labor and diligence, and humans were fallible.

"What about your coworkers?" Kowalski asked. *"Any suspicious activities?"*

Trine didn't like that question. "That's not the kind of thing I look for," she said slowly. A sense of allegiance to the rest of the construction team slowed her words. It would be too easy to mar someone's work record with a casual comment or clumsy turn of phrase. Besides, qualifying for orbital duty was a long and arduous process. It was hard to imagine that anyone could achieve it without genuine devotion to duty.

"The only thing out of the ordinary is you, a visitor, without escort, sir," she said. "Are you expecting trouble?"

"Nothing specific," Kowalski said. His features were largely hidden by the Ultima's filtered visor, but the expensive suit was responsive enough that Trine could actually

see a minute change in his body language. The man had relaxed.

For whatever reason, Trine had the feeling that she had passed a test. Her responses had pleased him.

She checked her helmet clock. "Six hours now," she said. "Until embarkation, I mean."

"Yes," Kowalski said. This time, when he laughed, it was warmly. *"But they won't leave without me. They wouldn't dare."* He seemed amused at the idea.

He had returned his attention to the view. The Sun had moved completely from behind the Earth now, and they were both bathed in it stark radiance. Trine's right earphone had begun to report steadily climbing temperatures, and Kowalski's Ultima was no doubt reporting the same.

Trine wondered at his fascination with the view. She liked it herself, but that was one of the things that made her suitable for her line of work. She would have thought someone like Kowalski would more likely prefer the comfort and security of his quarters and a remote view.

"It looks different from here," Kowalski said. *"Smaller, but bigger, too."*

"Yes," Trine replied. The observation didn't make much objective sense, but he had neatly articulated something she had felt more than once.

He looked at her again. *"Things are going very well here,"* he said. *"The Old Man will be pleased."*

CHAPTER 1

"GOD," Erik said, and fell back on the couch, as if struck. "Good God, no." His words sounded distant in his own ears, and the world seemed to recede, as well. The things that he had spent so much time and credit securing for his quarters, the real-wood paneling and objets d'art that he had imported at scandalous expense, all seemed to retreat until they hovered at the periphery of his vision. Along with them withdrew the nearly unconscious sense of security and reassurance that a man felt in his home. All that remained was the image of Sylva Taschen, the third of his ex-wives.

Twelve years or more had passed since he had spoken to her. As time tended to be, the decade-plus had been both cruel and kind. Sylva looked older. There were tiny crows-feet at the corners of her eyes and mouth. For whatever reason, she had not corrected them, so that they were cruelly evident in the high-resolution depths of Erik's Mesh display-wall.

If Sylva looked older, however, she looked lovelier as well, her features more strongly drawn and better balanced. The high cheekbones and aquiline nose complemented one another now in a way that Erik did not remember from his years with her. Her hair, in his memories the color of fresh-sheared copper, looked more like aged bronze now, and the color looked authentic. He would not have been surprised to learn that she wore no prosthetics or cosmetic appliances at all.

Erik's marriage to Sylva had ended a lifetime ago and literally a world away, but he missed her still. Not even the sick feeling of grief that raced through him now could blind him completely to that.

"I'm sorry, Erik," she said, after the seconds-long lag that stretched as his words raced back to Earth, and then her response journeyed to the Moon. "It was painless, but it was fast—too fast. There was no time for any rescue or medical aid or reconstruction."

Tears were bright in her eyes. Erik knew that they were genuine. When his marriage to Sylva had foundered, it had been in part because of the depths of her feelings and her readiness to express them. He knew that she mourned his sons as if they had been her own.

There were times when he had envied her that kind of compassion. This was not one of those times.

"How?" he asked. The word was barely a croak.

Even with the infrastructure buildup of the last few years, real-time Mesh links between Earth and the Villanueva lunar colony remained very expensive and not entirely trustworthy. Even though Sylva's tears came freely now, she still knew Erik too well to either spare words or mince them. In clean, precise sentences that made the most of the precious connection, she told him what had happened.

It had been a hang-gliding accident, off Australia's eastern coast. Rod and Todd, there for their wives' family reunion, had misjudged their own skill, or misunderstood the weather conditions that had been reported to them with complete accuracy by local sports wardens. (Sylva, not waiting for Erik's prompt, confirmed that she had verified the wind-speed reports.) They had been flying without Mesh assist, however, using muscle and mind and skill to guide their frail craft. They had been blind to the sudden wind shift that slapped them down from the sky.

Erik wondered about that. He wondered what had truly killed them. Had it been the overconfidence of the twins' relative youth, or the desperate courage of midlife crises? What specific foolhardiness had taken his sons from him?

He would never know, he realized. There were things beyond knowing.

"I'm sorry," Sylva said again.

Unable to speak now, Erik waved at her, in acceptance or dismissal or resignation. He didn't know which, and he didn't care. Even before he could complete the gesture, he lost control. The same hand moved to cover his eyes, shielding him from Sylva's worried gaze. Instantly, his fingers went wet with tears, as racking sobs shook his body. He slumped farther into the couch's accepting embrace and moaned softly, rocking back and forth in some animal spasm of denial. He seemed to have become disconnected from the world.

Sylva's words were coming to him from a world away, but they felt even more distant. He felt as if he were experiencing the entire conversation once removed, as if it were happening to someone else. He knew that was wrong. He knew that it was happening to him.

Sylva started to say something, but the apartment housekeeping system interrupted her. The brainware had detected his distress, and it had extrapolated an embarrassment that he did not feel. *"Shall I break the connection?"* his apartment asked. A long-ago whim had prompted Erik to configure the system with a faux British accent. That accent grated now. *"Do you wish me to implement mirage filters for privacy?"*

"No," Erik said. He choked out the word. His throat seemed to have closed.

"Erik," Sylva's Meshcast presence said, with urgent compassion. "If you want, I can—"

Still sobbing, he gestured again, the same hand wave of silent acquiescence. Sylva had seen him cry before, after all.

The real-time Mesh link remained open for long, expensive minutes before he could compose himself enough to lurch to his feet. Shock stripped away long years of acclimatization, and he lurched like a newcomer in the low gravity as he staggered to the refreshment nook. He snatched up a fistful of disposable napkins and blotted his eyes, then cleared his nose.

As his vision cleared, the nook's two dozen distinctly shaped and labeled bottles dominated his field of view. The array was a precise match for a favorite venue of his youth. He stood without moving for a moment, just long enough to trigger the housekeeper's automated prompts. Without any formal request on his part, the housekeeper presented him with a cut-crystal old-fashioned glass, already loaded with three logo-decorated ice cubes.

Erik ignored the offer. Still dabbing at his eyes, he gazed back at the Sylva's Mesh image. "And Veronica?" he asked, the words coming more easily now. Veronica was Erik's second ex-wife, Rod and Todd's mother.

"She's in seclusion," Sylva responded. "I haven't spoken

to her." Again, she paused. "Erik," she said. "You should be with someone. You aren't still alone now, are you?"

His hands were shaking. With conscious effort, he forced them to stop, and some part of him was grateful for the challenge. He reached into the bar's recesses and found a bottle of processed water. It chilled in his hand as he thumbed the top open. He held it without drinking.

Ever attentive, the housekeeper took the hint. The glass and ice receded again below the bar's perma-glossed surface.

"I live by myself," he said. "If that's what you mean." Sylva's silence told him that it was not, but she chose not to press the issue. "She asked you to call?" he continued. His voice sounded dead now, even to his own ears. He passed the still-cooling bottle back and forth between his hands. For some reason, he was acutely conscious of the tiny droplets of water that splashed his skin as bubbles formed in the carbonated water and then burst, splashing him with their spray.

"I'm the primary executor," Sylva said. It was less an answer than an explanation.

That made sense. He remembered that Sylva had been a very good stepmother during some difficult years. It didn't surprise Erik that the three had remained close, in whatever capacity. He nodded, despite a vague feeling of having been displaced.

"They've been cremated," Sylva said, reverting to her earlier, more neutral tones. "The memorial is late next month, in Haiti. At the summer house."

Ashes. His sons were ashes.

"They'd have liked that," Erik said. Speaking, even about such a horrible, incomprehensible matter, made the pain microscopically less severe. It was as if his mind held only a limited amount of mental energy and any that he could divert from the central issue left less for hurting.

Seconds later, Sylva nodded in agreement. "Will you attend?" she asked gently.

Erik's features went blank as he considered the question. It took him by surprise. After another moment that seemed to stretch interminably, he shook his head. "No," he said.

She said nothing.

"I don't think I *can*," he slowly continued. "I'm too old, and it's been too long."

Erik had lived on the Moon for nearly twenty years, and more than ten had passed since his last visit to Earth. Even with gene therapy and rigorous exercise, that long a stay in low gravity worked changes on the body. Bone mass and density, muscle tone and patterned reflexes—all changed as the body adapted to its new environment. As always, age made things worse.

A trip to Earth now would pose serious health challenges. Such a trip at his age and in his condition would require months of genetic therapy and aggressive exercise, and even then, he was not sure it would be possible. Whether he liked it or not, Erik was almost certainly on the Moon to stay.

Sylva didn't seem to understand that, though. Her wallpaper image looked infinitesimally less sympathetic as she responded. "The dedication ceremony is next month, also, isn't it?" she finally asked. "The museum? I've screened the Mesh reports."

Erik stiffened in mingled shock and offense. The coincidence had not even occurred to him, but the idea that Sylva could even imagine that he would make such a choice hurt him deeply. "That has nothing to do with it, Sylva," he said. "Nothing at all. And it's not a museum, only an exhibit."

There came another pause, one that stretched to an uncomfortable length. When Sylva spoke again, it was with a quality he remembered well from their days together. She seemed to project reasonableness and concern, even as she hinted at disapproval. Hearing that quality in her voice reminded him of the last, dark days of their marriage. "Of course not," she said. "I'm sorry. But I do wish you could come."

"I wish I could, too," Erik said, with absolute sincerity. There was no place in all of existence that he would less rather be than at his sons' funeral, but no place that demanded his presence more.

"You'll audit, at least?" she asked. "I can arrange the feed."

"I should be there. I would be, if I could be," he said, and his voice broke again. "But watching it, from so far away—I don't now. Probably. I'll make arrangements." He stared at her for a long moment, unable to say anything more.

"I understand," Sylva finally said, and this time she sounded sincere. "We'll talk again, then. We'll talk soon." She looked at him levelly. Abruptly, for a brief moment, she seemed mere inches away, rather than so many hundreds of thousands of kilometers. It was as if she were in the room with him, then, there, so close that he could smell the scent of her hair and feel the warmth of her breath.

Memories, he knew. Sensory echoes, summoned from his subconscious as much by stress and despair as by her familiar voice. His mind remembered stimuli that his body had once known.

"You shouldn't be alone, Erik," she said again.

"I know," he said.

"Call someone," she said. "Anyone. A professional. A friend."

"I will," he said, but it was a lie.

Sylva closed her luminous eyes and then opened them again, slowly. The action was another reminder of his days with her, a silent indicator of doubt and disbelief. "You need to be with someone," she said.

"I will," he repeated, more forcefully. "I promise."

"I hope so," Sylva said. "We'll talk. Call me, if you have to."

Then the connection broke, and her image was gone. The wallpaper reset itself to its idle view, a superhigh-resolution image of a Frederic Remington painting. Erik had seen the original once, in his teens, at the second Louvre. The picture's fidelity was absolute, down to the microscopic level. It seemed to promise the coarse texture of old, brush-stroked paint in return for a fingertip caress, but the promise was false. The painting, the paint, was not there at all. It was only an image, only as real as a memory. It was a phantom, like Sylva's presence.

In his command voice, he said, "I want to talk to Inex Santiago."

Sotto voce, unctuous and unchallenging, the house-keeper reminded him that it was well past duty hours and that Inex was likely to be asleep. Erik had opted for a consideration subroutine in the system.

"Make the connection," Erik commanded. He paused, suddenly aware of his own pajamas and general dishabille, of his still teary eyes and clogged voice. "Mirage me," he continued. "Give me something informal but businesslike. And make me sound nice."

He had spoken just in time. The Remington simulation faded and then redrew itself as an attractive Hispanic woman, his personal assistant. Inex Santiago was less than half Erik's age, with flawless dark skin and perfectly straight black hair that had been pulled back and set for the night. The image showed her in bed, wearing a translucent nightgown that was cut low to reveal the smooth curves of her breasts. As the connection finalized itself, she hastily adjusted a sheet to provide some modesty and said, "OH!"

Erik wasn't fooled by the charade. A discreet telltale in one corner of the wallpaper image reported that Santiago's feed was miraged, just like his. Her home system had overlaid her true appearance with brainware imagery. If he could see her like this now, over a Mesh link, it was only because she wanted him to.

"Hello, Inex," he said. "I'm sorry to call this late."

The lie was a reflex action, courteous rather than considerate. He had other things on his mind, more important than consideration. Erik wasn't particularly sorry at all, and she probably didn't mind, either. One of the perquisites that came with authority—one of the symbols of authority—was having a personal assistant. There was little Inex could do for him that high-end brainware couldn't do better, other than impress. Inex benefited, as well. Being a status symbol carried a certain status of its own. Most of his assistants had found some kind of personal validation while working for him, as well as the professional experience that had led them to new roles within EnTek's hierarchy.

"Please," Inez said. "I don't mind." She spoke with a slight accent that Erik found affected and even annoying, but he had never bothered to tell her so. "Do you need something? I can—"

"I need you to cancel all of my appointments tomorrow," Erik said. His voice sounded hoarse and thick in his own ears, but he knew that the housekeeper's Mesh filters would correct that. "In-person and Mesh, both."

Inez blinked. There seemed to be nothing artificial or deliberate about her surprise. "Tomorrow is a very busy day, sir. Kowalski is due back from Ship Site, and the staff conference—"

The world beneath Erik's feet felt rubbery now, and he sagged against the refreshment nook bar. His self-control slipped a bit, still keeping the grief from his words but allowing irritation to slip through. "I don't care," he snapped. "Something more important has come up. I won't be in the office at all tomorrow."

"Is something wrong?" Inex leaned forward, closer to the Mesh camera's lens. The concealing sheet slipped, and one tawny shoulder came into view. She looked worried, and that was understandable. Erik was famous in professional circles for his busy schedule, and for his strict adherence to it.

Now, at last, he took a sip of the manufactured "spring" water. It was bitter cold. He had held the bottle too long without thumbing the bottle's *off* symbol. Chips of ice clicked against his teeth and made them hurt.

"Just cancel the appointments," he said, swallowing. The water did nothing to soothe his aching throat, but he forced himself to continue.

Relying on his own memory rather than on a housekeeper prompt, Erik delegated the next day's highlights. He told Inex who she could meet with and what she could say, told her whom to apologize to for his absence and whom simply to tell. Some sessions were to be postponed; others, canceled outright. Briefing Inex only took a few minutes. It was diverting enough to blunt his pain, but keeping his composure was very difficult. By the time he finished, he was completely drained. "And I'm not to be disturbed for any reason," he said in conclusion.

"What about the evening?" she asked, surprising him. "The candidate crew banquet, remember? It's the second one."

He looked at her blankly. "That's tomorrow?" he asked. When she nodded, he reviewed his mental list and flinched. She was correct. He had never attached great importance to the gathering, and now the shock of Sylva's news had driven it completely from his mind.

"You really should attend," Inex said. "Even by Mesh."

He shuddered. Nausea swept through him at the very thought of attending the meeting with them while his sons' ashes awaited their journey home. He couldn't do it.

"My apologies, then," he said. "Attend in my place if you'd like." He paused. "No, attend as my representative. Take someone. You've been working a heavy schedule lately. Relax and have a good time. That's an order."

"I shouldn't," she said. "You're supposed to—"

"I won't be in attendance," Erik said sharply.

"But what about your remarks?" she asked.

"You can deliver them," Erik said. "You're representing me, remember?"

Inex blinked. She nodded in acquiescence and slumped back slightly in her bed. The Mesh screen image presented the full complement of facial and body cues that announced agreement without protest. Fleetingly, Erik wondered if it were Inex who sent those signals or the brainware. Then, with a muttered nicety, he broke the connection.

"Give me Haiti," he said in his command voice, setting aside the bottled water. "Give me the beach vista. You should have it in your files."

Obediently, the available wall space faded and blurred. When it came back into focus, it was as a beach scene, with too-blue sky and gray-foamed waves that pounded on sun-bleached sand. Incongruously interrupting the image were his treasured decorative accessories that hung on the wall-papered walls and physically blocked their feed. The real world overrode the illusory one, as it usually did. He looked past he accoutrements of his present life and at the shore he remembered from his old one.

Erik nodded. "Music now," he continued, "Something local." Steel drums and flutes played, soft but insistent. "Good," he said. "That's fine." He reached for the bourbon.

And then he was crying again.

CHAPTER 2

THIRTY-TWO hours later, Erik's mind was reasonably clear, but the world seemed wrong. Everything had taken on a greasy, rubbery feel. The corridor floor seemed to slide and yield beneath his feet as he trudged from the Bessemer Conduit commuter rail station to his suite of offices in the ALC's primary sector. The men and women who shared that corridor seemed equally wrong and unreal, strangers with familiar faces rather than coworkers and colleagues. Their respectful greetings sounded like more ambient noise.

Even his body felt wrong. For the first time in literally years, Erik had taken motorized transit for the entire commute, forgoing the walkways and laddered foot-shafts that most Villanueva residents used. His body missed the incidental exercise and let him know. His knees didn't flex in quite the manner that they usually did this time in the morning, and his breaths came less deeply. Even his coordination suffered, and among the few things that penetrated the sorrow clouding his mind were the concerned glances of his fellow commuters.

He didn't care.

The corridor took a sharp left turn, and Erik half-stumbled, half-slid into the side passage that led to a private executive entrance that bypassed the receptionist. Immediately, the herd surrounding him thinned to near-nonexistence as he approached the discreet but impressive portals. The doors were three-meter-high panels of lunar stone laid over steel frames. Perma-glossed and etched with the five interlocking rings that were the official ALC logo, they recognized him and swung open silently.

Erik's movements were defined more by habit than by conscious thought as he made his way to his personal office and settled into the spun-steel spiderweb chair behind his desk. He rested his hands on the polished stone surface. Its stability, cool and solid, was oddly reassuring.

The surrounding wallpaper came to life. It presented his preferred view, a real-time image of Earth that had been fed to the Mesh by cameras on the orbiting construction satellite installation. The Sun was rising.

Erik supposed that the Sun was always rising, somewhere.

"I won't need that," he said in his command voice. "I won't need anything." The office walls became gray and stark as the image promptly faded. To Erik's immediate right, a mug of steaming new-coffee paused in mid-entry and then retreated into the desk's mechanisms. Only its aroma lingered.

"Inex," he said. Even to his own ears, his voice sounded dead. "I'm here."

Almost immediately, she was there, too, standing at easy

attention in front of his desk. She held her personal mug of new-coffee and a neatly folded computer. With a courteous nod, she settled into the guest chair.

"I have your schedule and the notes from yesterday," she said without preamble. Her hair was elaborately coiffed, and she wore a coordinated slacks-and-blouse outfit that could have stepped from a Mesh drama production.

"Never mind the schedule," Erik said. "I won't be seeing anyone today."

She looked at him, puzzled. She was an attractive woman, almost always well-dressed and utterly composed, but appearance was not why he had chosen her as his assistant.

That would have been a perfectly reasonable basis for selection, of course. He knew that, and knew that she did, too. Someone of his standing could select his personal staff using any criteria and never be questioned. More than a few of his fellows expected their support staff to serve, at least in part, as ornaments. Erik expected competence and adaptability instead.

"The report, then," she said. She unfurled her computer and began to read from the flexible plastic sheet. "Per your instructions, I met with—"

"Just send me the file," Erik said, interrupting. "I'll look at it later. I'm sure you did fine." Coming to the office was already beginning to feel like a mistake, but he did not want to be home and he did not want to be alone. He drummed his fingers slowly, a nervous habit that he had thought he had long since conquered. "Tell me about the banquet."

"I discuss it in the report," Inex said. She was watching him carefully but seemed neither nervous nor particularly ill at ease. "Everyone attended. Everyone except you, of course." She paused. "People asked questions. I made a list. That's in the report, too."

Erik nodded. That was to be expected. The second of five, the banquet was an exercise in prestige and recognition. It would be as much for the benefit of ALC executive staff as for the one hundred candidate crew members who where ostensibly the guests of honor. It was very much a chance to see and be seen. Invitations were eagerly sought by lower-line staff. He had probably done Inex a great favor by sending her in his place.

"The next one is next week," he said, half-asking.

Ultimately, the ship's crew would number some two hundred and thirty, to be selected from a candidate pool of five hundred highly qualified individuals. All deserved recognition, if only for coming so far in their career tracks. Erik's idea had been to manage the larger number incrementally with a series of events. His goal was to fete personnel in groups that were small enough that they would at least seem personal. The idea had been a good one, but logistics were proving complicated.

"Yes," Inex said. She finally took a first sip of her new-coffee, then she drew one silver-finished fingertip along the surface of her computer. "I've scheduled the Mesh links for Earth management already. Horvath's family wants to audit, remember?"

The question was rhetorical. She had to know that he hadn't forgotten. The late Janos Horvath had been an En-Tek senior regional director and Erik's superior and sponsor in the corporate ranks. Inex wasn't asking if he remembered Horvath; she was asking if Erik intended to attend.

"We'll be honored to have them," he said. "And I'll be in attendance. Janos was very important to my career."

Inex managed to look interested. He had told her the official version of story several times before, Erik realized, but he could not help delivering the account again. When

his career within EnTek had soured, Horvath had facili-
tated what had technically been a promotion, albeit to a
largely powerless office on the Moon. What had been
meant at least partly as a punishment had become a last-
chance opportunity. Erik had never forgotten.

"Liaison with Earth," he said. "Make certain that the
entire Horvath family is extended every possible courtesy."
He glanced at her. "Are you recording this?"

She nodded. "Of course," she said. She always recorded
their morning meetings.

"Then stop."

Inex looked startled. She was a woman who almost always presented a carefully controlled face to the world; on
her, the look of surprise was itself a surprise. The expression only lasted a split second, however, and then Inex's
silver-tipped fingers moved again. They touched the silver
dragon brooch she wore. "There," she said.

Now she was studying him even more carefully, he realized. She wasn't being particularly subtle about it, either.

"Did you enjoy yourself?" Erik asked. He leaned back
in his chair, half-wondering why he asked. "At the banquet, I mean."

She nodded.

"I hope you took a guest," Erik continued.

Again, she nodded. "Dawg, from EnTek Accounts."

"Someone you're seeing regularly?" he asked. The question sounded odd even in his ears. He wasn't known for
asking that sort of thing. Inex didn't seem to mind, though.

"Occasionally," she said. "You met him at the Founders
Day party."

Erik sifted through his usually excellent visual memory.
He was able to find only the vaguest of images, a picture of a
squat Hispanic man with laughing eyes and too many teeth.
Had that been Dawg? He didn't suppose it really mattered.

"I remember," he said. "I hope he enjoyed himself."

The perfect arches of Inex's eyebrows moved upward a fraction of a centimeter and then settled back into place. "We both did, I think," she said. "So many new people. They were very impressive. The crew candidates, I mean."

"They should be," Erik said. "We've spent enough getting them ready." He paused. "Did you make any contacts with the other guests? In a professional sense." He chose the words with some care. His subordinates would tend to their own career interests, he knew, but even to suggest that he suspected her of job-hunting would have been an insult.

"They were many impressive people there," Inex told him again. She shrugged and smiled slightly, but offered no additional detail.

"Good." Erik nodded and paused before continuing. "Inex, I'll be working an abbreviated schedule for the next few weeks. Half days, I think. I'll be here, but I want an absolute minimum of callers and guests. You can tend to anyone and anything I don't."

This time, her surprise was obvious and profound. He was offering Inex a degree of authority unprecedented in their relationship. She said, "But—"

Erik gestured dismissively. "I'm sure you can manage things," he said, interrupting. "I'll post you the details later today."

"Sir, the calendar is very full," she said. She fidgeted. He had never before seen the cool, composed woman look so uncomfortable. "There are decisions that *you* have to make. I don't have the authority—"

"I'm giving you the authority, Inex," Erik said firmly. "You've worked on this series long enough."

Inex smiled nervously. He could understand why. She was ambitious, but he was offering her a chance to succeed or fail on a grander scale than ever before. Worse, he was offering that opportunity without allowing her to decline.

Erik continued. "The ones that need my personal approval, I'll review and sign," he said, watching her. "You'll do fine, Inex. Consider it career development."

She took a deep breath. "Is something wrong?" she asked.

It was easier to pretend not to hear the question. "I'll provide a list of authorized callers," Erik said. "You can deal with everyone else." He reached for his cup of new-coffee, realized it wasn't there, and composed his hands neatly again. "It will be a short list," he said. "Expect to see me no more than four hours a day, and not every day."

"Is something wrong?" Inex asked again, more emphatically this time. Strain colored her tone. She was either worried about him or about herself. Perhaps it was both. Inex's career depended very much on Erik's, at least at the moment.

"I need to address some personal issues," he said, finally answering her.

"This is an important project," she said, pressing the issue. "You can't just walk away—"

"That's all you need to know, and no one else needs to know even that much."

"I hope everything is all right," she said. "If there's any way I can help—"

"Yesterday," Erik said, interrupting her. "Do I need to know anything about it?"

Secure on more familiar conversational ground, Inex glanced at her computer. He could tell that she was about to deliver her entire report and gestured for her attention. "I'll review the details later," he said. "Was there anything major? Any callers? Any issues? Any action items of note?"

"Business as usual," Inex said. "But the Proxy called and requested an appointment."

"I've told you not to call her that," he said sharply. The sudden surge of anger felt good. "It's rude."

Inex surprised him again. She blushed, plainly embarrassed, and bit her lower lip. "I'm sorry," she said. "*Enola Hasbro* called, and then she called again. She had messaged you at home, but your housekeeper bounced it to the office system."

"What does Enola want?" Erik asked, nearly as unhappy to hear the proper name. Enola Hasbro was never his favorite topic, and one that he especially did not want to deal with now.

"An in-person appointment," Inex said. "She didn't indicate the subject. But she asked about the banquets and about guest lists. I think she wants an invitation."

Erik considered that for a long moment. If Enola Hasbro was asking for an invitation, it wasn't for her. It was for Wendy Scheer. Very little that Enola did these days was not on behalf of the other woman.

Scheer was the past and present head of Project Halo, the scientific research project that operated from the federal government's Armstrong Base. Despite her status, and the importance of Halo to the deep-space exploration Ad Astra project, Scheer was persona non grata within Villanueva proper. That had been part of an agreement struck between the ALC and the federal government more than a decade before. It had been a necessary deal, making coordination between the two organizations possible, if at times extraordinarily difficult. Enola was a partial work-around. She served as Scheer's personal emissary, a unique and dedicated envoy that Erik had recruited to her service.

Sometimes, he felt guilty about that.

"I'm still unavailable," he said. "If she tries again, tell her I'll contact her as soon as it's convenient." He paused. "If she should happen to call in person, I'm not here."

His assistant blinked. Flat-out lies, even polite ones of convenience, weren't typically part of Erik's stock-in-trade. "I can do that," she said slowly. "But, if you'd prefer, I could—"

"I'll contact her," Erik said again. He was beginning to wish that he had accepted the new-coffee. The dead feeling inside of him was reasserting itself, no matter how hard he tried to focus on business. "I'm unavailable," he emphasized. "To anyone."

Inex nodded. Her features, ordinarily a cool mask of professional composure during working hours, showed concern. He could tell that she wanted to pursue the issue and was relieved when she didn't.

He gestured, waving toward her office. "Thank you, Inex," he said. "I'll let you know if I need you."

Even before the door to the outer office whisked shut behind Inex, Erik had accessed his personal Mesh directory and thumbed the day's files to life. Images, numbers, and words flowed through the surface display in a river of information, slipping away even as he tried to focus on them. He gritted his teeth. He slowed the feed and forced himself to read.

It hurt to be here, but there were things that had to be done and issues that had to be addressed. He had already discovered that it was impossible to work at home in his current state of mind. Here, it was possible, if difficult. His mind felt clogged.

His sons were dead. Nothing could change that. The world went on, however, and Erik needed desperately to think of other things.

Duckworth, the ironmongering conglomerate that supplied most heavy construction services and coordinated the smaller companies that provided the rest, reported supply chain difficulties. Recent accidents at a remote lunar mining site had allegedly slowed the production of key alloys. Erik had his doubts; the numbers didn't make sense. More likely, the alleged situation was a ploy to justify cost increases. He made notes, flagged the file, and closed it.

Dynamo, the energy giant whose proprietary cold fusion process had done so much to make the lunar colony practical, was facing yet another court challenge regarding its local monopoly. Erik snorted in derision. Lawyers never learned. Dynamo engineers had spent literally generations discovering and refining the process, only to be locked out of Earth markets by competing utilities. Know-nothing public safety advocates had had their opportunity. The company had earned its lunar exclusivity, and the ALC would fight to keep it. Erik made his suggestions for counsel, made notes of the potential impact of litigation on Ad Astra's final outfitting, and routed them to the appropriate stakeholders and decision makers.

Zonix reported increasing competition from visiting entrepreneurs. Erik found it hard to be concerned. The lifestyle services corporation had always been the most vulnerable of the five ALC systems, at least on certain fronts. The company had an absolute lock on official media feeds, but the ratio of official to unofficial had shifted in recent years. There was simply no way to control the tide of visiting entrepreneurs who came to Villanueva. So many of them came incognito as tourists, with portable equipment and plans of their own, and at least some freedom of expression considerations remained in play, even here and now. He could provide no meaningful comments about the situation. He limited himself to noting, yet again, that Zonix accepted healthy franchise fees from foodstuff, dining, hostelry, and sex service subcompanies and could anticipate their continued increase as tourism grew.

Slowly, he fell into the rhythm of the review, opening

and closing files, murmuring comments, and flagging problematic items for later consideration. It wasn't his best work, but he was confident that it was basically sound. After three hours thinking about matters far more mundane than the terrible news about his sons, he felt nearly normal again.

The sudden resurgence of thirst and hunger surprised him. "Coffee break," he said. "And I think I want something to eat."

He had to look up to claim the small tray that his desk obediently presented. That was when he saw that the guest chair was again occupied. Where Inex Santiago had been now sat Hector Kowalski. The director of Security Operations was gazing at him silently, with an absolutely neutral expression on his face. The effect was like seeing a ghost.

Erik half sighed, half gasped, and sipped new-coffee to cover his surprise. He took in too much, and the hot liquid nearly scalded his tongue.

"How did you get in here?" he asked, bluntly but without any particular hostility.

A member of Erik's personal line staff, Kowalski was a man of precisely average height and build. Overall, he was nondescript to the point of near-total anonymity. In the years since Erik had first met him, Kowalski had carefully cultivated that nondescript quality, selecting hair color and style, cosmetic appliances, and wardrobe that deflected attention rather than demanded it. Even his body language and facial expressions enhanced the effect. Erik had seen Kowalski thread his way though throngs of staff and visitors nearly unnoticed, even by people who knew him well. He made an impression only if he wanted to.

The skill was a useful one for a security specialist, Erik knew. No one should have been able to appear without notice in this of all offices, however.

"I have ways," Kowalski said. Even his voice was nearly without character, but whether from effort or artifice, Erik could no longer tell. The cool and reserved Hector of today reduced the brash and abrasive young man he had met years before to a faded memory.

Erik sipped more new-coffee. He glanced at what the desk had provided to accompany it, then shuddered. The pseudoturkey wrap was the desk dispenser's least objectionable option, but the idea of eating it now appalled him. His appetite had fled once more. The new-coffee was good and welcome, however, and he found its warmth curiously reassuring.

Once it had become obvious that Erik did not intend to press the issue, Kowalski continued. "There's an anomaly Ship Site," he said.

"Oh?" Erik asked. He leaned back in his chair and gestured at his desktop display. "Is it already in the reports?"

Kowalski shook his head. "I'm not going on Mesh with this," he said. "I wanted to report it directly to you, in person."

"Privacy, then," Erik said, speaking in his command voice for the office Gamma's benefit. "Don't record—"

"It won't," Kowalski interrupted. "It can't see me. Or hear me. That's how I got in." From a pocket, he drew a palm-sized slab of polished plastic and set it on the desk before Erik. "Suppressor," he said. "It radiates a field effect that interrupts the brainware protocols of systems in close proximity. Your office manager can't see or hear us, but doesn't know to be alarmed."

This time, he actually smiled. Kowalski liked his gadgets and toys.

Even in his current state of mind, Erik was impressed. He was no technician himself, but he had been an EnTek man long enough to have some idea of just how complex a task Kowalski had accomplished. "What about records?" he asked.

"If someone reviews them, they'll show a gap," Kowalski said. "But we're working on ways around that."

Erik sipped more coffee. "You said we had a problem," he prompted.

"Not a problem," Kowalski said. He returned the suppressor to its hiding place inside his tunic, but when he brought his hand back out, he held a data pod. He set it beside the suppresser. "The specifics are here, but use a dedicated reader. I don't want it on the Mesh," he stressed.

Erik waited patiently. Kowalski did things his own way and on his own schedule. That extended to answering questions, even his superior's questions.

"I just spent six weeks in low orbit," Kowalski said. "I got back early yesterday." He gazed pointedly at Erik's unclaimed sandwich. "Some interviews, general inspections. I pulled tissue samples from the core Gummis, too."

When Erik nodded in agreement, the other man construed it as permission. Kowalski scooped up the sandwich with an easy, fluid motion and thumbed its heating element. One aspect of Kowalski that had changed not one iota was his amazing capacity for food. As the air filled with the fragrance of warm quasiturkey and melting cheese, Kowalski continued.

"Factors are present in the ship's main processors that don't belong there," he said. "We found foreign alleles in the primary strains." He bit into the sandwich and chewed, watching for Erik's reaction.

It was bad news, potentially disastrous. Gummis were semiliving computer processors, painstakingly grown under exacting factory conditions. Each embodied thousands of generations of directed evolution. They were imprinted with brainware engrams that flickered along their strands, processing information, executing commands, and, in general, making the world work. Those engrams were composed to work with specific Gummi strands. The purity of those strands was essential to proper function, especially for more complex systems. In low-end devices, such as Mesh readers or personal computers, a damaged or incorrect processor might still be able to do its job well, but in high-end systems, such as life-support monitoring or navigation, there was vastly less margin for error.

The Ad Astra systems were second only to Villanueva's in complexity and refinement.

"How could this have happened?" Erik demanded. He leaned back in his chair, considering the implications of Kowalski's quiet announcement. As bad as the news was, at least the information was something new to think about. "How bad is it? And why didn't we find out until now?"

He caught Kowalski in midswallow. In rapid succession, the security chief shrugged, pointed at the data pod, and gulped. "I'm working on finding out," he finally said. "I don't know how bad it is. And as to why we didn't find out earlier, well, I don't think that we were introduced until very late in the production cycle."

Erik looked at him in surprise. He had spent many years working directly for EnTek, the ALC sister that held key Gummi patents. Never a true technician, he had nonetheless spent enough time guiding quality-control programs to be very knowledgeable in every phase of the process. "The primary strands should have been locked down years ago," he said, irritated. "And everything says they were. Even allowing for drift—"

"The problem's not in the primaries," Kowalski said, interrupting. "Not really."

"But you said—" Erik started.

"They're in the primary strains, but not in the functional

segments," Kowalski continued. "We found them in the junk, where the coding strands go to die."

Erik looked at him blankly. Structured viruses were engineers' most important tool suite. After countless generations of splicing and resplicing to create validated stock, technicians imposed the final tailoring on Gummi cultures with various classes of virus. The processes were as proven and consistent as anything at that specific molecular level could be. Even the genetic debris they left behind was consistent and predictable.

"That doesn't explain why this wasn't found sooner," he said. "I don't like surprises, especially not this late in the project."

"Apparently, there are quality-management issues," Kowalski said.

"Apparently."

Kowalski had finished the sandwich. For as long as Erik had known him, the other man had been an eater, constantly snacking and nibbling and cadging meals. It was a wonder that he wasn't that rarest of things on the Moon—fat.

"These things are ordinarily not my purview," Kowalski said. "But I wanted to run some systems checks, to look for tampering. We've had problems before, remember."

Erik remembered. The deep space exploration program had not been embraced with equal eagerness by all world governments or political factions. Over the decade and a half that he had helped shepherd the program along, there had been major and minor incidents that served to illustrate the opposition's viewpoints. He thought of them as he asked the question that had hung in his mind throughout Kowalski's report.

"Sabotage?" he said.

Kowalski shrugged. "Deliberate, at least. Occurring this late in the process, it has to be deliberate."

"That's not an answer," Erik said, but he knew what Kowalski meant. He had a solid understanding of the developmental processes involved. Gummis underwent scores of genetic audits as they developed. Issues like the one Kowalski had discovered would have been noted many cycles back.

"I believe the corruption is deliberate," Kowalski responded. "But I don't think that it's sabotage." The words were surprising, coming from such a deeply suspicious man, and he amended them smoothly. "Or, if it *is* sabotage, it's stupid sabotage. The changes are in the junk code. They can't do any harm."

"Could that change?" Erik asked. "You said they're mixed in with the coding strands. Could they be some type of rewriting medium?" He was no geneticist, but his work had given him a basic understanding of the manufacturing process.

Again, Kowalski shrugged. "I don't see how. None of the people I use can see how, either." Noticing Erik's sudden concerned expression, he continued. "I parted out the analysis. You and I are the only ones with the whole picture. But there's no likely way to do damage with junk like this. It's sequestered debris, partitioned off from the rest of the processors."

"It doesn't belong there," Erik said flatly. He had finished his new-coffee, and the desk knew it. When he set the mug down for the last time, a fresh one was waiting for him.

"No, it doesn't," Kowalski agreed. "It doesn't belong anywhere, really. But there it is."

"Find out why," Erik said. Kowalski would almost certainly have done so, anyway, even without direction. "Bill the hours to my discretionary management account and give the work reasonable priority. Try not to draw any attention to yourself."

Kowalski surprised him by laughing softly at the concluding directive. Erik almost found it in himself to smile.
The prohibition had been unnecessary. It had been a long
time since Kowalski had deliberately drawn attention to
himself.

He picked up the data pod. It was a shielded model,
heavy and cool in Erik's hand. For another long moment,
he considered it, before meeting Kowalski's gaze again.
"How important is it that I review this?" he said. He
wanted to work, but the idea of reviewing complex bio-
engineering files seemed daunting. "Is there anything specific I need to know?"

"It's raw data, mostly," Kowalski said. He clasped his
hands loosely together and set them in his lap. "I was going
to use it to provide more detail in case you had questions
about my findings, but as it is . . ." His words trailed off
into an eloquent silence.

"Good," Erik said, relieved. Another murmured command, and his desk's safe compartment popped open. Erik
dropped the compact cartridge inside and locked it shut.
"I'll look at it later. Anything else?"

Kowalski took a breath. The cool and neutral mask
dropped, and a look of gentle concern replaced it. "I'm sorry
about your sons," he said. It was as if someone else entirely
had taken his place.

Erik flinched. He started to ask what Kowalski knew
and how he knew it, but he bit back the words. Nearly
twenty years had taught him that Kowalski knew everything. Instead, he said, "Thank you. I didn't make any announcement for a reason, though."

He hated talking about it. Talking about it made it
worse. Talking about it made it real.

"I haven't spoken with anyone," Kowalski said. "But you
need to know that it's no secret, either. It hasn't made the

Mesh feeds, but you're too well-known for your family to be off-limits. People will hear."

Erik nodded, grudgingly. "My family's lives are their own," he said. He remembered rumors that had surrounded him during his earliest days on the Moon. "I don't want them to be topics for gossip and idle chatter."

"Their lives are their own, but not their deaths," Kowalski said. He spoke with a simple directness that took the sting from his words. "And your own celebrity these days won't make privacy any easier."

"I know," Erik said. The world had gone cold again.

"It's not like surveillance brainware," Kowalski continued. "You can't suppress it completely. But you can manage and direct it. I can help you with that."

Incongruously, Erik remembered a fishing trip he had taken with his sons Earthside, long decades before. In southern Alaska, Todd had hooked a trophy-sized trout and hauled it into the boat, but the fish had somehow freed itself. The two boys had tried hard to recapture it, but it had been Rod who made the mistake of gripping the big fish too tightly, squeezing it. The trout had used the pressure against him, squirming free to disappear into the cold river waters. By holding too tightly, his son had lost the control he sought so eagerly.

"Thank you, Hector," Erik said. It was all he could think to say.

"I have contacts in most Mesh providers," Kowalski continued. "A discreet feed now will help more than hurt."

"Thank you," Erik said again. He was unsure how to respond to the display of consideration.

"I have some good contacts Earthside, too," Kowalski said. "I'll do what I can to control the situation there." He paused. "Do you want me to investigate?"

"Why?" Erik asked. The word felt rough in his mouth.

"You have to consider the context. You're an influential man strongly identified in the public mind with Ad Astra," Kowalski said. "Not everyone wants it to succeed." He paused, then spoke carefully. "There are ways of influencing influential men."

The idea that the deaths could have been anything other than accidental had never occurred to Erik. Now, it struck like a thunderbolt. Rod and Todd had pursued careers of their own and had never been part of his public life. More, he was acutely aware now of how small a part of his private life his sons had been, especially in recent years. But to a stranger, or even to a moderately well-informed strategist, things might have seemed very different.

"I don't know," he said. "I never considered that."

Kowalski reverted to his professional mode, speaking with matter-of-fact dispassion. "You should," he said. "I would."

Erik sighed. This, too, was something he desperately did not want to think about. "There were no threats, if that's what you mean," he said. His voice caught. "No warning."

Kowalski said nothing, but waited.

After a long moment's thought, Erik nodded. "See what you can find out," he said. "But be discreet. Passive data collection only. And I don't want any official record. To begin with, at least, bill it to my personal budget."

"You're key to the project," Kowalski reminded him. "If I do find anything, the matter will become official."

"And if you don't, it won't," Erik said sharply.

Kowalski nodded. "I can accommodate that," he said. "You'll need to make plans for managing the situation. I can recommend some media specialists—"

"I don't need that kind of help," Erik said. "I spent years as EnTek's on-site communications director, remember? I can manage a Mesh relations program."

"I remember," Kowalski said. Now, he sounded nearly clinical in his dispassion. "But you shouldn't be doing it yourself. You need to consider the impact this will have on your decision-making ability."

Erik glanced at his desktop display, which was still live. With a single glance, he took in the list of files and action items, the ones that he had acted on and the ones flagged for later consideration. The more crucial issues all fell into the latter category.

"I'm well aware of that," he said brusquely. He thumbed an icon, and the view scrolled down, offering new items for his consideration. "I appreciate the advice, but I won't need you anymore today, Hector. Let me know what you learn."

Kowalski rose to leave. As he turned toward the door, he looked back and said, "You shouldn't be by yourself." They were the same words that Sylva had spoken. "If only for the sake of the project, you shouldn't be alone."

"If only for the sake of the project," Erik echoed. He knew himself reasonably well. He knew that Kowalski's argument was one of the few that might work with him, and it seemed only reasonable that Kowalski knew it, too.

CHAPTER 3

VILLANUEVA was very nearly a closed ecosystem. Imported goods, tourist traffic, and immigration all contributed to its growth, but the colony created the vast majority of its own energy, processed its own waste, and grew its own food. Water ice might be fantastically scarce on the Moon in absolute terms, but enough existed to yield oxygen aplenty for Dynamo's proprietary cold-fusion systems. Vast greenhouses and hydroponics farms, populated by genetically tailored, high-yield species, did the rest. Enough biomass capacity existed even for limited production of meats and other animal foodstuffs via tissue cultures, and extensive fisheries allowed for fresh fish.

The investment of time and effort, energy and ingenuity, had been tremendous. It was nearly enough to make Erik feel guilty about the sautéed prawns that sat, uneaten, on his dinner plate. With a fork, he toyed with one, dabbing it in chili-plum sauce while trying to convince himself to eat it.

"Is the food to your satisfaction, sir?" the waitperson asked. Lean and attentive, he had appeared without warning to Erik's left. He moved with effortless elegance as he refilled the half-empty water glass that waited beside untouched wine. Erik could not help but notice that he had the arm- and finger-bones that marked lunar natives. He might speak with a French accent, but he had been born to the Moon's gravity, one-sixth that of Earth's.

"It's fine," Erik said.

"If there is—" Enola Hasbro started to say. Seated across from him in the secluded dining niche, she was almost as attentive as the restaurant staff. She was very attractive, a petite woman of Asiatic descent, whose minimal concessions to age were remarkable in their graciousness.

"It's fine," Erik said again, interrupting. More gently, he continued. "It's excellent."

With a nearly inaudible *hmph* of skepticism, the hovering attendant glided to Enola's side. He filled her glass, too, then reached for her nearly empty plate. She shook her head in disagreement, and he *hmph*ed again, then excused himself.

When they were alone, Enola said, "You haven't eaten anything since the consommé." Her voice was low and musical, but she sounded more analytical than concerned. Her own plate held only the slightest remnants of a meal, just enough that she could keep it before her for politeness's sake. She was too courteous to be a spectator at another's meal. "This is a very nice restaurant," she continued. "We thought you would like it."

Erik turned the fork and brought its edge down hard on a prawn. Metal clicked against porcelain as he neatly bisected the inoffensive shellfish. He dabbed one half a second time into the bright purple sauce and popped it into his mouth. He chewed and swallowed and forced himself to smile.

"Very good," he said, but he let the fork fall. He knew that he wasn't going to eat any more of the expensive entree. Two bites, following half a bowl of soup, were all that he could manage.

His dining companion sipped her Lethe water. Before she could return the glass of mild euphoric to the tabletop, the waiter had appeared again. This time, both she and Erik nodded, and he gathered up the plates. He made a tiny head-shake, just emphatic enough to indicate his disapproval that Erik's plate remained nearly full.

Enola's comment had been accurate. This was a very nice restaurant, and an expensive one. A less-expensive one would have had substantially politer service. A cheap one would have had no live table staff at all, its patrons forgoing the modest prestige of making other persons serve them.

"I'm just not very hungry," he said.

She gazed at him with disconcerting directness, confusion, and even concern evident. When he had first met Enola, some fifteen years before, she had combined poise with a contrasting girlishness. He had encountered her more than a few times in the ensuing five or so years and always found her to be pretty much the same—a bit naive, somewhat flighty, and almost always at least a little flirtatious. The subsequent ten years, spent in the service of Wendy Scheer, had done much to change that. But for her name and essential appearance, she was very nearly a different person entirely. One thing about her that had not changed, however, was a reluctance for forego life's pleasures without good reason.

"They raise their own fish," she persisted. "Engineered to the chef's standards. He works with designers from Biome to tailor the fish and the other ingredients for one another. If something is wrong—"

"Really, Enola, there's nothing wrong," Erik said. He forced himself to relax, or at least to seem relaxed. "The food is fine. I'm just not hungry. But I appreciate the thought that went into choosing this establishment, and I promise to visit it again."

The waiter had reappeared, bearing a dessert tray. Enola always seemed younger than her years, but she seemed younger still as she made a coo of pleasure and considered her options. Enola selected an elaborate cream-topped pastry, but glanced pointedly at him before accepting it. Erik, after a moment's thought and some careful inspection of the available wares, opted for cheese and port. She obviously wasn't going to eat if he didn't, and he knew that he needed the calories.

Besides, the complex and delicate flavor of sauced prawn still lingered, just enough to pique his slumbering appetite.

"They're famous for these," Enola said. The pastry had been served with a cannikin of liquid caramel and she poured it now, laying down dark amber liquid in loops and swirls. To Erik, they seemed overly elaborate and ornate for something that would be consumed immediately, but Enola was something of an artiste. She had come to Villanueva as a holo-designer for architectural elevations, after all. The artistic bent had never left her, despite the odd course her career had taken.

"Oh?" he asked. "I didn't know that."

She looked up from her food and fixed him with a glance that included, again, a remembered impishness. "I'm surprised, then," she said. "Usually, you can tell me the chef's name, or at least the autochef brainware sequence. Didn't Kowalski have time to do the research?"

Erik said nothing, but studiously examined his own dessert.

"Did Wendy recommend this establishment?" he asked.

If so, it was a misstep. Erik was in no mood for seduction, and this place was designed for dalliance.

She shook her head. Her hair rippled like black water. A forkful of pastry shell, whipped cream, and frothy meringue rose to her mouth. Strands of congealing caramel trailed behind it, and she had to use her tongue to catch them all. Raising her hand in front of her chin for manners' sake, she chewed as she spoke. "I'm not the doxy," she said, and giggled. "I'm the Proxy."

Erik flinched. He didn't like the term. "I've asked people not to call you that," he said. With easy, practiced movements, he sliced the Stilton that had been served him, paring wafer-thin shavings of nearly machine-quality precision. He arrayed a half-dozen neatly on his flesh plate and went to work on the cheddar. Erik's hobby was cooking, and working like this with his hands was a comfort.

"I don't mind," she said. "Smile for me."

Erik didn't feel like smiling. Enola's relationship with the Halo chief was unique and sometimes troubling, and one that he'd had a hand in arranging.

"You've changed," Enola said, in vague accusation. She ate some more. Erik began to wonder about the contents of the tart.

"We both have." Then, to change the subject, "What does Wendy want?"

"Wendy Scheer would like to attend at least one of the candidate crew banquets," Enola said. She set her fork down next to her half-eaten dessert. Her tone of demeanor shifted, as if something inside her had been reconfigured. "Wendy would like to meet some of the fine young men and women who are going to contribute so intrinsically to Ad Astra's success."

"I appreciate your—*her* interest," Erik said. It was the precise request he had dreaded. Too many key personnel had already been invited to one or more of the celebrations for Wendy not to be interested. "But I can't grant permission." He paused. "I'm sorry," he said, meaning it.

"You're being silly, Erik," Enola said. Casually slumped over her tart a moment before, she sat now with near-military posture. Her voice and the cadence of her words took on new qualities. Very slightly, a Pacific Southwest accent colored her words. The effect was unnerving.

Ten years of working closely with the head of Project Halo had done things to Enola's persona.

"We're all working together now," Enola said. She seemed to have forgotten her pastry. "She has a right to see the fruit of her labor."

The cheddar cheese was tart and sharp, and the Stilton made an excellent counterpoint. Erik's guess was that both were local products, but of the highest quality. The wine, however, was certainly an import, robust and tawny. No doubt it was ruinously expensive. He rolled it on his tongue a moment before swallowing.

He was surprised how good all of it tasted now. He had eaten very little in the preceding forty-eight hours, and appetite might still be a stranger, but his body had suddenly decided that it needed food. He ate more before continuing.

"*You're* welcome to attend, Enola," he said. He was gentle but businesslike. "But Wendy knows the rules."

Scheer had been born with what some called a "wild talent." As near as Erik and his personnel had been able to determine, she represented some kind of mutation, though EnTek's best analysts had been unable to find anything anomalous in her DNA. Whatever the source of her gift, however, its effects were undeniable.

To know Wendy Scheer was to like her.

She exuded a subtle charm, not specifically sexual, but one that induced the desire to please. No one seemed

completely immune to it. An in-person encounter made one
subject to her allure, and any subsequent real-time communication enhanced the effect. Mesh audits, person-to-person
calls, even text feeds—all were vectors for influence and re-
inforcement. The affection did not always express itself in
sexual terms, as lust or desire, but once felt, it forever colored the subject's judgment.

The process was as fundamental as a child's imprinting
on and bonding with a parent. People who knew Wendy
Scheer had a predisposition to do things that they thought
would please her.

"Fifteen years is a long time, Erik," Enola said. She
leaned back in her chair and gazed at him, without any particular hostility that he could see, but also without warmth.
"Those are old rules."

In all but the specific pitch of her voice, she sounded
precisely like Wendy Scheer.

"I prefer to think of them as value-proven," Erik said.
He ate another slice of cheese. Cheese, even local cheese,
was a dairy product. It was rich in calcium and good for
the bones, which tended to shed mass in local gravity.
"You're welcome to attend for her. Inex will be happy to
make the arrangements."

In years past, Scheer had used her glamour to build a
clandestine network within Villanueva, a system of opera-
tives and informants who had monitored ALC activities on
behalf of the federal government. Wendy had run the network personally, using a variety of cover identities, both
fabricated and borrowed. Many who had worked for her
had done so unknowingly, but careers had been destroyed
in the process of dismantling the arrangement. Enola's had
been one.

Now, Scheer was unwelcome within the commercial
colony except under the most controlled of circumstances,

and with advance authorization. That permission was Erik's to give, and he had no intention of doing so in this instance.

"Wendy doesn't want to talk to Inex," Enola said. "She doesn't like her."

"I strongly hope that Wendy doesn't know Inex well enough to dislike her," Erik said. "That would be a gross violation of our agreement."

"*I* don't like Inex, then," Enola said. "She's rude."

"She's very polite," was all that Erik could think to say. He wondered what had happened between the women and promised himself to find out.

"Wendy would prefer to attend in person," Enola continued. "She says that fifteen years is a long time to spend in Coventry."

"Lady Godiva lived in Coventry," Erik said. The Proxy had invoked the term during their last visit, and he had done some research since. "Everyone liked *her,* too."

Suddenly, briefly, Enola was herself again, and no longer an echo of Wendy Scheer. Cool reserve fell away, and Enola laughed. It was a sound like silver bells. "When did *you* become a history student?" she asked.

Almost despite himself, Erik smiled. It felt good to smile, even if the feeling did not last.

"We're all working together now," Enola told him again, all business again as she pressed a perceived advantage. "She'd like to be there in person. She'd like to see you again."

"I'd like to see her, too," Erik said. He sipped wine. Warmth rushed through him. He had eaten nearly nothing in many long hours, and his body absorbed the alcohol eagerly. "That's why I can't."

Enola rolled her eyes. The effect was fetching, and a good reminder of how charming she could be, both as Wendy's envoy and as herself. She took another forkful of pastry, and crumbs clung to the pink curve of her lips for a long moment before her tongue retrieved them.

This was the Enola Erik remembered, girlish and with a pragmatic flirtatiousness. He had always liked her. She was someone who coasted through life on her own charm and appeal. If she didn't offer the magic allure that Wendy could, her own charm was undeniable.

"I don't think Wendy's physical presence is appropriate," Erik said. This was one policy area in which he had near-total authority. "She's welcome to audit, but I cannot extend a full invitation. Even the audit is a great courtesy."

It was also a risk, but Erik chose not to make that point explicit. The truth wouldn't make anyone any more appreciative.

"She's seen the list of attendees," Enola said. "She's never met any of them."

"She's welcome to audit," Erik repeated doggedly.

"We're supposed to work together on this," Enola said. "This is a joint effort, private and public."

He shrugged. "It's a joint project, based on a private-sector infrastructure and derived from a private-sector discovery," he said. "If Hello—if *Halo* wants complete control of a deep-space exploration, the Feds should have funded production facilities for Armstrong Base."

She actually scowled at him. The expression looked utterly foreign to her features, which were ordinarily either tranquil or smiling. Even her body language changed, as she shifted in her seat and sat more erectly. "It's been argued that the federal government did essentially that, in the form of tax breaks decades ago and production contracts more recently. Villanueva is here because of a federal charter."

"Villanueva is here because the old United Nations needed money and decided to issue land-grant leases on

Luna," he corrected her. The argument was an old one, reassuring by its very familiarity. "We're here because the Moon offered new opportunities, and because the ALC sisters wanted to make use of new processes that weren't approved for use on Earth. And most of that happened before you were born."

"So the ALC is willing for forego billions of new-dollars in federal contracts and the business growth driven by federal approval?" she asked sharply.

She sounded like Wendy again, a Wendy who was angry. If the actual Wendy Scheer had been seated across from him now, Erik knew he no doubt would have been frantically trying to make amends for his own, perfectly reasonable words.

"That's not the point," Erik said, with patience that was still forced. Money was a perfectly reasonable club, but he didn't like seeing it used so clumsily. "It won't happen, not at this stage and not over something as trivial as this. And even if it did, budget cuts wouldn't make as big a difference as you think. The ship *will* sail, Wendy."

His mistake startled them both. Enola's demeanor shifted again, as the almost military bearing seemed to ooze away and she slumped slightly in her chair. She half-smiled, but it was bravado. "I'm doing it again, aren't I?" she asked.

She was entirely Enola again. The Scheer mannerisms had fallen away, like a canceled mirage overlay.

He nodded, wishing that he could take back the wrong name, but knowing that regrets were futile. It was a mistake that he made only rarely, but invariably at the worst possible moment.

"I'm sorry," he said. He sipped port and tried not to look at her. At times like this, it was too easy to talk *past* Enola and try to engage directly with the woman whose words she spoke.

He had forgotten his dinner companion and spoken to
the Proxy, instead. It was a terrible thing to do to a woman,
to a friend, calling her by someone else's name.

"You know me too well for that," Enola said. "You've
known me too long."

He nodded, still embarrassed by the gaffe. Sometimes,
with Enola, there was a certain lapse in individuality that
made such mistakes easy, but that was no excuse.

"I met you before you met her," Enola continued. She
spoke with faint sadness. "I remember the first time."

Erik didn't say anything.

"Do you?" she asked.

He did, but only vaguely. "At Duckworth."

"At Duckworth," she agreed. Duckworth was the heavy-
industry member of the ALC, an iron foundry that had
expanded into a broad range of large-scale construction services. In a very real sense, Duckworth or its subsidiaries
had built most of Villanueva. Enola had worked for them as
a design rendering specialist until circumstances had dic-
tated her transition to the federal sector. "I was in the banquet area. You were on a courtesy call, a meet-and-greet,"
she continued.

Erik didn't remember the specifics. His early days on
the Moon had been hectic and not particularly happy, and
he had no doubt he had forgotten many chance encounters.

"I'm sorry, Enola," he said. "It's just—it's just, I've heard
Wendy make those points in person."

She sipped Lethe water. "This isn't always an easy job,"
she said.

"I don't imagine that it is," Erik said.

"There are benefits, of course," she said. She smiled. "Ten
years ago, I was eating soy-elves three times a day. Now—"
She moved her hand in a circular gesture that indicated not

only her place setting but the tastefully appointed dining niche and, presumably, the restaurant beyond.

"Ten years ago, you were looking for work," Erik said.

"You helped with that," Enola responded.

There was a double meaning to her words. Indirectly and inadvertently, Erik had been responsible for her being displaced from Duckworth, through his actions as an En-Tek manager. To make it up to her, he had introduced her to Wendy Scheer.

"Sometimes I regret that," he said. He regretted the introduction, too.

"Now you're being silly," Enola said. "It's important work." She took a deep breath. "Should I tell her that there is no chance of an invitation?"

"You're not recording?" Erik asked. That was a surprise. He had expected her to do so and had even considered bringing countermeasures.

"I can if you want me to," Enola said. She reached for the ornate bit of jewelry that hung from one of her earlobes. The only such item she wore, it was obviously an accessory in more senses than one.

Erik shook his head. "The answer is the same either way. You're welcome to attend as her envoy, and Wendy is welcome to audit on the Mesh, but she can't come in person. I won't permit it."

He had made exceptions in the past and authorized carefully monitored visits by the head of Project Halo, but not this time. Even setting aside the issue of Scheer's wild talent, and the key personnel she would certainly encounter, there were the Gummis to consider. Earlier generations of the semiliving brainware processors had proven sensitive to Scheer's presence and had tended to fail and reset themselves. The newer systems were supposedly immune, but Hector Kowalski's report was too fresh in his mind to allow any additional hazard.

It was almost a relief to wrestle with issues like these, he realized. It was easier to think about Enola and Wendy, about brainware failures and organizational protocols, than it was to think about his sons.

"She will appeal," Enola said. "She'll push Earthside management and try to contact you directly."

"Is that a warning?" Erik asked. He wondered again why Enola's sponsor was so insistent.

"Just facts," Enola said. "I know how she thinks."

It was an understatement.

"Why are you so sad, Erik?" Enola asked. She leaned closer and tilted her head slightly as she considered him. "You're very sad tonight. Have Wendy and I made you unhappy by asking? Have I?"

"No," Erik said, shaking his head.

"Usually, we enjoy these meetings. We have fun," Enola persisted. "Don't we?"

"It's nothing you've said or done, Enola, I promise you," Erik said. He pushed the remnants of his dessert aside and gestured for the waitperson.

As if of its own accord, Enola's right hand drifted across the space that separated them. Five cool fingertips pressed gently against Erik's left cheek and brow. Enola's eyes, at once dark and sparkling, took on new depth.

"You've never smiled very much, but this is different," she said. "You seem so very sad. She said you would be sad. She told me to be gentle with you, and I wasn't."

He nearly told her. He could feel the words well up within him, rush to his lips, and demand release. Just in time, however, he pulled back from her touch.

It was as if a circuit had broken, for both of them. His

own professionalism fell back into place and Enola seemed to relax, as well.

"I'm fine," he said again. "Tell Wendy what I said. I'll deal with any repercussions."

At some point, the waiter had gathered up their place settings and carried them away. Now, he stood and moved to help her with her chair. She half-giggled at the old-fashioned gesture.

"The Bazuki Brothers are playing at Ricardo's, in the Mall," she said. "They all have the new-series cranial interfaces. They're supposed to be remarkable."

"I'm sure they are," Erik said. "Perhaps sometime we can see them, but not tonight."

"Your quarters, then?" Enola asked. "I haven't seen them since you remodeled." A sidelong glance made the words an offer.

Enola had never been very subtle, Erik realized yet again. "Not tonight," he said again. "But I'll see you to your door."

CHAPTER 4

SEATED behind the small and spotless desktop that hung between two heavy steel support members, Wendy Scheer could have been a portrait downloaded from an esthetics text feed. She had amber eyes today and honey gold hair that offset them nicely. She had dressed with casual elegance, in a loose blouse and midlength skirt that seemed to flow one into the other. The ensemble was in earth tones that gave warmth to her fair skin, even under office lights, and she had selected modest personal jewelry that suggested excellent taste but not personal wealth. She looked every centimeter the well-groomed professional.

"It was worth a try," she said, as the last of Erik Morrison's recorded words faded away.

"I'm sorry," Hasbro said, seated in the guest chair across from her. She watched Wendy carefully as she spoke. "I did my best."

"I know, Enola," Wendy said gently. She sipped new-coffee from a mug with a cartoon cat on its side.

Enola sipped new-coffee, too, mirroring her host's movement. Her cup, taken from the office's guest service, bore the logo of Project Halo, the government-run scientific research that was Villanueva's neighbor on the Moon.

"It wasn't likely." Wendy continued. Her voice was low and gentle, and she tried very hard to keep the sadness she felt from coloring her words. Hasbro had a tendency to respond to Wendy's emotional cues more emphatically than she liked.

"I could try again. I like Erik," Hasbro said. "I like seeing him."

Wendy shook her head. Hasbro's head shook, too, almost too faintly to notice, reflexively imitating her boss. Wendy felt a frown forming on her lips and suppressed it, just in time.

Long association with Wendy Scheer had wreaked changes on the other woman's personality, changes that had been subtle at first but were more pronounced every year. Hasbro didn't seem to mind, but sometimes Wendy felt guilty.

There was nothing to be done for that now, however.

"He's a better man than he realizes," she said. Wendy was certain of that. "He's a more important man, too." Enola nodded agreeably, if blankly, and Wendy felt yet again the need to try to explain.

"There is a flow to history, Enola," Wendy said. "I don't mean economic cycles or political movements, but the underlying currents that shape them."

"Manifest Destiny," Hasbro chirped. The words were surprisingly appropriate, but Wendy was sure that they had arisen from no real understanding of the issue. Hasbro's mind simply didn't work that way. More likely, the other woman had been watching Mesh historical dramas again.

Wendy continued with a slight head shake of disagreement. "Not 'destiny,' really," she said. "But close. I think we have roles to play. I think we're here for a reason. I firmly believe that."

"Then I believe it, too," Hasbro said. She was eager to please.

She was always eager to please, Wendy realized with another twinge of sadness. She could find no happiness in allegiance so totally given.

Morrison was different. He was subject to Wendy's gift like any other man or woman or child, but he was aware of it and unafraid. He had always dealt with her in a spirit of wary pragmatism, and she admired that.

"Erik was given one of those opportunities," Wendy continued. "He's an important man. I don't think anyone will realize just how important until we're all long dead."

Hasbro looked at her blankly, unsure what to say. Philosophic discourse was not the Proxy's métier.

Wendy sighed. "How was the rest of the evening?" she asked. "Did you enjoy yourselves?"

"Should I have recorded the entire meal?" Hasbro asked anxiously. "I *knew* I should have."

"No, Enola," Wendy said, soothing the nervous woman. "You have a right to privacy. You have a right to your own life. I was just curious."

"Next time, I'll record everything," Hasbro said. She bit her lower lip.

"Don't." Wendy smiled, and smiled wider still as she saw the other woman finally relax. "You're my friend, Enola. We have to be friends to work well together. Please. Just understand that you're my friend and I like talking with you."

Hasbro beamed.

"Now," Wendy said. "Tell me what happened after you stopped recording."

"He escorted me home," Hasbro said. For the preceding ten years, Enola had lived in comfortable quarters in an upper-middle-class sector of Villanueva. The rent for that apartment was a line item buried deep in Wendy's annual budget. Wendy Scheer might be unwelcome in the commercial colony, but her envoy lived there. "He saw me to my door, and he kissed me good night," Enola continued.

Wendy nodded. "How was he?" she asked.

"He was very sad," Hasbro said. There was a detached quality to her voice as she concentrated on remembering the evening and communicating it clearly. "He wouldn't say why." She paused. "He looked different. He looked old." She made the comment with an air of mild disbelief. Enola could scarcely understand why anyone would allow himself to look old.

"Did you ask him to stay?" Wendy asked.

"I didn't ask, but he knew," Enola said. She showed no self-consciousness about the topic, no irritation at the rejection. "You said he would be sad. What's wrong?"

The spring steel basketwork of her desk chair shifted as Wendy leaned back. "Death in his family," she said. "Erik has—*had* two sons, back Earthside. They died recently in a sporting accident."

"Oh. How terrible," Hasbro said. Abruptly, she looked older, too, the perpetual youth of her features aging as sorrow touched them. "I didn't know he had sons. He never told me."

"He didn't tell me, either," Wendy said. She thought back, recalling her few in-person conversations and the countless hours that she had audited. Morrison's advent on the Moon had come hard on the heels of a personal and professional scandal. His restraint in those days had been Wendy's first clue to how much he valued privacy. "But they're mentioned in his backgrounders and Mesh profiles."

They were mentioned in the way that famous people mentioned their private lives, in passing and with little emphasis. She had researched them more than once, over the years, but never in any great detail. There had seemed to be no need.

Hasbro sat silently, trying to digest the information. Wendy could understand her confusion. Hasbro had spent far more time with Morrison than Wendy. Now, she was clearly realizing that she really didn't know him very well.

Because she felt she should say something, Wendy continued. "I met Rod once, six years ago. I was on Earth, for business, and the opportunity presented itself. He seemed to be a very nice man, if a bit unfocused. He didn't know who I was." She paused, remembering again Morrison's penchant for privacy. "Erik doesn't know about that, Enola. I don't want him to."

The younger woman nodded obediently. "Should I extend our sympathies, at least?" she asked.

Wendy thought about that for a long moment, then chose her words carefully. "You may extend yours, Enola, if you wish," she said. "Call him. Not on my behalf, but on your own."

Enola looked confused again.

"He shouldn't be alone now," Wendy continued. "He's never been a man with many friends, and he needs more now."

"You're his friend, aren't you?" Enola asked.

Wendy shook her head. "I don't think *friend* is the word," she said, with a trace of sadness.

SIX months had passed since Trine Hartung's last visit to Villanueva, half a standard year spent at the nearly zero-G Ship Site. Her entire body insisted on reminding her of that, but her legs and feet spoke the loudest as she trudged along a Mall concourse.

Despite her diligent maintenance exercises and the best gene therapy credit could buy, they hurt. She knew that it would have been much worse if she'd chosen to spend her downtime on Earth instead of the Moon.

She settled into a convenient padded bench, long and low, and dropped her parcels next to her feet. They fell in what an Earth native would have considered slow motion, but they fell, nonetheless. She had spent enough time Ship Site that she found the effect novel.

Around her surged the endless tide of human commerce that was Villanueva's lifeblood. Tourists and natives, staff and patrons, they blurred together as they milled about the cavernous space. The chatter and ambient noise and the aroma of countless human bodies in close proximity filled the air. The effect different from Ship Site's most heavily trafficked work areas: different, yet similar. The olfactory landscape was at once less intense and more complex.

Trine ached all over, but her calves had taken the worst of it. The muscles had tensed and knotted. She prodded and kneaded them with her fingers. Hard work had kept her hands strong, even in low-to-no gravity, and Trine had received training in physical therapy. Slowly, something like normal sensation began to reassert itself.

The muscles were intact, she knew. She had followed the medics' directions, but no exercise program, however rigorous, could fully compensate for half a year in near zero-G. The most the regimen could do, even in tandem with genetic therapies, was to ensure her the ability to recover. The discomfort was only temporary and would pass.

The stress to her body would be far greater if management selected her for the final crew and sent her on the Long Voyage. Therapists said that she'd likely never be able to readapt. Despite the warning, she hoped to find out for herself.

Trine had done what she could for the aches, at least for now. She slid her feet back and up, out of the low shoes she wore, and leaned back on the bench. Her business could wait for a moment while she watched the world go by.

The Mall was the heart of Villanueva's commercial sector, and like a real heart, it surged with turbulent life. It was thirteen levels of shops and theaters and restaurants and galleries and brothels. Merchants, restaurants, service providers, and galleries lined the walls of the great cylindrical shaft that once had been Villanueva's central launch and landing facility. Every storefront and facade bore the name of an ALC company or an ALC licensee or, at the very least, an ALC tenant. The largest single concern, the Zonix casino, had operated for long decades under multiple trademarks since the founding days of the colony. It stretched across three levels and fully a quarter of the space's circumference. The vast majority of consumer-class commercial transacting took place in or was serviced from the Mall. When travelers spoke of going to Villanueva, they generally meant the Mall.

It was absurd, really. Trine couldn't imagine leaving the planet of her birth, traveling hundreds of thousands of kilometers, merely to go shopping. She wasn't blind to the Mall's allure, but she liked to think that her sites were set higher.

The world went by. A doyen in designer attire spoke sharply to the attendant of a freestanding cosmetics kiosk. A paunchy man in poorly fitting clothes gobbled soy-dogs daubed in plum sauce as he gawked at the licensed sex workers who prowled among the crowd, living advertisements for the delights that could be had behind this door or that. A little girl wailed because her parents refused to purchase some cheap souvenir that had caught her eye.

Being surrounded by strangers was a novelty. She knew the men and women of Ship Site well, some of them intimately. If she qualified for the Long Voyage, some of those same individuals would make up the majority of her world. The thought made her more appreciative of the madding crowd. As the men and women of Villanueva went about their lives, Trine watched with casual appreciation, never staring and never making eye contact.

That changed, abruptly. It changed as she saw someone she recognized, not from personal experience but from official documents and news feeds and even history programming. He was a man very late in middle age, who had allowed his hair to remain gray and his features to become worn. He was a tall man, built wide, and Trine could tell by the way he walked that he had lived in the Moon's lesser gravity for a very long time, but that he had been born on Earth.

She stood hastily. Too late, she remembered that her feet were halfway out of their shoes, enough to make her stumble. She gasped and smothered a curse as her soles met the bare floor, with only a sheer layer of stocking between them.

"Sir!" she said to the man who was still moving vaguely in her direction. "Sir! You're Erik Morrison, aren't you?"

He turned and faced her squarely. He didn't look good. His eyes were hooded and bloodshot, and dark bags hung below them, and his skin had an ashen quality, like packing film. He looked ill or old or very unhappy, and the expression of mild confusion he wore didn't help things.

Trine didn't care. She could scarcely believe her good fortune.

"Yes. Yes, I am," he said. If he looked frailer than Trine would have expected, his voice still carried power. It was a familiar voice, one that she had heard countless times on orientation feeds and packaged Mesh productions. "Do I know you?"

"No, sir!" Trine said. Without conscious thought, she drew herself to attention and extended one hand, thumb cocked. She could not keep the enthusiasm from her voice. "I'm Trine Hartung, sir! It's an honor!"

Morrison had been shopping and held a woven carryall in his right hand, filled with bottles and boxes. He had to move the bag from right hand to left before he could accept Trine's offer. When he did, when their thumbs hooked, Trine could feel the easy confidence that came from a long career of great power. Whatever the big man's circumstance, it had not affected his grip.

"I'm pleased, Trine," he said. He looked at her with cool appraisal. Something about Trine, her stance or her slightly passé attire or her utilitarian haircut, told him what he wanted to know. "You're crew, aren't you? Back from Ship Site?"

Trine nodded. Now that she had introduced herself, she wasn't sure what to say next. "I had downtime, sir," she began.

Morrison interrupted. "Not 'sir,'" he said with a tired smile. "Erik. Are you here for one of the banquets? I hope their not charging you downtime for that."

Trine liked that. The scuttlebutt on Morrison was that he had a common touch, at least with people outside his immediate circle.

"Erik," she corrected herself. "No, sir. I'm not scheduled for another three weeks. But I had downtime, and I thought I would try to get my land legs back." She winced slightly.

"Not as easy as you thought?" Morrison asked. He spoke lightly, but there was no happiness in his tired eyes.

"No, sir," Trine said. She winced again as she realized she had misspoken.

Morrison didn't seem to notice. "It's not a bad idea, though. And it's easier when you're young," he said, suddenly looking very old. "What's your billet, Trine?" he asked.

"I work for Biome," she said eagerly. "Company bones. Environmental systems specialist, first class."

"They'll keep you busy," Morrison said. He rocked back on his heels and swung the shopping bag slowly, like a lumpy pendulum. Now, at last, he smiled, however faintly, and the new expression took years from him. "Do your feet hurt, Trine? You're not wearing shoes."

Trine had half-forgotten, but he had noticed. She blushed furiously, something she had not done since adolescence. "Yes, sir," she said, embarrassed back into formality.

"Proper footgear can help with that," he said.

She knew what he meant. Landing port vendors sold smartboots with built-in massagers, Gummi-controlled systems designed to do the therapeutic work that had occupied her fingers minutes before. Trine didn't like them. She was stocky and squat, and the knee-high boots made her legs looks look even shorter.

"I'll have to try them, sir," she lied.

"Call me Erik," he told her again. His smile faded as a more serious expression took its place. "Don't undervalue yourself. You people on Ship Site are the ones who get the job done."

She blushed again, more deeply this time. "Thank you, sir," she said. "Thank you, Erik, I mean."

It felt very strange to stand here, in stocking feet, talking with such an important man, and especially strange to be shown such courtesy.

It was Morrison who had brought the *Voyager* find to ALC management, and it was Morrison who had occupied increasingly prominent roles in the subsequent initiative to explore deep space. Trine was well aware that her personal interest in project history was far stronger than most, but even so, she was surprised that no one else seemed to take notice of Morrison. He was no Mesh star or head of state, but a very real celebrity, nonetheless. In Trine's circle, at least, he was very famous.

"I mean it," he said. "I'm glad we had a chance to talk." He paused. Evidently, the big man was not very skilled at small talk. "Trine, will you be Moonside long?" he finally asked.

"A standard week," she said. "Then back again for the banquet." She grinned, relaxing at last. "Just long enough to confuse my feet."

"That's long enough," he said. "This is a busy time for me, you know. In addition to the banquets, I'm supposed to participate in a dedication ceremony next month, for a museum exhibit that might interest you. I hope you'll consider attending."

"The Ad Astra museum?" she asked eagerly. Mesh event calendars had mentioned the ceremony with tantalizing frequency, but Trine had never thought she would be able to attend. It was by invitation only.

She had just been invited.

"I—I'd be honored," she said slowly, her mind racing. There wasn't much opportunity for spending Ship Site, but Trine sent much of her compensation home for the benefit of her parents. Her accounts were in good shape for most expenditures, but an event like this called for a new ensemble at the very least. A complete makeover would be better, if she could afford it.

"Good. But it really is just an exhibit," Morrison said. "Message my office, and I'll see to it that you're invited. Perhaps we can talk again, then." His grip on his parcel tightened, and his stance shifted. He was getting ready to go.

"I would like that, sir," Trine said. Eager to extend the conversation, she continued. "I met a friend of yours recently. Ship Site."

"Oh?" Morrison looked at her again. "Who was that?"

"Hector Kowalski," she said.

Now Morrison seemed genuinely surprised. His gaze hardened slightly. "I hope it was a pleasant encounter."

"We spoke only briefly," Trine said. She wondered how best to sum up her short conversation with the security chief. "By chance. We were making our rounds, both of us," she said. She told him about the hull encounter. "It was a bit of a surprise," she said. "I didn't expect to see anyone there, much less someone from off-ship."

"Hector is very thorough," Morrison said, "and likes surprises." He paused, then amended the comment. "He likes *being* a surprise."

Trine nodded. "He seemed very happy with operations Ship Site," she told him. "He said that the Old Man—"

Too late, she bit off the words. "He said that *you* should be pleased," she concluded.

Now Morrison surprised her. He laughed, not a guffaw or a chortle, but a rolling chuckle that boiled up from somewhere inside him. If his smile of a few minutes before had taken years from his shoulders, laughter took a decade. The effect was pronounced enough to make Trine wonder how anyone could call him *old,* even as a term of affection.

"That's good," Morrison said. "That's very good. Thank you for that, Trine." He paused again. "And I'll have to thank Hector for it personally."

"Please," she said. "Please, I'm sorry. I don't want to offend or cause any trouble."

She heard a slight edge of panic in her own voice. Men like Morrison and Kowalski moved in vastly more rarefied orbits than Trine, after all. She could have just cost herself the invitation to the dedication ceremony, or even damaged her career. To have worked so hard, and come so far—

"I'm sorry," she said again.

Still smiling, Morrison shook his head. He clapped his free hand affectionately on her shoulder. "I told you, don't undervalue yourself," he said again as he released his grip. "I've had some dark days lately, Trine, and you've just given me a little bit of light. Thank you."

ERIK took the path of least resistance home. Rather than the walkways and rung-lined vertical access tubes that encouraged muscle tone, he took the motorized tram that tourists preferred. Seated on the hard plastic, his purchases in his lap, he let the kilometers between the Mall and his quarters roll by without any effort on his part.

That was a mistake, he knew. Exercise was as essential as gene therapy and a good diet to a long healthy life in the Moon's lower gravity. He didn't care. The inadvertent moment of brightness that the young woman from Ship Site had given him had faded quickly, and pervasive sorrow had reasserted itself. At the moment, he didn't care much about living healthily, and he wasn't entirely certain that he cared much about living at all.

The apartment entrance sensed his approach and opened without being asked. The door whisked shut behind him, but the housekeeper system said nothing; he had ordered silence the night before and done nothing to countermand the command. Any messages could wait, perhaps forever.

The groceries couldn't, though. Erik set the mesh sack on the kitchen counter and opened it. One by one, he unpacked his purchases and stowed them away.

Shopping in person really hadn't been necessary. He had bought nothing but basic foodstuffs, with no indulgences like imported beef or fresh fish from the local hatcheries. He had made the trip primarily out of a vague belief that seeing people would help and seeing people he didn't know would help more. He had been right, but not as right as he had hoped.

The last item in the sack was a package of fresh fettuccini noodles, soft and supple as silk. He hefted the pouch for a moment, considering it. He had bought pseudoolives and anchovies, and plum tomatoes waited in the produce drawer.

He should eat, he knew. He wasn't hungry, but he should eat, and cooking would give him something to do. Pasta puttanesca would take only a few minutes, and he might even enjoy preparing it, but it really didn't seem worth the effort.

He shrugged and stowed the noodles away and took down a package of soy-elves instead. He pulled two bottles of budget beer from the refreshment nook, then let himself drop into an armchair's embrace.

He should have been exercising, he knew. Exercise was important, even vital. At the moment, however, the long-term benefits didn't seem worth the effort.

Nothing seemed worth the effort.

He thumbed the container's release catch and freed the elves from their prison. The top receded, and the little creatures beckoned at him cheerfully, eager to be eaten. He was relieved to realize that he had bought the silent variety.

He didn't like soy-elves. They were novelty food, bland and forgettable, bereft even of any interesting texture. Erik kept them on hand only as emergency rations, or for the convenience of the rare guest who liked them. Four of the squirming things were all he could force himself to eat before he set the container aside and opened the first beer.

Inexpensive drink was almost always a better value than

inexpensive food. Even budget beer did its job. Sorrow and loneliness receded just a bit, and he could think with what seemed like clarity.

Erik surveyed his domain. The living room was a wreck. More than a week had passed since Sylva's call, and entropy had taken its toll. The furniture was in slight disarray, with rumpled cushions and misaligned ruffles. The paper-and-ink book of poetry, antique Longfellow, left to him by his father, lay open and forsaken on an end table. A caddy of data pods hung from the entrance utility hook, instead of being stowed away properly. Empty bottles and half-empty vessels littered every flat surface.

He was drinking too much, he realized. That could become a problem. Vaguely pleased with himself for the observation, he finished the first beer and opened the second.

"Messages," he demanded in his command voice, and then he listened without comment as the housekeeper system told him of his calls.

None were of particular import. Between his own half-days of concentrated effort and Inex's diligence, deadlines were being met and challenges resolved. Things were going better than he had expected.

He was going to have to keep an eye on Inex, he realized. He had always insisted that his personal staff be ambitious, but there was a difference between ambition and competition. If Inex became much better at her work, she could become a problem, as well.

"—*confidential from Sander Adkins*," the housekeeper said. "*Priority.*"

"Pause," Erik said, coming to attention.

He hadn't heard Adkins's name in at least seven years. Adkins was a psychiatric therapist, affiliated with EnTek Personnel Services. The counselor had been appointed by Over-Management to counsel Erik during his recovery from injuries sustained in an incident of sabotage directed at the Ad Astra project. Erik had been badly hurt in a foundry explosion and its aftermath, but psychological and emotional issues had proven more challenging than the physical ones.

Why the hell was Adkins calling now? Erik's sense of career preservation stirred and reminded him of the obvious answer.

"Play it," Erik said. He drained the second beer, heaved himself up out of his chair, and shuffled to the refreshment nook.

The wallpaper was set to an Amazon jungle motif, images of trees and vines and bright-colored birds, ghosts of species long dead. A segment of the flora faded away, to be replaced by a lean man with bushy eyebrows, looking studiously compassionate. Sander Adkins looked exactly has he had looked long years before, but whether that was the result of good genetics, facial appliances, or mirage brainware, Erik couldn't tell.

He opened his third bottle and held his thumb on the opening tab long enough for the bottle to chill thoroughly before half-draining it. He supposed that Adkins was good enough at his job, but Erik had no happy memories of their association and had never particularly liked the man.

"Erik," Adkins's recorded image said. *"I hope you're well and that you'll forgive my presumption in calling."*

Erik scowled at the image.

"Media Relations has brought something to may attention," Adkins continued. He paused. *"It was about your sons, Erik. I'm very sorry to hear of your loss."*

The third bottle was empty now. Erik didn't even remember raising it to his lips. He passed the vessel back and forth between his big hands nervously. A fourth called to him from the nook cooler, but he ignored it for the moment.

Erik worked for Over-Management now, but EnTek still

had a claim on him. He wondered which functionary within Media Relations had reviewed the data-sieve reports and made the connection between a hang-glider accident off Australia and a high-ranking EnTek alumnus. Clearly, whoever it was had acted on the insight.

Adkins continued, with professional earnestness. *"Erik, I know it's been years, but I hope you'll regard this as coming from friend—"*

Erik snorted softly. Adkins had never been his friend. He drew another beer from the cooler.

"I'd like to speak with you at your earliest opportunity about grief management options," Adkins said. He could have been reading from a prepared statement. *"If we could meet in person, all the better, but Mesh will do."*

Adkins had been an ardent believer in personal presence, Erik remembered, at least for professional sessions. The counselor had maintained that the seeming intimacy of Mesh conferencing was a lie.

"I remember how resistant you were to some of our sessions following the foundry incident, but I think you'll agree that they helped you return to full duty," Adkins said. *"And I think we've both learned a lot since then."*

Despite Adkins's compassionate tones, Erik felt a rush of irritation that verged on genuine anger. Adkins didn't care a minute's compensation about him. EnTek management did. Someone high in the hierarchy was concerned about his prominent role within Over-Management and worried that he might not represent the company well.

"Let's meet soon, and consider the options," Adkins said. *"At the very least, I can put you in contact with an appropriate support group."*

"I don't need a support group," Erik muttered. "I don't need your help."

The recorded message continued. *"I know that these*

*are hectic times for you and that your professional obliga-
tions are considerable,"* Adkins said. *"But the early stages
of grief are critical. I would appreciate it greatly if you'd
respond within the next day or so."* He paused. *"And,
again, Erik, please accept my condolences, and the sympathies of everyone at EnTek."*

The image froze and then faded. The jungle reasserted
itself. Erik gazed at the wallpaper for a long moment,
thinking.

Even on a nearly empty stomach, even with the soothing haze of alcohol, his thoughts came with surprising clarity. Adkins's call hadn't been one of condolence, and the
decision to make it probably hadn't originated with him.
Adkins's final words had been the clue.

The call had been an order, and it had come from high
in the EnTek hierarchy. Adkins might have gotten the news
and might even have run the psychological model personally, but someone else had made the decision to approach
him directly.

Someone was concerned about Erik's job performance.
Someone was concerned and had enough authority, formal
or otherwise, to act on that concern.

Erik thought back to his sessions with Adkins, in the
months that had followed the Duckworth Foundry disaster.
Reluctantly, he had to grant that they had been helpful, but
that seemed like a lifetime ago and a world away. Injuries
were something that could be dealt with, even corrected.

Nothing would bring his sons back.

"I need some things," he said in his command voice. His
words were clear, and his voice was strong. "Run a search on
available feeds pertaining to grief management, all media.
Focus on personal and family and charge the top three to my
personal accounts. Make it an open search; I don't care who
knows."

If Adkins, or anyone else, decided to research the matter, their knowledge would be worth the trifling expense.

"Find out which therapy groups are available on-Mesh,"
he continued. "Research them. Use my security protocols
to profile memberships by education, career, demograph-
ics, and loss. Enquire about joining procedures, but do it
discreetly. Don't use my name, but don't bother with privacy protocols, either."

He nodded, pleased with himself. Adkins was almost
certainly monitoring his activities and behavior now. If he
wasn't, someone else was. Either way, the buys and queries
would give them something to think about.

A banded constrictor, scaled and sinewy, slithered along
a drooping tree limb in the wallpaper jungle. The movement
was so smooth and continuous that the reptile's body could
have been liquid, rather than living flesh. Only the snake's
triangular head, moving rhythmically to this angle and that,
seemed to demonstrate animal purpose. The snake was
hunting.

"Contact Adkins's office," Erik continued. He still spoke
clearly, but the adrenaline that had come with irritation and
defensiveness had begun to ebb. "Not Adkins; his office."

"Business hours have concluded," his apartment said.
"His office manager brainware extends its apologies."

"Thank him for his courtesy call. Promise him that I'll
return it. Make it polite but pro forma," Erik said.

*"Message received and acknowledged. Response
logged,"* his housekeeper said.

"Good," Erik muttered. The minor discourtesy of a return
call by brainware proxy would probably irritate Adkins, but
that was all to the good. It was fair payback for Adkins's presumption in calling and a subtle reminder of the counselor's
place in the overall scheme of things.

"Now, see if you can find Sylva for me," he said. The words were still in his command voice but came without conscious thought. Once spoken, though, he didn't try to call them back. Instead, he waited, wrapped in thought, as his housekeeper worked to obey.

It took long seconds, as much for protocol reconciliation as for signal transit, but the wait paid off. Where Adkins had been, where the snake and jungle had been, Sylva's image loomed instead. It was prerecorded, Erik realized with disappointment.

"*Hello, Erik,*" his third wife said. She was dressed in black, seated on a rose granite bench in her personal garden. Behind her were roses and hyacinths, and beyond them were prism-cut greenhouse panes that filtered and enhanced the afternoon sun.

"Hello, Sylva," Erik said reflexively.

"*I'm happy you called, but I'm sorry I'm not able to talk with you,*" the recorded message continued. "*The service and travel arrangements have proven unexpectedly demanding, and I need what little private time I can make available to myself. Veronica has been a dear, but she's really not very practical, and . . .*"

Her words trailed off, and she paused. Her mouth made a little moue of disgust, and she shook her head, almost too slightly to notice. "*I'm sorry,*" she said. "*I shouldn't have said that. I should go back and edit it out, but I'm not going to. You know that Veronica and I have never been particularly close, and I have more of these to record, and I have to meet the shuttle, and I really don't have time to do things again and again.*"

The words came in a torrent that was very uncharacteristic of Sylva, who had always combined easy pragmatism with an even easier composure. The situation on Earth must have been even more difficult than she indicated, Erik realized.

"I'm sure you're calling about the memorial arrangements," Sylva said, back in control. *"The details aren't finalized yet, but I'll speak with you soon. Until then, I hope you're well, or as well as you can be. I hope you're not lonely, but I'm very worried that you are."*

The image faded, and Erik blinked. The jungle was back, but the snake was gone. A flash of color flickered though the verdant display. It was a parrot.

"Give me ambient," Erik said sadly. "Low volume."

Softly and as if from a great distance, the sounds of the jungle filled Erik's living room. Wind-blown leaves rustled, and insects buzzed. Birds sang warnings to one another, marking their territory. They were the sounds of life.

"Direct contact information for Sylva Taschen is available, on a priority-override basis," the apartment said.

"No," Erik said. "No, leave her alone. She has enough work." Now, at last, he opened the fourth beer and returned to his chair.

The moment had passed, but he wished that he could have spoken with Sylva. They might have set each other at ease, at least to some degree. She had always understood him, perhaps too well.

"I hope you're not lonely," she had said. *"But I'm very worried that you are."*

She was right. Adkins was right. He needed someone to talk to. But Sylva was unavailable and Adkins was likely an enemy, and he would never present his personal life to the anonymous members of a support group.

He needed someone, and he had no one.

ZONIX Hospitality operated an employee hostel within ten minutes of the Mall, and candidate crewmembers had use of it. More precisely, a Zonix subsidiary had subcontracted the management of an austere quasi-residential enclave to an entrepreneur from Earth. The agreement in place stipulated that certain franchise fees would be satisfied by complimentary staff use. The rooms were small but clean, scarcely larger than the beds they held, bereft of wallpaper and smelling of disinfectant.

Trine didn't mind. She had never been one to spend unnecessarily, and her tastes were modest. Perched on the edge of the bed, pondering a barebones Mesh terminal, she was perfectly at ease. The self-heated basin of water that soothed her bare feet had been her single indulgence.

The Mesh workstation was cheaper than cheap. Even the most basic features, such as a vocal interface, were available only at extra charge. If you wanted to access the Mesh for anything other than passive viewing of the hostel's endless commercials, you had to use the keyboard, which looked shiny and new. Trine wondered if she was the first to use it.

She didn't mind typing. She had been a data technician in her childhood, and the mechanics of the process were familiar and reassuring. Moreover, Trine didn't think she was very good with words and found that typing gave her more of a chance to tinker and revise.

The smartbucket pinged. Her authorized credit had run its course. Trine sighed and, reluctantly, pressed a toe to the key that would give her another ten minutes in the soothing bath. She leaned back and reviewed her work in progress.

Dear Erik:

I met you in the Mall today. I liked meeting you. You might remember me. I am the girl from Ship Site. I am writing you because you invited me to the museum opening, and I would like very much to attend. If I need to provide any information

or undergo any procedure, please tell me so I can prepare.
Thank you again for your time and your invitation.

Trine scowled. She moved the second sentence so that it
followed the greeting, and nodded. That was better. It still
wasn't very good, but it had a certain mechanical effective-
ness. She was a technician, not a wordsmith, after all.

Morrison likely wouldn't read it, anyway. She had gotten his address from a public directory, so someone on his
staff would see it first. She added her contact information
and pressed the Send key. Instantly, the Message Received
icon flashed.

Her feet felt better now, and the throbbing in her calves
had finally faded. The smartbucket had done its work and
would need no further payment.

The first day back on surface was always the worst, but
she felt better already. The human body was a resilient instrument, and the human body as modified by genetic therapy was even more forgiving. If she intended to attend the
exhibit opening, however, she might do well to extend her
current stay and build up some stamina.

A thought struck her, daring and impudent but with undeniable allure. She opened the public directory again (at
no charge) and entered a name into the query field. Again,
the Mesh's response was immediate. Access codes appeared, along with a surprisingly short backgrounder and a
single image of a man who was nondescript but not unat-
tractive. Trine took a deep breath and began to type.

Dear Hector Kowalski:
   I met you on Ship Site recently. You might remember
me . . .

CHAPTER 5

"IT looks like what happened to your sons was an accident," Kowalski said. He leaned back in the steel spring-mesh of the spiderweb of the guest chair in Erik's office.

Even delivered in Kowalski's utterly matter-of-fact tones, the words were enough to make Erik's world, if not brighter, at least less dark. He nodded.

Kowalski continued. "The local authorities owed me a few favors," he said. "They provided copies of official forensics reports, and I did some research of my own." He paused. "It was an accident," he said again. "A random cross-current, just like the initial findings said. I've sent you the substantiating files, but that's the essence of my conclusions."

"A cross-current that no one saw coming," Erik said. His sons had died by misadventure, not because of any attempt to influence or respond to their father's actions.

The information made things easier in some ways and more difficult in others. A move by a business rival or enemy might have lent a twisted sense of order to the situation. It would have given Erik someone to hate, but it would also have given him someone to blame.

Himself.

"We can't see everything in advance," Kowalski said. "We can't even determine everything after the fact. Believe me, I know." He smiled faintly and uncharacteristically. "I've tried."

Something about the security chief was different today, Erik realized as he looked across the desk at Kowalski. Early in Erik's tenure on the Moon, when the two had first met, Kowalski had been brash and aggressive, even obnoxious. That had changed, as Erik had become his supervisor and advocate within the corporate hierarchy. Bit by bit, the younger man had remade himself, becoming subdued and remote.

Today he was different, however. Today he seemed edgier and less formal, and a hint of animation colored his voice and features. It was like seeing an afterimage, faint and faded, of the man Kowalski had once been.

"I appreciate your diligence," Erik said. He toyed nervously with the mug on his desktop. It was difficult to even try to look at ease.

Kowalski shrugged. That was atypical behavior, too. "There are limits. But it's difficult to see why anyone would have moved against them without approaching you first, or afterward," he said. He looked at Erik levelly. "*Has* anyone contacted you?" he asked.

"No." Erik shook his head, raised his mug to drink, realized it was empty, and set it down again. "No one has. Not like that."

"My office hasn't received any overtures, either," Kowalski said. "And if this were hostile action, I'd expect to." He paused. "Of course, mistakes get made. There was that business in France."

"The other Erik Morrison," Erik said in acknowledgment.

Years before, another man with Erik's name had met a violent end during an anti-ship demonstration on the grounds of an EnTek facility. The parties responsible, an activist group opposed to deep-space exploration, had apparently acted on faulty information. It had been a case of mistaken identity, all too possible, even given the Mesh's prodigious data management resources.

"But I don't think anything like that happened in this case," Kowalski said. "I'm not closing the file, though. If I hear anything more—"

Erik nodded. He waved one hand in dismissal. "I trust your judgment," he said. "And I appreciate your help." He paused. "And your concern," he said.

Kowalski didn't seem to have a response ready for that. He sat in silence for a moment. "You're not popular in certain circles," he said. "On the corporate front, I mean."

"What do you mean?" Erik asked. He felt surprise again, not from the information but from the announcement. It was unlike Kowalski to volunteer such an observation without prodding.

"You're prominent. Since you—since we moved to Over-Management, you've been involved, at least peripherally, in almost every major decision that's gotten made around here," Kowalski said. "People notice that, and they remember it."

Erik grunted. There wasn't much he could say in response to such obvious truths. He had always tried to be considerate of others' situations, but he had also always done what was best for the enterprise. Sometimes, the two priorities came into conflict.

"I thought at first there might be an element of revenge," Kowalski continued.

"I don't think that's likely," Erik said sharply.

"I don't think so, either," Kowalski said. "Now. But it was

a possibility I had to consider." He leaned forward now, making the metal of the guest chair sing faintly. He drained his mug and set it on a low, convenient table. "Most of the work I do for you isn't gathering data," he said easily. "I have too much of that, really. Most of what I do is draw lines between one event and another, or one individual and a second, and see if I can substantiate them. What happened to your sons seems to have been blind chance."

Erik nodded again, oddly reassured, but puzzled at Kowalski's persistence in arguing the point. "I didn't think I had that kind of enemies," he said.

"But you do," Kowalski replied.

Erik had heard the expression about blood running cold before, had even used it in conversation, but he had never experienced the actual effect. Kowalski's tone was nonchalant, but his words were ominous.

"You really do," Kowalski continued doggedly. "You do, and I don't think you realize it. Especially now. You were sent here as a punishment, Erik."

He almost never used Erik's first name.

"That's not a good memory," Erik said.

More than twenty years before, a career misstep had led to Erik's exile to the Moon. Those had been very different days for the colony. To fend off challenges in Earth's world courts, the ALC had worked hard to maximize the population of Villanueva, to establish the colony as thoroughly as possible. Work/scholarship agreements, lowered professional standards, and compensation incentives had been used to fuel the growth. The Moon had become a dumping ground for midlevel management, once-promising individuals who had not met expectations, or who had made mistakes along the way.

Men like Erik Morrison.

"People remember, though," Kowalski said. "It's part

of—part of your myth, your legend. You were driven into exile, but ended up in top management. They're opening a museum about you. People remember and notice things like that."

"It's not a museum, it's an exhibit. Not about me, about the *Voyager* find," Erik said. "And I really don't think I am a legend."

"People notice, and they resent it," Kowalski continued, as if Erik hadn't spoken. "If they didn't, you could take back half my budget."

Erik grunted again. There had been issues over the years.

"But the rank and file seem to like you," Kowalski pressed. "You have a good reputation with them. People like Hasbro think well of you, and the word spreads. The candidate crew members think you're some kind of visionary."

Erik thought back to his chance encounter with the young woman from Ship Site. He remembered the look in her eyes, the eager respect in her voice. "Why are you telling me this?" he asked.

"Because you need to know that, even with what's happened, you're leaving a legacy," Kowalski said.

Erik looked at him blankly. It was as if someone else entirely sat in his guest chair. He could never have imagined hearing words like those coming from Hector Kowalski.

The younger man continued. "Think about it," he said. "Think about me. Twenty years ago, I was a kid playing with Mesh gameware. I was good at my work, but working for you made me better. You can't lose sight of that."

The shift in Kowalski's overall demeanor abruptly made sense. He was nervous.

Kowalski had been one of the very few constants in Erik's tenure on the Moon. Line staff had come and gone, and his ascent though the corporate hierarchy had cost him more friends than it had made for him, but Kowalski had been a direct-report from nearly the first day. For the first time, as if discovering a new land, Erik wondered at the impact he must have had on the other man's life.

"I—" Erik paused. "Thank you," he said.

There was nothing else he could think to say.

"There is one more factor, though," Kowalski said. "I'm not entirely certain, but it seems barely possible that Rod encountered Wendy Scheer about six years ago, at a symposium on applied genetics."

Erik looked at him in shock. Scheer's status, her very existence, had long been a point of contention between the two men. In the not-so-distant past, the Halo chief had run an espionage network within Villanueva, made up of men and women who had met her and were eager to please.

"How is it possible that you hadn't brought this to my attention before?" Erik asked slowly. As with most of the emotions he had experienced of late, his anger was blunted by grief. Even so, it was still too strong to be denied.

She had gone after his family.

"Didn't know," Kowalski said. "The correlation arose when I was reviewing his activities." He paused. "Did Rod ever say or indicate anything that might reflect her influence?" he asked.

"I didn't have much contact with either of my sons since transferring here," Erik said. "Our careers took us in different paths, and we didn't talk much."

Ashes. His sons were ashes. He would never be able to speak with them again.

"I can't see any advantage she could derive from the encounter," Kowalski said. He was deeply suspicious of Scheer and her motives and always had been. The words of potential absolution came slowly. "It may—*may* have been simple chance."

Erik said nothing.

"There seems to have been no subsequent contact," Kowalski continued. "No message traffic, either. I can't identify any corporate decisions that he might have influenced at her behest, but I can continue the investigation if you want."

As if of its own accord, Erik's hand came up in a dismissive gesture. "No," he said. "Let the dead rest. It doesn't matter now."

Kowalski nodded, visibly relieved to be done with the topic. He continued his report. "To other things, then," he said. "I met with Santiago regarding security for the banquets," he said. "I'd like to make some revisions to media coverage . . ."

On familiar territory again, Kowalski continued. In a cool tone of voice, he outlined minutiae and major concerns alike. Erik only half-listened to him. Focusing was difficult, and, in any case, he knew from experience that Kowalski would provide written reports as backup. Even so, there was a certain comfort to be taken from the familiar business routine.

Kowalski paused. He slid back his right tunic sleeve and inspected the wristband unit, then glanced at Erik. "Were you expecting a visitor?" he asked.

"No," Erik said. "I'm working half-days. No callers, except for you."

"Someone doesn't know that," Kowalski said. "Whoever he is, he's carrying a full complement of surveillance equipment."

A discreet light on Erik's desk flashed. Inex was trying to reach him. He ignored it.

Kowalski did something to his portable display. "It looks like medical gear," he continued. "Remote electroencephalograph, electrocardiograph, respiration product analyzer, and voice/stress analyzer. It's all professional-grade equipment."

"You can tell all that from here?" Erik asked. He was impressed.

"Most of the operating brainware resides on the Mesh, and I'm monitoring data traffic." Kowalski looked up. "No whois ID, but I'd guess it's your doctor."

Erik made a sound of disgust. He leaned close to his desktop unit and opened an audio-only link to Inex in the outer office. "Inex, Sander Adkins is out there, isn't he?"

"Um—yes, yes, he is," came the reply.

He had surprised her. That was to the good.

"Tell him I'm getting ready to leave. I can see him for five minutes, but he'll have to wait five minutes for that, all right?"

The reply was in Adkins's voice. *"That's fine, Erik,"* the counselor said. *"I was hoping we could have lunch!"*

Rather than reply, Erik broke the connection. "What can he learn with a rig like that?" he asked.

"It depends on what he wants to know," Kowalski said. "You've had a recent tragedy, and he wants to know how you're dealing with it. The breath-tester will tell him if you're using psychotropics, or drinking to excess—"

Erik flinched, however slightly.

"—but he'd need several sessions to get a meaningful read, I'd think," Kowalski said. He stood, letting his tunic sleeve fall back into place. "The real question is *why*," he continued. "You're not friends, are you?"

"No," Erik said. He sometimes wondered if he had any friends at all.

"When was the last time you had a session with him?" Kowalski asked.

"Seven years ago," Erik said. "A follow-up, after the foundry incident."

"Someone's put him on you, then," Kowalski said. "Do you want me to deal with him?"

"Not now," Erik said. "Not here." He drew his slim briefcase from its recess beneath his desk and opened it. Sheets of plastic foolscap and data pods lay within. He scooped them out and set them on his desktop, creating the illusion of work. "But look into it. And if you know some way to block his equipment, find it for me. I didn't come this far to live in an ant farm."

"Ant farm?" Kowalski asked, confused. "What's that?"

"Never mind that now," Erik said. "Get back to me when you have something."

"ERIK," Adkins said, his booming voice a mismatch for his slender frame. "It's so good of you to make time!" He extended his hand, twisting it at the last moment so that it came in up and under Erik's. Instead of hooking thumbs, the two men shook hands, the old-fashioned way.

It was a presumption, but one with a reason, Erik realized as the counselor's hand enclosed his. The psychotherapist wore rings on each finger, mesh circlets that were discreet but still readily noticeable. They were likely part of the personal sensor array that Kowalski had detected.

There was so much of human communication that occurred nonverbally, Erik realized yet again. Even the best Mesh links gave only a small percentage of the information available to a skilled participant, or a well-equipped one.

"I don't think you gave me much choice," Erik said. Deliberately, he allowed both indulgence and irritation to color his words. "I have a busy calendar, Sander," he said. "You should remember that from the old days."

He pulled his hand from the other man's, just emphatically enough to underscore his point.

Adkins nodded. "I know, I know," he said. He waved both hands in mock surrender, and the mesh of his rings glinted in the office light. "But I had an appointment in this sector, and I wanted to talk to you. I truly am glad you agreed to see me," he said.

"Five minutes," Erik said. "I have appointments of my own." He made a minor drama of repacking his briefcase, filling it again with the plastic printout and data pods that he had scattered about his desk. Kowalski had left before Adkins had entered, and Erik had made the counselor wait ten minutes rather than five. He wanted very much for the doctor to carry away the impression of a man dealing with grief by focusing on work.

The impression of productivity was nearly as important as the real thing.

"You didn't return my call," Sander said, with mild reproof. "Not personally."

"I've been very busy," Erik said. His desk drawer held a small stockpile of disposable personal computers. He rolled up a half-dozen of the ephemeral things and stowed them in his valise. He was careful not to meet Adkins's gaze as he worked.

"Erik," Adkins said gently. "I'm a professional. I know the symptoms of transient depression."

The words stung. Erik's head came up as if on a string. "Transient?" he snapped.

"'Incidental,' if you prefer," Adkins said agreeably. Without asking permission, he settled into the guest chair that Kowalski had vacated. He eyed Erik. "Sleeplessness," he said, then half-smiled, briefly. "Or excessive sleep; it's a paradox. Moodiness. Difficulty in focus. Withdrawal from certain kinds of personal contact. Substance abuse." One by one, Adkins ticked them off on his ringed fingers.

"I'm coping," Erik said. He settled on to the edge of his desk. The fixture's top was a beveled slab of polished gray stone, quarried from one of the ancient lava flows that dappled the Moon's surface. Even in low gravity, his weight made the stone's sharp edge dig into his fundament, but he stayed where he was. He wanted to appear as at ease as possible.

"Are you?" Adkins asked.

Erik nodded. "I'm better at these things myself," he said.

"No, you aren't," Sanders said. "I know you, Erik. Not well, but well enough. Remember our sessions after the foundry incident?"

"Not as well as you seem to," Erik said sourly. More likely, the counselor had reviewed his notes from those days.

"You did what you're doing now," Adkins continued implacably. "You pulled back. You buried yourself in work. You didn't confront the situation."

"That's not true," Erik said. This time, he managed not to snap the words. "I remember that much, at least."

The foundry incident had been a disaster. It had happened during the initial pour for the casings of the great engines that would drive the ship to the solar system's outer reaches. Terrorist sabotage had resulted in a spill of liquid metal and multiple injuries and deaths. One of those deaths had been of Sarrah Chrysler, a woman whom Erik had slowly been coming to love.

The culprit who had placed the bomb that caused the spill had been Enola Hasbro, according to the initial investigation.

Adkins nodded. "But not for months. It was months before you spoke to Hasbro directly."

"Everyone thought Hasbro had done it," Erik said. He had thought so, too. It wasn't a pleasant memory, but being wrong almost never was.

"She didn't," Adkins said. He settled farther back into the chair's springy embrace, half-reclining. He crossed his legs so that the soles of his big shoes confronted Erik. He seemed utterly at ease.

That was the point, Erik realized. He had taken enough organizational management studies to realize when he was being manipulated.

"She knew she *hadn't*," Adkins continued. He spoke calmly. "I think *you* knew, too."

His words stunned. They hit Erik with almost physical force. He stiffened in response. "I testified against her," he said. Anger and adrenaline made him feel more alive than he had in days. "I would never have done that if—"

"Not if you knew it consciously," Adkins said, still agreeably. "I think part of you did." He looked at Erik steadily. "Or, a part of you had difficulty believing in her guilt. And a review of our sessions from those days tends to support that conclusion."

"A man with your responsibilities must have other demands on your time," Erik said. "I know that I do."

It was a warning.

Adkins continued, speaking as if Erik had not. "It's a basic truism of life that people are conflicted, Erik. They spend time and effort to avoid confronting trauma and associated emotions. You wanted resolution on the Chrysler woman's death and your own injuries. You want *closure,* to use a word I don't much like. If Hasbro hadn't kept asking to see you—"

"Why are you here?" Erik asked. His own facade of affable hospitality dropped away completely now. "Who set you on me?"

"I know you, Erik. I've studied you. I'm here because I think you need help," Adkins said. His bushy eyebrows moved closer together. "You need to deal with the emotional impact of your sons' deaths, and I think you need help doing that."

"Who set you on me?" Erik asked again. He stood and closed his briefcase. It was the concluding act of his busy-work charade, a signal to Adkins that he was preparing to leave. The two halves sealed themselves together with a re-assuring hiss.

"I hear things, Erik," Adkins said. His eyes were bright and attentive as he watched Erik carefully. "You would be surprised to know the names of some of the people who talk to me on a regular basis."

"I might," Erik agreed.

Not at Erik's behest but with his permission, Kowalski had periodically attempted to research personal medical data on highly placed members of management. His success had been minimal; such files were sacrosanct, espe-cially for people in positions of power. Despite the high security, however, Adkins's name had come up more than once on appointment calendars and meeting logs.

"I urge you to consider getting help," Adkins said. "These are momentous times, and you need to be at the peak of your decision-making ability. I'm here as a coworker—"

"I'm Over-Management now," Erik interrupted, re-minding him.

"You're an EnTek man at heart," Adkins said. "And my services are available though Over-Management, at any rate. You know that."

Erik said nothing.

"If not me, then," Adkins resumed. "Consider joining a grief group. At least access some interactive Meshware. I can make recommendations—"

Erik interrupted again. *"Sorrow as a Discontinuous Process?"* he asked. The titles of the feeds he had pur-chased came up easily from his memory, but he hated say-ing them. *"Good Things End? Pain Has Its Reasons?"*

Now, at last, Adkins seemed taken aback. He blinked, surprised by the ready citations. "Those are good choices," he said slowly. "*Discontinuous* is especially good. But you can't do it on your own."

"I'm dealing with the situation," Erik said. He allowed some warmth to enter his voice. "Sander," he said. "I appreciate your concern. Truly, I do. But I'll be fine."

HE looked better than Trine had expected. He looked younger and more handsome than he had in the directory photo. She wasn't at all sure that he was attractive, at least not in the usual sense, but he looked interesting.

Hector Kowalski, perched on the corner barstool, looked up from the menu screen and glanced at her. "You're studying me," he said, and then began to read again.

Trine blushed.

Kowalski, still apparently working his way through the selection list, continued. "Don't be embarrassed," he said. "People study one another. It's what they do. But it works better if you're not obvious about it."

"Oh," Trine said. With a finger-stroke, she starred her tentative selections, a soy-burger with new-bacon and radish salad. They were familiar foods, the kind of fare she could have ordered in the Ship Site mess.

"You're in your early thirties," Kowalski said. He spoke without looking up again. "You're well educated. You make a good salary from your work, but you have a tendency to scrimp. I'm not sure why. You're not cheap, but frugal, and tend to buy quality goods."

Trine felt her features flare again, this time from anger. "You've been back in my personnel file," she said sharply. "That's not nice."

"No, it wasn't," Kowalski said. Now he glanced at her

again, making eye contact. His gaze was coolly appraising, but unchallenging. "I could tell by the way you dress, and by the restaurant you suggested, and by what you've selected." Now, at last, he smiled. "It's my treat, by the way."

They were in an out-of-the-way Fargoes! Colony planners had tucked the restaurant into a corridor bend near the Bessemer Conduit's terminus. Rents and traffic were both lower there, and the restaurant prices were lower, too, even if the food was precisely the same as what would have been served at the Mall outlet.

Fargoes! was a chain that catered to the casual diner. It wasn't Trine's favorite place to eat, but her experience was that men liked it, because of the masculine decor or the attractive waitstaff, or both. She and Kowalski had commandeered a corner of the long bar, private enough for easy conversation but open enough to keep things casual.

"Oh," she said. "Thank you." Two more taps of her fingertip and the soy-burger was de-opted, replaced by broccoli florets in a light cream sauce. Fargoes! served excellent broccoli and priced it accordingly. "What's wrong with the way I dress?" she asked lightly.

She was wearing parachute pants that flattered her stubby legs and a knit top that fit snugly enough to keep things interesting but not obvious. She had pulled her dark hair back and clipped it into place with silver-finished barrettes that were at least as ornamental as functional.

"Nothing," Kowalski said. "You dress well, in fact. But you buy for quality rather than trendiness or false economy." He looked up from his menu-screen. "Ready?" he asked.

She nodded, and he placed orders for both of them. It was an old-fashioned gesture that she found oddly charming. Her father had ordered meals for her mother that way.

"Why did you call on me, Trine?" Kowalski asked.

Trine blinked. That wasn't the kind of question she had ever heard her father ask. She wasn't entirely sure how to answer it.

"I mean, no one *ever* calls me," Kowalski said. "Not socially, at least."

A lazy grin lightened his features some more, and for the first time Trine realized that he probably wore facial appliances. She wondered which was the real Hector Kowalski: the nondescript functionary in the Mesh directory or the slightly boyish character seated at cross-angles from her.

"I like meeting new people, and I don't get to very often," Trine said, not entirely truthfully. The candidate crew Ship Site was very nearly a closed social set, but visitors weren't uncommon. "And you seemed interesting."

In that, at least, she was 100 percent honest.

"Interesting, or potentially advantageous to your career?" Kowalski asked. Again, Trine could hear no particular challenge in his voice, just professional curiosity. The question seemed to be his idea of a pleasantry.

"Interesting," Trine said, without offense. There weren't very many men in her experience willing to linger on a Ship Site hull, just to see the sun rise on the Earth. For most of her fellow candidate crewmembers, the novelty and awe had long since faded away.

"Good," Kowalski said. He sipped beer from a self-frosting stein at his elbow. The dark amber liquid left a white froth on his upper lip. "So," he said. "Tell me about yourself. Tell me things that I don't know."

"I don't know what you don't know," Trine said. She surprised herself by half-giggling.

"Pretend I don't know anything," Kowalski said.

He proved to be a skilled listener, paying close attention,

as Trine told him about her life. She told him about her childhood in Hawaii's relocation camps and her parents' insistence that she find some way to attend school in their native Alaska. She alluded just strongly enough to her brief, failed marriage that he would know had happened, even if he knew none of the details. She told him about her decision to compete for a candidate crew slot, and about the program of psychological and genetic testing that had followed, all in answer to gently probing questions.

At some point during the discourse, their food arrived and they began eating. By the time Trine started to tell Kowalski of her assignment to the extra-vehicular activity crew, she had finished the salad and nearly consumed the broccoli. The cream sauce was thicker than she had expected, but good.

"I've been talking a long time," Trine said suddenly, toying with the last of her food. "You tell me something. Why are you here? I really didn't expect you to call me back."

"Hmm?" Kowalski asked, still dividing his attention between her and his meal. Trine had never seen a man order and consume so much food in a single sitting. Already, he had eaten two soy-burgers with quick, methodical bites, then an entire tray of Thai nachos. Now he was eyeing the breadbasket that had come with Trine's entrée. It was a wonder he wasn't fat.

"What do you mean?" Kowalski asked.

"You're a busy man," she said. "An important one. I didn't realize how important until after I messaged you."

That had been an adventure, in and of itself. Trine had spent nearly an hour sorting through a morass of automated replies and testy queries from Kowalski's underlings. Messaging Morrison had proven easier.

"If you didn't expect me to respond, why did you query?" Kowalski asked. He made it sound like the most reasonable question in either world.

Trine shrugged. She had no ready answer.

Kowalski took a croissant from the breadbasket. Flakes sifted between his fingers as he broke it. "I don't know why," he said. "No. I do. I wanted some perspective."

"Perspective?" Trine asked.

He nodded. "You're right, Trine. My work keeps me busy, and most of the people I meet in my work aren't the best." He ate half the croissant with two bites. "It wears on me, sometimes. It affects how I see things—"

"Excuse me," their waitperson said, interrupting. She pushed a dessert cart closer. "Can I interest you in something for after?"

Trine had been focused so tightly on Kowalski that she hadn't noticed the trim young woman approach. She was everything that Trine would like to be, lean and willowy (whatever willows were). She wore the Fargoes! uniform du jour, what looked like a cartoon of welder's gear. Trine managed not to make eye contact with her.

"So I thought it might be nice to chat with someone who asked to see me," Kowalski said. He had chosen something with many layers and an absurd amount of gooey filling. "I thought it might be *fun*," he amended.

He shoveled countless calories into his mouth. Trine refrained from shuddering as she watched.

"I met someone who knows you," she said.

"Oh?" Kowalski's fork paused in mid-trajectory.

"A coworker," she said. "Erik Morrison. I'm supposed to see him next week."

The fork, still laden with food, returned to Kowalski's plate. His expression became neutral, polite but remote.

"Oh?" he asked again, but in professional mode now. "How did you happen to encounter Morrison?"

Trine told him of her visit to the Mall and about recognizing the site coordinator. She told him about Morrison's casual invitation to the dedication ceremony, and something about Kowalski's eyes told her that he planned to verify her account.

"He looked very unhappy," Trine said. She was careful to make her words an observation and not to sound like she was prying. "He seemed sad."

Kowalski had relaxed some fractional degree. "He's had some bad news," he said, but didn't elaborate.

She nodded. Another detail of the chance encounter presented itself to her and demanded to be told. "Um," she said, then continued slowly. "I told him I'd met you. I told him you referred to him as 'the Old Man.'"

Again, Kowalski surprised her. He snickered. He reclaimed his fork, emptied it into his mouth, then chewed and swallowed. "How did he respond to that?" he asked.

"He laughed," Trine said. She thought back. "He seemed pleased."

"Good," Kowalski said. "That's good." He began to eat again.

CHAPTER 6

"ATTEND in my place," Erik said again, this time more forcefully.

"I don't feel comfortable doing that," Inex said. She didn't look comfortable saying so, either.

They were in Erik's office, with Erik behind his desk and Inex standing stiffly at attention before it. When she had entered the room, she had been relaxed and at ease. Now, frustration and irritation colored her voice and affected her stance. Yet again, Erik was struck at how personal presence affected human communication.

"People are beginning to ask questions," Inex said, after a deep breath. "They asked questions at last week's banquet, and they've been asking since. About your absence, and about other things. You have no idea what my message traffic is like."

"I can get you assistance," Erik said. Inex's words seemed to come to him as from a great distance. He supposed that her general air of confrontation should have concerned him, but he couldn't bring himself to treat it seriously.

It was cool and comfortable in his office. He had selected each of the suite's furnishings and personally configured its ambient environmental parameters. He had made it a place that would impress visitors while ensuring him that his own long days passed as easily as possible. He should have been happy here, or at least at ease.

He wasn't happy now. He felt dead inside.

"I don't need assistance," Inex said, still with some heat. "I need *you*."

She really was very attractive, Erik realized anew. She was lean and graceful and dressed with easy elegance. On more than one occasion in his personal experience, she had made a wonderful dinner companion.

"You'll do fine," Erik said.

"I wish that you would at least remote-audit tonight's function," she said. "Being there by Mesh would be better than not being there at all. This series was your idea, and you're supposed to be part of it. They're coming to see you, not your assistant."

"They're coming to see a presentation and enjoy a meal, and to receive some recognition for their hard work," Erik said. He had insisted on that. Each member of the candidate crew hoped that he or she would be on the craft, come launch day. Half of them would not. Erik continued, "They'll have all that. I'm unavailable."

He toyed with an ornamental document weight at the very periphery of his desk's work area. It was an irregular lump of meteoric iron, dark gray except for where handling had made it gleam dully. He took it up in one hand. He liked the way it felt, substantial and cool.

Why was Inex behaving like this? The opportunity he

had assigned her was a major step forward. Busy hours during the day and some glad-handing in the evenings seemed a reasonable price to pay. She could meet business contacts that would last her for her entire career.

Inex sighed. She relaxed, however slightly, and Erik knew that he had won. "I'll do my best," she said. "But when guests inquire—"

"I'm unavailable this week," Erik said.

"The Horvath party will want to reschedule, then," Inex said.

Erik flinched. He set down the lump of metal but kept his fingers curled loosely around it. "They're auditing tonight?" he asked.

"I messaged you yesterday," Inex reminded him. She seemed subtly pleased with herself. "You flagged it as having been reviewed."

He didn't reply. She had caught him in an untruth. Resentment flared. A supervisor had the right to make minor untruths.

Inex pressed the point. She was all too familiar with his usual attention to detail. "I appended it to the audit feeds of the event," she said. "Have you watched them? You said you wanted to see the event itself."

"I haven't," he said shortly. "I will."

Inex took another deep breath. She eyed him for a long moment. When she spoke again, it was more gently. "Erik," she said. "Are you seeing anyone?"

He looked at her.

"Are you seeing anyone to help you deal with your loss?" she asked. "Your sons?"

"Who told you about that?" he demanded. Did everyone know?

"People talk," Inex said. "You know that. You used to ask me to bring you up-to-date office gossip."

"That's different," he said. Gathering office scuttlebutt was simply good internal intelligence. Talking about him was something else entirely.

"Adkins says—"

"I don't want you talking to Adkins," Erik interrupted. His earlier sense of detachment boiled away, and the world jumped into sharp focus. "More to the point, I don't want Adkins talking to my staff. I hope he hasn't been." The idea was deeply offensive.

"He's concerned about you," Inex said, taken aback. She seemed to realize that her last jab, however inadvertent, had awakened the tiger.

"When?" Erik asked.

The single word of the question was enough. Inex blushed. "While he was waiting to see you," she said.

"What did he ask?" Erik pressed.

"I—I didn't record," she said. "Perhaps I should have, but—"

"What?" Erik asked.

"It was small talk," she said. "He was very solicitous. He wanted to know your state of mind."

"Did he mention anyone else in management?" Erik asked.

She shook her head.

"*Hmph,*" Erik said. He lifted the document weight again, raised it, and let it fall. The lump of iron was small and dense enough that it fell quickly, but not as quickly as it would have on Earth. Inex's eyes—an electric green today—tracked the descent. When it clicked against the desktop, her eyelids fell, too, briefly.

"I'm sorry," she said, looking at him again.

"It's not an issue," Erik said. "But remember it in the future."

He wondered what she was thinking now, what mixture

of concern and self-interest filled her mind. He knew all too well that he had been moody of late. Inex was a competent and confident young woman, not like some whom he had recruited to his line staff, but even she had her insecurities. She must be wondering now if she had damaged her status in his eyes.

"I want you to represent me at the banquet," he said. His tone was gentle but firm. "It seems I have some materials that I haven't reviewed, but need to. I don't think I'd be a good host, in any case." He paused. "You know the material better than I do."

"Most of it's canned," she said. The briefing that was the heart of each banquet had been laboriously prepared in advance. A phalanx of writers, image modelers, and audience-response specialists had worked together under her close guidance. Erik had reviewed and approved the process, but Inex had lived it.

"I know," he said. "I delivered the first, remember?"

She nodded.

He forced himself to smile. "And I'll deliver the next one, too, all right?"

She nodded again. "Erik," she said. "I really am sorry about your sons. You should have told us."

"I know you are," he said.

HEURISTIC Genetech was a joint venture between EnTek and Biome, funded by a federal contract and staffed by a brain trust of organic systems management specialists. For contracting reasons that Hector Kowalski didn't understand completely, Heuristic had been awarded the privilege of finalizing the Gummi processors and associated brainware that would serve as the central operating system of the deep-space ship, when launched.

Status as a priority contractor alone had been enough to justify keeping a close eye on the operation. The discovery of junk alleles in Heuristic's product had made a closer review mandatory.

The facility was remarkably mundane, or at least very, very typical. In reasonably secure spaces in the lowermost levels of Villanueva, white cabinets, long and low, hummed in controlled environments. They were each of them a closed system; within their confines, genetically engineered semiliving long-chain polymer compounds replicated according to painstakingly built-in guidelines. Equally complex servitor quasi-organisms shared their boxed realities, depositing brainware engrams in the form of coded molecules. Matured, inactivated, refined, and validated, the complex strands would be the beginning of the ship's final Mesh.

The nanomachine revolution predicted in the previous century had never truly come to pass. Hector, who prided himself on pragmatism, wondered sometimes if something better hadn't been found, instead.

He glided among the cabinets with a smooth, steady pace and the easy presence of someone who was absolutely certain he was precisely where he belonged. He wore the white laboratory jacket that was a scientist's equivalent of holy vestments. They were required wear in the sensitive environment.

He carried a passive recording device. Lines and values flickered on the device's viewer as it accessed and recorded the breeding cabinets' diagnostics. Everything seemed fine.

Pym's office, when Hector found it, proved to be more of the same. It was as different from Morrison's as Hector could have imagined, and the idea of working in such a space set his teeth on edge. It was white on white, with the only hints of color being the furnishings. They, too, were white, but human contact had made them less sterile-looking.

"Who are you?" Pym asked as Hector entered his sanctum without asking permission and dropped into the guest chair. "Do I know you?"

"Security," Hector said easily. He used the recorder screen to flash the current EnTek logo. He worked for Over-Management now, but EnTek management was cooperative on such matters, and Heuristic staff would be more likely to talk if they thought they were talking to ownership representatives. "I messaged you earlier," he continued. "Did you receive it?"

Pym was the darkest thing in the room and seemed to suck light toward himself. He had skin the color of boiled new-coffee and black hair, cropped short and close to his skull. His eyes were dark, too, as he referenced his computer. Whether it was real or enhanced, he had the kind a face that could have belonged to a man of nearly any age, but Hector knew that he was sixty-three.

"Oh," Pym said. "Yes. I'm sorry. It was a hectic morning, and I am still somewhat behind." He extended one hand. "Dailey Pym."

"Hector Kowalski," Hector said as they hooked thumbs. He generally used his own name unless there was a reason not to. "I'm running some background checks, Dailey," he said.

Pym smiled. He had the largest, whitest teeth Hector had ever seen, and the smile seemed competently sincere. "Again? Here? I thought you folks did most of that work on-Mesh," he said.

Hector shrugged. The observation he had made to Morrison a few days before came back to him. "We can't track everything," he said.

"I can understand that," Pym said. "Can I get you something to drink, Hector?"

His easy use of Hector's given name was a good sign. Rapport was important to any interrogation.

"Milk would go well," Hector said. "If you have it." It was a safe bet that Pym did. High-calcium beverages were a staple. They helped retard loss of bone mass in the Moon's low-gravity environment.

The processor that Hector carried was large for its type, with a surface area that was roughly equivalent to that of his two hands combined. It had leaves, like an old-style book, and Hector opened it now. Even as Pym set the self-cooling glass before him, Hector had opened the files he needed and was reading the information they presented.

"You're site manager, right?" he asked.

Pym nodded. "I'm pretty sure you already know that," he said easily. He spoke in a deep baritone and with a rolling drawl, the mark of a childhood spent deep in the United States South. It was the kind of voice that would make almost anyone feel welcome.

Not even Hector was immune to its charm. He leaned closer as he nodded. "It's a formality," he said, and opened some more files. "Dailey, if you have the time, I'd like to talk to you about some of your staff."

Dailey had the time. For nearly an hour, Hector asked him questions. Heuristics held holiday parties regularly; had Pym noticed any attendees drinking to excess? The new data shepherd, Douglas Huong, had left Biome proper to come here in a lateral move, and had he ever said anything about his reasons? Hector couldn't help but notice that Callie Aims had secured her career in genetic manipulation from the University of New Sacramento. Did Callie attend reunions, and if she did, had she ever voiced any opinions about her classmates? Most of them worked for other companies, after all.

For the most part, they were junk queries. He made such queries more to build a relationship than to elicit hard data, but the responses were useful, nonetheless. Hector's processor recorded each reply (with Pym's ready permission) and monitored various associated metabolic responses that might indicate veracity or lack of same (without Pym's knowledge).

"Were you part of the bid team?" Hector asked. He sipped from his glass. The milk was cool and soothing and could have come from an actual cow. "For the ship processors, I mean."

Pym nodded. "Hell of a thing. We put the proposal together back on Earth," he said. "I relocated ten days after contract award."

"EnTek had previously held the contract directly, without any intervening subsidiary or joint venture," Hector said. "I assume your superiors told you of the opportunity? I know it was a small-business set-aside."

Now Hector shook his head. "No," he said. "I'd been keeping any eye out for it. Or something like it. I was ready to jump."

"Oh?" Hector asked. He sipped his milk.

"I'd followed the colony news pretty closely for years," Pym said. "When Morrison found *Voyager,* I knew that there were sure to be opportunities."

Voyager had been one of Earth's earliest deep-space probes. The unmanned craft had exited the solar system decades before. With it had gone elaborate scientific instrumentation and information about Earth and the people who lived there. Forces—persons?—unknown had sent it back. The public at large thought of Erik Morrison as the man who had found the thing's broken fragments, when all he had really done was bring them to the attention of the ALC.

Pym continued. "I wanted to do work like this, ever since I was a child, though," he said.

"Why?" Hector asked. The ALC had designated deep-space exploration as a potential profit center during the period that followed the *Voyager* find. The Feds' interest in defense and "pure" science had underscored that designation. From what Pym said, he had taken an interest much earlier than that.

Pym took a long breath. "Have you ever heard of the Gaia Hypothesis?" he asked.

"No," Hector said, shaking his head.

"It's a theory from the last century," Pym said. "It looks at the Earth as a single organism, with a life and death cycle of its own. Even a reproductive drive."

Hector was usually very good at hiding his thoughts, but this time he must have failed, because Pym laughed.

"I know," he said. "Said like that, it sounds silly."

"I find it hard to think of planets having sex," Hector said. He made a mental note to review Pym's psych profile.

"Not like that," Pym said. "More like germination and seeding."

"And the seeds—?"

"We're the seeds," Pym said. "That's the theory, anyway. We seeded the Moon. It's time to move on. I thought that, even before the *Voyager* find."

"That was almost twenty years ago," Hector said.

"The federal procurement process is complex and wondrous," Pym said. "And I had to wait years after I joined EnTek before I could bid on that kind of contract, anyway."

Hector made a show of referencing his file on Pym. "That's right," he said, musing. "You were a Fed, until you job-hopped." He paused and shook his head with feigned rue. "I'm sorry," he said. "I don't mean to be rude."

"I don't mind," Pym said. "I always wanted to work in the private sector—who wouldn't?—but there was a quarantine period. Insider information and all that."

"Why did you make the move?" Hector asked. The entire interview had led to the question, by a route that he hoped Pym had not noticed. "To Villanueva, I mean."

"I believe in space travel," Pym said simply. "I wanted to be part of the process."

"You could have relocated earlier," Hector said. He made the statement a light one, as if it were of no import. "You could have come to the Moon before."

"Hah," Pym said. "The Moon isn't space travel. It's visiting an off-shore derrick. Trans-Plutonian exploration is what interested me. We should have been there decades ago."

"You're not in the candidate crew," Hector said. "Did you compete to join?"

His host laughed again. "No, of course not," he said. "Too old, not smart enough. But I could be part of the process. I could make my contribution."

Hector closed his processor unit, as if preparing to leave, but he left it live. Casually, he said, "So, the *Voyager* find came as good news to you?" he asked.

"Of course it did," Pym said. He chuckled with evident warmth. "When I was a *Fed,* to use your term, I used to hope and pray that someone would find something like that Morrison fellow found. I was a Census Agency systems administrator, but they couldn't keep me busy. I time-shared with other agencies, maybe too much. My wife left me because I spent three evenings a week helping out at Hello."

" 'Hello'?" Hector said, speaking more sharply than he had intended. The word was a nickname that he heard often, but didn't like. It sounded too friendly.

"Hello," Pym said, with a nostalgic expression on his broad, handsome features. "Some of my happiest hours were doing grunt work for the planning committees that steered Project Halo."

CHAPTER 7

THE apartment housekeeper greeted him by announcing the receipt of fourteen messages during Erik's afternoon absence and began listing them by category.

"Later," Erik said in his command voice. He dropped his briefcase on his workstation table and moved to the refreshment nook. He had taken the hard way home today, and his body knew it. More than a week of greatly reduced activity, and the walkways and ladders had taken their toll. The long muscles in his arms and legs hurt, and he needed something to sooth them.

It made a good excuse, at least.

"One is personal priority," the housekeeper said.

"Later," Erik said again. A bottle on the lower shelf held imported Earth bourbon, the same make and proof that he remembered from his years in Australia. He broke the seal, poured himself a generous portion, and placed the glass on a serving tray. He flanked it with the bottle and a second glass. This one he filled with what was the Mall shop had claimed was spring water, imported from Earth and sold at absurd expense.

The refreshment nook had auto-serve capabilities, but he almost never made use of them. There was comfort in serving himself. His father had followed the same ritual, and Erik remembered it well watching him in the early evening, when long hours had stretched between work and dinner.

The housekeeper persisted. *"Personal priority from Sylva Taschen,"* it said.

"Later," Erik said again. The night before, he had wanted very much to speak with her. Now, perversely, he did not. She asked too many questions and made too many suggestions.

He set the little tray on the workstation table, next to his briefcase, and seated himself. The fluids slopped a bit in their receptacles. Low gravity gave their surface undulations a hypnotic quality.

Inex had given him the coverage from the banquet that she had attended in his stead. It was raw feed, taken from a dozen cameras that had roamed the hall under brainware guidance. At some point, EnTek Public Relations would assemble programming based on it and on the coverage from the other events, for review by management and, ultimately, Mesh release. For now, however, Erik was one of the few with access to the material. He jacked the first of the data pods into his workstation.

One privilege of rank was that his home personal brainware complement included absolute state-of-the-art media capabilities, in an age when the difference between consumer- and professional-level was nearly nonexistent. With the ease of experience, he set his personal preferences. Viewpoints, editing style, sound quality, enhancement options—he entered them one at a time, guided by the gentle prompting of the system Gummi and based on the data available.

It was easy work, but getting it right took time. Nearly fifteen minutes had passed before he finished the configuration process, and the level of dark amber whiskey in his glass had dropped noticeably. Without leaving the workstation, he sipped "spring" water and replenished his drink.

"Play," he said in his command voice, and the wallpaper came to life.

"GOOD evening," Inex Santiago said. She was blond tonight, with her hair in long braids, and she had done something to her skin. The tawny gold that was the legacy of her ancestors had given way to a fairness that bordered on alabaster. In a white evening gown and tasteful silver jewelry, Inex could have been a Norse goddess rather than a child of the Brazilian meritocracy.

"I'm pleased that all of you could join us tonight," she said in warm, welcoming tones. "I'm very sorry to say that Erik Morrison is unable to attend, but I hope you'll accept me in his place. I don't believe that your program materials have been updated yet; I'm Inex Santiago, Erik's personal assistant and deputy for this series of events."

She stood where Erik should have stood, alone on the interactive dais before an attentive audience that numbered some two hundred. Behind her, Mesh display screens stretched from floor to vaulted ceiling, awaiting live input from remote locations or recorded feeds. Despite Inex's professed reluctance to serve as hostess, she seemed utterly at ease as she spoke.

The audience liked her. Polite applause swept through the hall, mingled with murmured questions and comments.

Thirty tables nearly filled the seating area of the Zonix Hospitality hall. Multiple steeply raked levels rose high behind one another to provide unobstructed views both of the dais and of the wallpaper displays. Seated at the tables, sipping cocktails and nibbling canapés, were the men and women of the candidate crew, along with representatives of upper management. Waitstaff drifted among them, refreshing the drinks. Live service was a horrendous expense for such a large function, but also an emphatic demonstration of respect and recognition. All attendees faced Inex.

"I'd like to welcome the members of upper management who've joined us here," Inex continued. "Welcome them, but not introduce them, at least not now. They can wait." Inex's lips parted in a smile, revealing perfect teeth. "I think we can all agree that they've already had their share of recognition, can't we?"

The joke had been written for Erik. Delivered by him, it would have been dry and witty and even self-deprecating, but delivered by his subordinate, it sounded wry and barbed.

Even so, the audience laughed. The best-dressed of the attendees laughed politely, their smiles artificial and deliberate. These were the celebrity guests, the upper management members and shareholders and media figures who were here to be seen. They laughed at their own expense because they could afford do, and because it simply wouldn't do to have a reputation as a poor sport.

The majority of the attendees, however, were the men and women of the candidate crew, and they were more heartily amused. They were the workers, the technicians and programmers and specialists whose labors gave Ship Site life. This was their night, and they knew it. More to the point, they had accepted Erik's assistant as one of their own.

Inex smiled again, more widely this time, and made a mock-curtsy. *"Good,"* she said. *"Then, if no one minds, I'll continue to focus on you, the candidate crew, for the moment. Then, I hope you'll enjoy the excellent meal prepared for you, and after that, we'll all mingle. The Very Important People can hook thumbs with the Very, Very Important People, and we can all argue about who is which."*

More laughter followed, mingled this time with applause. It faded as Inex raised one hand for silence.

"Please," she said. *"I'd like you to do something for me. I'd like each of you look to your right, then to your left."* She paused as her audience obeyed. *"Good,"* she said. *"I'm sure you know what I'm about to say. We're all educated people, and we've all had instructors tell us to do that. We all know the point I'm about to make."*

She took a breath before continuing, in a slightly more serious tone of voice. *"Unless you had the good fortune to be seated next to one of our distinguished visitors, you just looked at two of your coworkers. I'm sure the faces were familiar. According to the current payroll, candidate crew members stationed Ship Site number five hundred and seven. That's really not very many people, is it? Not when you work together for months at a time, in the confines of Ship Site."*

Again, she paused, this time for effect. *"In six months, management will announce the final crew assignments,"* she said. *"In seven months, five hundred and seven will be cut to two hundred and thirty-four, more or less. Your neighbors tonight may not be among that number. You may not. Less than half the personnel here will receive billets."*

The audience murmured. Men and women leaned close to tablemates and whispered to one another. Hope and apprehension mingled on young features. The members of the candidate crew had worked long and hard to attain their current status, but they knew all too well that final selection was beyond their control. Lottery selection, psychological profiling, and genetic factors would work together in an unpredictable equation to determine the choice.

"In twelve months," Inex continued, *"the ship will leave lunar orbit and begin the journey to deep space. Some of you will be on that inaugural crew.*

"The assignments won't be without risk. Even the best and most optimistic projections say that many of you will not return. The earliest possible return date is fifty years in our future. Fifty years is the shortest projected duration of your journey, and fifty years is a long time. The hazards you will face during that half-century are many." She paused. *"Even so, I know that each of you wants to make that journey. I'd like to, too. I wish that I were going with you."*

Those words had been intended for Erik, too. They had been written by him, to be delivered by him. He had insisted that they remain in each successive draft, despite impassioned arguments of staff writers and media specialists who were reluctant even to fantasize about losing such a prominent figure to adventure's call. Erik was all too aware that, in some ways, he had become a management figurehead.

Erik had intended the words to be a morale builder, a gesture of camaraderie, but their import had grown with each review and rehearsal. Now, even spoken by Inex, they seemed to ring with sincerity and passion.

"But I'm not," Inex said. She managed to sound sincere. *"You're the ones who will get the job done. And we all salute you, and celebrate you, and offer you all our heart-felt thanks."*

A dignified-looking man at a front table was the first to stand. A Mesh callout labeled him as a Duckworth

Foundries account executive, with three years experience administering a major construction contract. He stood, and the others at his table stood with him, driving their hands together in applause as they turned to face the rest of the audience. Then, one by one, the dining parties at neighboring tables followed suit, applauding the candidate crew in attendance.

It was a rare thing to see ALC movers and shakers cede the spotlight to what so many called "the little people." Even though it had been carefully planned and coordinated by Inex and her task team, the demonstration seemed sincere and heartfelt. The future crew of the deep-space probe had become media darlings in recent years, as a group if not as individuals. For the moment, at least, they commanded considerable respect from in increasingly fickle public, and management was eager to share in that respect.

That would change soon, for so many in the crowded hall. The glory would pass. Once selection had been made, more than half of tonight's attendees would lose their special status. Celebrity would fall away as they were reabsorbed into the colony workforce, to go on with lives that had been brushed briefly by greatness. Down-selected, they would remember this event as a high point of their professional lives, a story to tell children and grandchildren.

After a long moment, Inex raised her hand again and gestured for silence. Another moment passed before she got it.

"Please," she said. "Please, please. This is an evening for recognition, and not just by those of us able to attend in person. As our first Mesh speaker, I introduce to you now—"

ERIK fast-forwarded through the remainder of the recorded feeds, pausing only sporadically to review them in real time. There was little new to see. But for the novelty of Inex delivering his remarks, he could have been watching a replay of the first banquet, which he had overseen himself. The specific names and faces differed, but the homilies they mouthed were all too familiar.

The Duckworth account executive segued from praising the candidate crew to a testimonial for a Duckworth specialty alloy, never mentioning that he had joined Villanueva management only recently. Lawrence "Buck" Alcatena, division manager for Zonix Infotainment, rambled on at length about the packaged programming Zonix planned to make about life onboard the ship. Harriet Tyler, of Biome Specialty Products, waxed eloquent about her subcompany's exponential growth over the course of the primary Ship Site contract. Casper Hauser of Dynamo explained how proud his company was to have created Ship Site's internal power systems.

Erik let the images scroll past. Through it all, the editing system he had so painstakingly configured cut away, again and again, to the feted guests, who smiled and nodded as they worked their way through catered meals.

There was a sameness to the gathered multitude, as well, but it was a good sameness. They were all of them young, the eldest of them no older than forty-five, if Erik recalled accurately. Some had been young children at the time of the *Voyager* find. Even factoring in the possible effect of facial appliances and other cosmetics, they fairly radiated health and vitality. They were healthy and well educated, and they stood at the threshold of what could very well be their best years.

He could not look at them without seeing his sons. He could not consider promise without being reminded of promise cut short.

By the time he had sped through the last of the ceremony,

the bottle of bourbon was half-empty. He stood, stretched, and signed. He was drinking too much.

"Load *Sorrow as a Discontinuous Process,*" he said in his command voice, then filled his glass again. He took the bottle with him as he shuffled from workstation to lounge area and then dropped himself slowly into the sofa's thickly padded embrace.

An older man with rugged features and bright eyes smiled at him from the wallpaper. He wore a bulky sweater that was the same rusty color as his bristling moustache. He looked familiar and friendly, like an affectionate uncle.

"Hello, Erik," the brainware simulacrum said. *"I want you to know that I'm very sorry to hear about your loss. Let's talk about it, shall we?"*

Discontinuous was an interactive grief management tool, a low-option artificial intelligence system that had been programmed to meet highly specific needs. His housekeeper had loaded it with his personal usage preferences and basic backgrounder data, to give the thing a context in which to work.

Erik sighed, annoyed by the process but willing to give it a try. The package had come highly recommended, by critics as well as Adkins.

"I can call you Erik, can't I?" the imaged counselor asked.

"That will be fine," he said. "Thank you for your consideration."

The image fairly beamed. *"Your feedback has been logged and will be forwarded,"* it said. *"Thank you!"*

Erik made no reply. He drank more whiskey and let the world became a softer place.

"Now, as I understand it, you have an engineering background, correct?"

"That's right," Erik said. He'd begun his career as a systems engineer for EnTek, what seemed like a lifetime ago.

He had worked with designers and fabricators and marketing specialists for years before realizing that management and corporate vision were his true interests.

"That's good," the image said. *"That's very good. Engineers tend to think in terms of processes. Did you know that, Erik?"*

"A bit less interactivity, please," Erik said in his command voice. "A bit less personal familiarity, too."

The system complied. The imaged counselor spoke in slightly more formal tones as it continued. *"Central to the human mind is its ability to heal and adapt,"* it said. *"And core to that ability is the process of grief. Now, if we consider grief as a rough analog to . . ."*

It continued its routine of discourse-and-question for another twenty minutes before Erik decided that he'd had enough. That thing had said nothing but polished psychobabble, tailored for his personal consumption. Such an approach might work for others, but it wasn't working for him. He ordered the housekeeper to shut down the program and gazed at the blank wallpaper in silence long after the image faded.

"You shouldn't be by yourself."

Sylva had said that. Kowalski had said it, too, and Adkins had said something similar. Even Adkins thought he needed someone to talk to and had recommended the canned brainware packages only as a last resort.

They were right, he realized. Being alone was a mistake. He needed someone to talk to, someone who would listen sympathetically and try to make the pain go away.

The bourbon bottle was nearly empty when the name at last came to mind.

SHE was in her kitchen when the call came. A simple salad had served as a late, light supper, and she was cleaning the remnants away. The bowl and utensils she stowed in the washer and the last of the dressing went into the refrigerator. That left the avocado pit to deal with.

The kitchen was small and modestly appointed, but included a hydroponics nook for growing spices, herbs, and other garnishes. She dropped the seed into an appropriate vessel, using a small rack insert to keep it from submerging completely. The water rippled slightly as it accepted her gift. She smiled.

"Erik Morrison would like to speak with you," her housekeeper said. She managed to keep the surprise from her voice as she said, "Accepted."

The image was raw and unfiltered, received and processed without mirageware masking. Her caller looked awful, tired, and worn. It had been some ten years since she had seen him in person, but he seemed to have aged twice that. His skin had a graying tone, and his eyes were shot with blood.

He had been crying, she realized sadly, and he mumbled his greeting. When she recognized the slurred tones of a man who had been drinking heavily, she realized why he had called. Despair could make people do surprising things.

"Hello, Erik," Wendy Scheer said gently. "I was beginning to wonder if I would ever actually speak with you again."

CHAPTER 8

ERIK ran. He leaned into the concave treadmill's mechanism, and he ran, his hands tightly gripping its instrument-loaded handlebar. The smartshoes that he wore alternately clung to and released the curved track of the treads. The effect prevented the force of his stride from sending him flying. The Moon's low gravity made it impossible to run without artificial assistance.

He felt better than he had in days, physically and emotionally. The exercise made him feel better still. The numbers on the handlebar display crept upward, and as they did, so did his general sense of well-being. Heart rate, respiration, blood oxygenation, and neural activity all demonstrated immediate benefits from the session.

He was near his office, in a wellness facility that Over-Management maintained for executive use. He rarely came here, preferring to work out at home, but something about the place had called to him as he entered the facility.

He felt alive again. He felt as if some great weight had been lifted from his shoulders. The air seemed cleaner, and colors were brighter. The sadness of days past had, if not vanished, at least receded, and the world had become a happier place. Here, alone, putting himself through rigorous paces, he felt better than he could remember feeling in years. He focused on the instrument display and ran some more, picking up the pace.

"We need to talk," Hector Kowalski said.

Erik looked up from the handlebar, startled. The security chief was perched on the housing of an inertial trainer directly opposite the treadmill and was eyeing him coolly. He had not heard the other man enter.

"How'd you get in?" Erik asked, slowing his run so that he could speak more easily. "How did you find me?"

"You weren't in your office," Kowalski said. "And as for the rest of it . . ."

A shrug was his only answer, and the only one that was needed. Generally speaking, Kowalski could find anyone, once he set his mind to the problem.

"Talk, then," Erik said, settling into a steady pace. The exercise felt too good to forego for conversation with a functionary, even an advisor as trusted as Kowalski.

"Do you know a man named Dailey Pym?" Kowalski asked.

Erik shook his head. His feet went up and down. "No," he said.

"He's a site manager for Heuristic," Kowalski said. "I'd like to get rid of him."

That was enough to command Erik's attention. He released the treadmill's throttle. As the rolling treads slowed and stopped, so did his footfalls.

"Why?" he asked.

Years had passed since Kowalski had made such a comment, and it brought back troublesome memories. In their early days of working together, one of Kowalski's primary duties had been to dismantle what he had called the Scheer Network. One by one, he had identified those Villanueva personnel whose first loyalties had not been to its federal counterpart, Project Halo. One by one, they had gone back to Earth. Many careers had been destroyed in those dark days, and Erik had been part of that destruction.

"Heuristic grew the Gummis that I found problems with," Kowalski said. He seemed utterly at ease, but his attentive eyes were trained directly on Erik. "They're growing the next generation now, and samples show the same corruption. Pym runs the project."

"What are his qualifications?" Erik asked. "Have you accessed the quality assurance logs?"

"I don't need to. I have reason to suspect that Pym knows Wendy Scheer."

Warily, Erik wondered just what Kowalski was thinking. The security chief was a deeply suspicious man, but there had to be limits. Very few personnel within Villanueva were permitted any direct contact with Wendy Scheer. Erik was one, and all others required his authorization.

"When did he meet her?" Erik asked. He stepped off of the treadmill and kicked off the smartshoes. He hated the things and would wear them only when necessary. "Hand me my robe, will you?" he said, gesturing.

Kowalski retrieved it from a nearby hook and tossed it at Erik in a slow-motion trajectory. It was big and loose, and a five-ring logo—the ALC trademark—stretched across its back. Shrugging the thing into place over his gym suit, Erik felt like an advertising mascot. He would be glad when he could shower and dress.

"I'm not sure," Kowalski said. Despite the words, he sounded utterly confident. "Not recently. Not in years. On Earth, it looks like."

"On Earth?" Erik asked, surprised. "How?"

"Pym used to be a Fed," Kowalski said. He made a great show of inspecting the nails of one hand.

"Space Administration?" Erik asked. He was in his cooldown period now, and the porous cloth of the robe felt good as it drank up his perspiration. "And you hadn't flagged him already? I'm surprised."

Kowalski shook his head again. "Not Space," he said. "Not formally. But he worked for Census, and Census didn't have enough work for him, so they shared his hours with Space. That's how we—how *I* missed it."

"But you don't know that they've met," Erik said. The possibility that they had didn't seem particularly troublesome, but he decided against saying so. "Then, or since."

"*I've* met him, though," Kowalski said, lounging again against the inertial trainer. He scowled. Kowalski was a deeply suspicious man, at least when it came to certain issues. The Scheer Network was one of them. "He's a believer, a zealot. You should see his eyes light when he talks about deep space. I don't see any way a man like that couldn't have met Scheer, especially if they were working on the same project."

"But has he?" Erik asked, pressing the issue. Even after so many years had passed, remembering the forced reassignments, transfers, and even terminations brought pain.

Kowalski felt differently, he knew. Kowalski had few qualms when it came to such things.

Pym might be a stranger, but Erik had never been eager to damage even an adversary's career. Besides, dealing with Scheer did not necessarily mean dealing with the devil. He had told himself that only this morning, for some reason.

"I don't know," Kowalski said. He shook his head. "I can't know. I told you before, I can't know everything, even though a lot of this job is convincing people that I do."

Erik looked at him, wondering if the words had a second meaning.

Kowalski continued. "But Pym is running a project that grows custom Gummis, and the Gummis he grows have shown signs of deliberate corruption. His job history demonstrates at least the strong possibility that he's one of Scheer's people. That makes him the wrong person for the job."

Reluctantly, Erik nodded. "Get rid of him, then," he said. "Do it with discretion, though. Be gentle. Find a reason that won't raise any eyebrows."

"Can't," Kowalski said.

"Can't?" Erik asked, disbelieving. "We have friends in EnTek. They'll be happy to remove him, if we ask."

"There are chain-of-command issues," Kowalski said. "Heuristic is a joint venture between EnTek and Biome, for one. Pym himself is a minority shareholder, for that matter—"

"But that shouldn't buy him immunity," Erik interrupted.

"It's a joint venture, not a subcontract," Kowalski continued. "They deal directly with the federal government, and that makes things more complicated. Pym was part of the bid team." Kowalski's gaze became more intense. "These things don't work the way they used to," he said. "Ten years ago, we could have canceled his contract and closed his file like that!" He snapped his fingers. "Now, there are safeguards."

"Keep working the issue." It was all that Erik could think to say. "Find out what you can, and we'll do what we can. Talk with Legal."

"I want to talk to Scheer," Kowalski said.

"What!?" Erik snapped, taken by complete surprise. Kowalski had met Scheer and experienced her allure first-hand, but he had also been one of the architects of the policy that kept her in isolation. Erik would never have imagined that Kowalski would even consider deliberately encountering her again. If nothing else, the security chief's dedication to his job made such a scenario vanishingly unlikely.

"I'm going to set up an interview, and I'm going to discuss things with her," Kowalski said. He nodded for emphasis.

"No," Erik said. He pulled the robe more closely around him. "I don't think that's a good idea."

"There are countermeasures that can be taken," Kowalski said. "I've had a team working on defenses."

"And have you tested them?" Erik asked.

"No, but I will," Kowalski said, dogged now. "I need to find out what's going on." He half-smiled. "She keeps saying that she's not our enemy," he continued. "I'll give her a chance to prove it, by cooperating. She has the authority to waive the terms of Pym's contract."

"She knows about you," Erik said slowly, his mind racing. It seemed prudent to keep the security chief and the Project Halo director away from each other, but the situation demanded finesse. Too strong a protest would make Kowalski even more suspicious. "And she knows that you know about her. A direct query will put her on guard."

Again, Kowalski considered his words in silence.

"Use the Proxy first," Erik said. Even as he used the nickname, he wished he hadn't.

"The Hasbro woman?" Kowalski asked. He snorted. He had never cared for Enola. Not even her status as one of the few Scheer associates who had survived his various purges could make him respect her. "She's an idiot."

"She's Scheer's closest confidante, at least among

Villanueva residents," Erik said, pressing his point. "Talk to her first."

Finally, reluctantly, Kowalski nodded. "I can do that," he said. "But only as an interim measure. Scheer has too much to answer for."

INEX looked up from her work in surprise as Erik Morrison strode into the outer office, surprise both at his mode of entry and at his general demeanor. He had taken the main entryway for the first time in recent memory, and he smiled as he greeted her.

"Um," Inex said, blinking as she rose. "Good morning, Erik. You're early."

"It's the best part of the day," Morrison said cheerily.

Something about him was different, Inex realized. She could tell that he had exercised recently; his hair, iron gray and short, was damp from the shower, and his skin had a ruddy vitality. But there was more than that.

The melancholy that had been her superior's constant companion of late was gone. He seemed newly energized, and when he smiled, it was as if he were lit from within.

Inex wondered if he were using psychotropics.

"I'd like you to arrange an all-hands, Inex," Erik said. "I need ten minutes with everyone. In my office will be fine."

She felt her hackles rise. All-hands meetings were almost never good news. "What time?" she asked.

"Schedule it before lunch," Morrison said. He paused and did something else she had never seen him do. He stroked his chin, as if confronted with a sudden excess of energy. "Even better, arrange lunch, too," he continued. "We'll hold the all-hands here and then adjourn to somewhere nice for lunch. Charge the office account."

The words made her relax. A meal on the committee

budget meant that the all-hands meeting would be good news. Inex smiled. "I'll take care of it, Erik," she said. "I'm sure everyone will grateful."

Morrison nodded. "And schedule a one-on-one for the two of us," he continued. "I want to talk about some personal development options for you."

"Me?" she asked. She wondered what he meant.

"Yes, you," Morrison said. He smiled more broadly. "Inex, I want you to consider career growth. I reviewed the banquet feeds last night and saw how good you were," he said. "You're wasted here."

"I've very happy here, Erik," Inex said, suddenly worried again.

"Shhh." He waved at her and repeated his previous words. "You're wasted here, Inex. A good assistant is the hardest thing in all of business to find, but I don't believe in wasting resources. We need to find a new role for you."

"I like the work, and I like working with you," she said. "I hope that I've done nothing to—"

"You've done nothing but excel," he said gently. "But you can do even better, for yourself and for the ALC. We'll talk about that later, all right?"

"A—all right, Erik," she said slowly, utterly confused now. It was an unusual state of mind. Inex had always scored high in adaptability, but nothing in her experience had prepared her for this. Erik had always been a considerate supervisor but not an especially effusive one, at least not on a day-to-day basis. That had been Inex's experience on the job, and her predecessor had told her much the same during training.

What had happened?

ONE measure of rank and prominence within an organization was office space. Another was the privilege of directing a live staff rather than dedicated brainware. Erik was acutely aware of both truisms as he half-sat on the leading edge of his big stone desk and contemplated the personnel who stood before him. There were nine of them, and they didn't even half-fill the roomy space as they stood in formation, eyeing him nervously.

He knew their names. He knew their roles. He knew which analyst managed his accounts and which writer massaged his words into publishable shape, and who over-saw which accounts. He was slightly saddened to realize he knew little more than that.

"I'd like to thank you all," he said without preamble. "We've had a hectic few months, preparing for the ban-quets in addition to our regular workload. To make things worse, I've had some personal demands on my time and I haven't been here as much as I should. I'm sorry for that." He paused. "Last night I reviewed the recordings of last week's event, and I saw some things I didn't see before. For some reason, I couldn't see them before, during prepa-rations or when I presided at the first one."

They looked apprehensive, and he understood why. No one liked to be summoned to the boss's office and no one liked to be told that their supervisor wanted to discuss a re-cent review of their work product. Apprehension under such circumstances was human nature, pure and simple.

"Please," he said, and he gestured. "Relax. What I saw made me think. When I thought about Inex recognizing the hard work and dedication of the candidate crew, I realized that no one had recognized *yours*." He paused again, struck by how easily the words came. "So—thank you."

No one said anything for a long moment, and then the slender intern who pulled files for Over-Management Le-gal raised one hand tentatively.

"Sir?" he asked. "Are you leaving us?"

"No," Erik said, chuckling. That came easily, too. "No, no, no. There may be some changes, but I have no plans to leave."

"Changes?" the intern said. He looked frightened. Erik understood. This was the kid's first professional position. He simply didn't have the experience to face change with confidence.

"I think you'll like them," Erik said reassuringly. "Inex will be assuming some new responsibilities, but she'll still be part of our team, and there are some procedures I'd like to see changed. I hope you'll all share your thoughts with me."

The intern pressed the issue. "Well, sir," he said eagerly. "I have some ideas about file-indexing and—"

"I hope you'll share them later," Erik interjected smoothly, to good response. "Wait until after lunch, at least. Inex has made the arrangements, I think."

He looked in her direction. She nodded.

"But I won't be joining you," Erik continued. "I have some arrangements of my own to make." He smiled. "Arrangements for bonuses, as my thanks for jobs well done."

Now, at last, they applauded.

AFTER the applause, after the thanks and the backslapping and the glad-handing, Erik remained behind in his office. Alone behind the big desk, he opened a Mesh document and began to draft the bonus memorandum. It was easy work. He ran an efficient operation and had included a reasonable set-aside in the year's budget. That money had gone unspent thus far and was available on a discretionary basis. Procedures demanded that he document his rationale for the disbursal, but all that really mattered was deciding who got how much.

He was nearly finished when the office manager announced, *"Sylva Taschen would like to speak with you."*

Erik pulled up a Mesh mirror and eyed his own appearance. After running his fingers though his hair to tidy it, he grunted in approval. "I'll accept it," he said in his command voice. "No mirage filtering needed."

"Erik," Sylva said from the desk viewer. She was pale, and her voice was unsteady. Behind her were white walls, and he could hear background chatter. She was in a public place, calling on a public phone, he realized. *"Erik, is it really you?"*

"Of course it's me," he said, suddenly realizing that he had never accepted her most recent call. "What is it, Sylva?"

"Oh, thank heavens. The screen on this thing is awful, and I'm so tired of speaking with answerware." She turned from the video pickup and spoke to someone Erik could not see. *"In a moment,"* she said sharply. *"Wait your turn!"*

"Where are you, Sylva?" he asked, even as a Mesh screen call-out provided the answer.

"Where do you think?" she asked sharply. *"I'm at the spaceport. I'm on the Moon. Now come get me, or send someone to do the job!"*

CHAPTER 9

THE executive car on the spaceport train was nearly unoc-
cupied, with private compartments readily available. Erik
was able to secure one without difficulty, once he had shep-
herded Sylva through the final stages of visitor processing
at Chrisium Port.

"How was the trip?" he asked, once the compartment
door had whisked shut behind them. Despite her immediate physical presence, it was proving difficult to believe
that she was actually there.

She fixed him with one eye. "Dreadful," she said. The
word was not so much a complaint as a simple statement of
fact. "I don't believe that I'm meant for space travel. I was
nauseous nearly the entire time."

Erik thought back to his own advent on the Moon, some
twenty years before. He nodded. "Zero-G can do that," he
said. "Especially the first time."

Sylva said nothing. She was seated opposite him, on a
padded recliner that matched his own. Erik had insisted she

take the seat that faced the direction of the train's destination. He knew from experience that facing forward was less likely to aggravate motion sickness.

"You'd feel better with something in your stomach," Erik said. There was a cooler within easy reach. He opened it and reached inside.

"I don't think so," Sylva said.

"Some juice, at least," Erik said. He showed her a bottle of synthetic punch, thick with fruit sugars and electrolyte compounds.

"I said no," Sylva told him. She passed one hand over her forehead as he put the container away. "It will pass. I'll be fine, once I've had some sleep."

"There are medications—" Erik started to say, still concerned.

"I'll be fine," Sylva said again. Her eyelids drooped and half closed, a clear indicator that she considered the topic closed.

Erik gazed at her as the kilometers raced by. He didn't like seeing her like this. The finely drawn features he knew so well were pale and sallow, and her eyes were rimmed with shadow. She was a poor match for the portrait in dignity that she had been when speaking to him from Earth.

"Why did you come, Sylva?" he asked.

Her lips drew back in a faint smile. "I'm here for the exhibit opening," she said, in pointed reminder.

"That's cruel," Erik said. He spoke without rancor. "It's been a long time since we've been cruel to each other."

"I know," Sylva said. She sat upright in a sudden lurching motion. Her body had not yet learned the ways of the Moon's lower gravity. "I'm sorry. I shouldn't have said that."

"Why did you come, then?" he asked again.

"Hand me my bag," she said, by way of reply.

Erik stood. He opened the overhead storage compartment and drew out the reinforced suitcase that had been Sylva's only luggage. She had always been a light traveler, but she had outdone herself this time. The compact case was big enough to contain only a few changes of clothing at most. Erik set it on the low table between their seats.

"There," he said, gesturing.

Sylva leaned farther forward. She pressed her thumbs against the suitcase's locks. Once it had unsealed itself, she reached inside and lifted out a cylinder crafted of black plastic. She presented one of its end faces to Erik. It was marked with a Roman numeral *II,* the horoscope symbol for Gemini.

It was the twins, he realized sickly, and hoped that he was wrong. The container Sylva held was an urn for ashes.

"I spoke with Veronica at some length," Sylva said. She tried to hand him the black cylinder and looked annoyed when he refused. "It was her idea."

"But—but you were going to strew them in Haiti, at the summer house," Erik said. The words did not come easily.

"We divided the cremains," Sylva said. "Half for the summer house, half for here."

"No," Erik repeated. He pulled back from the container as she tried again to pass it to him, recoiling. "You didn't."

"They often spoke of following you here, Erik," Sylva said gently. "For a visit, for a vacation, if nothing else."

"Not like this," Erik said. His gorge rose. "Why are you doing this?"

"I told you, it was Veronica's idea," Sylva said. "But I think it was a good one, the right one." She glanced at the antique watch she wore on one wrist, an elegant bit of silver jewelry with several analog dials. "The ceremony is in ten days," she said. "That should give me enough time to adjust to local living. We'll audit the Earth ceremony together and scatter them together, too."

Erik gazed at the urn, still securely held in Sylva's hands. He shuddered. It was difficult to think about the thing's contents.

"Ten days?" he said. "And until then?"

"We'll spend some time together, you and I," Sylva said. "I still have some planning to do, but I can do it from here, and you really shouldn't be alone."

HECTOR nearly never used the interrogation room personally. Others in his service preferred the austere space, finding advantages both in its Spartan decor and in the complex monitoring systems built into its gray walls.

Not Hector. He had always found greater success conducting his interviews in person and on-site, at the workplaces of the individuals who were the objects of his investigations. There, he could make his inquiries with minimal disruption to productivity. Another advantage was that interviewees tended toward overconfidence on their home ground, and overconfident people made mistakes.

He made an exception for Enola Hasbro. She had no true workplace within Villanueva, and she knew him from past encounters. She knew him, and she disliked him as much as he disliked her. That made her almost impossible to surprise.

"Hello, Enola," he said. "Thank you for coming on short notice."

Seated across from him, on the other side of the oblong table, the comely Asian woman smiled. Her fingers toyed with the handle of a coffee mug with an advertising mascot imaged on its side. "Hello, Hector," she said. "Did I have a choice?"

"Of course you did," he lied smoothly. He had half hoped that she could refuse his summons and provide an excuse to intensify the investigation. Even better, he might have been able to revoke her special status entirely, if he'd found Erik in a properly receptive frame of mind. "It was a request, not an order."

The Proxy was very attractive, possessed of natural, healthy good looks, complemented by careful enhancements and cultivated poise. It was hard to draw a line from the Enola of now to the Enola he had first met, long years before.

Hasbro had been a minor image modeler working for Duckworth, no different from the thousands of other drones who prowled the corridors of the lunar colony. All that had set her apart had been a sequence of bad luck followed by good—falsely found guilty of murder and terrorism charges, she had found new employ by the federal enclave and new advocacy at the highest levels of ALC Over-Management.

Erik was her champion. It was one of the few ongoing points of contention between Hector and his superior.

The modern Enola was something different from what she had been. Better mannered, more elegantly dressed, she seemed to have stepped from the imageware of a Mesh fashion feed. Those were only surface changes, however, and easily explained.

What impressed Hector was subtler. She moved and spoke differently. She spoke in the same girlish tones, but the cadence of her speech had changed over the long years. Dealing with her as she was now, remembering her when they had first met, was like viewing a Mesh feed in which the mirage filters had gone out of phase. He could have been speaking to two women at once.

Perhaps he was.

"Remember when I worked for Duckworth, Hector?" Enola said. Her head tilted as she considered him. "You had already left EnTek for Over-Management by then, hadn't you?"

He nodded. "I'll work for EnTek again," he said. Corporate loyalties ran deep. "But I don't see you ever going back to Duckworth."

She continued. "When I worked for Duckworth, there was a saying about you. 'When Hector Kowalski makes a request, it's an order.' Isn't that funny?"

He laughed softly. "That was a long time ago. You've come up in the world since then," he said. "Things are different."

"Yes, they are," Enola said, still speaking with a confidence that he didn't remember. "You have only limited jurisdiction over me."

"I have enough," he said, before he could stop himself. He did not like challenges to his authority. "But I don't want to make things difficult—"

"Again," Enola said, interrupting his sentence and concluding it. She still smiled, but there was steel in her expression now.

He knew why. He had led the investigation into the Duckworth Foundry incident personally, and personally had gathered the evidence that had pointed to her guilt. He couldn't reasonably expect her not to remember that and not to resent it.

"That was a long time ago," Hector said again. "And I helped prove you innocent, didn't I?"

"At Erik's request," Enola said. She shifted slightly in her seat.

"At Erik Morrison's request," he agreed, nodding. "It's part of my job. We all had our jobs to do, Enola. And we still do." He paused. "And I truly do appreciate your coming here."

"What do you want to talk about then?" she asked, with

surprising directness. The sensation that he was speaking with someone else reasserted itself.

"We've encountered anomalies in the Ship Site Gummi prototypes," he said. "Nothing major, and it may simply be a manufacturing issue, but I've been tasked to investigate."

"I didn't realize that you worked Quality Control," Enola said.

He ignored the comment. "Do you know the name Dailey Pym?" he asked, watching for reaction.

Enola's face and voice were both smooth and calm as she replied. "He's a black man, handsome, but he lets himself look old. He's a manager on-site at Heuristic." She smiled. "He's very nice, very friendly. If I'd had a father, I would have liked one like Dailey."

"How do you know him?" Kowalski asked. "From Earth?"

"No, don't be silly," Enola said. She tapped gilded fingertips on the tabletop. "I was only a teenager when I left Earth. How could I ever have met someone like Dailey Pym? We didn't even live in the same part of the world."

Enola had been born in Eastern Europe. Her family's ties to the sequence of civil wars that historians called the Czech Challenge had been part of the evidence used to frame her.

"Here, then?" Kowalski asked. His hands were empty and the tabletop that stretched between them was empty, too, but for Enola's new-coffee mug.

"Here," she said readily. "He works on a federal contract, Hector." She surprised him slightly by pronouncing his name European style, with a guttural *ch* sound. It was a deliberate reminder of her background.

"He *manages* a federal contract," he said. "A very important one."

Enola nodded. Today she wore her hair short and tightly

styled, and it looked like a black metal helmet as it moved beneath the muted lights. "Site manager," she said. "I interface with him periodically. You should know that."

He talked past the last of her response. "Interface?" he asked.

"On Wendy's behalf," Enola said.

"I didn't know that you had an administrative role," Hector said.

"I don't." She shook her head slightly, but her eyes, deep and luminous, fixed on his. "You know that. That kind of information gets routed through Earth. That's part of the arrangement between the ALC and Hello."

"Then why?" Kowalski asked.

"Courtesy," Enola responded. "Morale. People need to know they're appreciated." She leaned forward and grinned, abruptly impish. "Do you feel appreciated, Hector?" she asked.

He didn't pull back. "I have what I need," he said. "Tell me more about Pym."

"He's nice, I told you," she said. "He likes Cajun food and Bahamian jazz. His staff likes him. He seems to be very good at what he does, even if I don't understand it entirely." Now, at last, she sipped her new-coffee. The cat on the mug gave a thumbs-up sign and winked. "He writes well," she continued.

"Oh?" Hector asked. "How do you know that?"

"I accessed the proposal archives. I wanted to see the winning bid," she said.

That surprised him, too. Nothing in his personal experience with Enola had ever suggested such devotion to duty or desire to know the barebones basics of the work she did. Hector made a mental note of the comment. It might indicate that Pym held a more prominent role than Enola said.

"Have you seen him socially?" Hector asked.

The temperature of her voice fell a few degrees. "No," she said. "Of course not. I'm not *that* kind of morale builder."

Kowalski nodded, unperturbed. "Has he ever said anything to make you doubt his loyalty?" he asked.

Her fingertips drummed again. Her delicately arched eyebrows came together, and she glared at him. "I'm supposed to cooperate," she said. "But I'm not going to help you destroy someone's career."

"It's a high-profile project, Enola," he said with deliberate patience. "It's a federal contract, yes, but he's working in ALC space, and Heuristic is owned by ALC sisters. You and I, we share interests in this."

She settled back in her chair, thinking very subtly. He could almost see the circuits open and close inside her head as she searched her memory. This kind of thing wasn't Enola's forte.

"No," she finally said. "I can't imagine Dailey doing anything to damage his project. He believes in what he does." She smiled faintly. "Sometimes he sounds like Wendy," she said.

Hector seized on the opening. "Like Wendy?" he asked. "How?"

"Yes," she said. "Like Wendy. She's wanted to go to outer space ever since she was a little girl, did you know that? Her father used to take her stargazing. Dailey is like that."

"Do they know one another?" Kowalski asked casually.

Enola smiled again. "Is he part of the Network, you mean?" she asked.

He hadn't fooled her.

"No, I don't think so," Enola said. She sighed. "We've told you before, Hector. There isn't a Scheer Network anymore. Nearly every Villanueva resident who has met Wendy

has relocated to Earth. I think that only Erik and I are left."
She paused. "The two of us, and you, I mean."

AFTER the interview, after an assistant had appeared to escort Enola from the premises, Hector remained in the interview room, alone with his thoughts. He replayed Enola's responses a dozen times in his mind, considering each sentence and phrase. She was a difficult subject. She said much but told little, at least not deliberately.

"I need an analysis and report," he said in his command voice.

The office manager acknowledged him. *"Working,"* it said. A snippet of background music played, too uninteresting to be definable.

"Review the recordings from this session," he said. "Research the archives and access prior sessions with the same individual. Use everything you can find—visual, audio, voice/stress, bioelectric activity, everything that's on file."

More music played as the Gummi checked its rainwear memory. *"Older recordings are incomplete,"* the manager said.

Hector ignored the caveat. New technology had made new classes of information available but didn't reduce the utility of the old.

"Break today's interview down into sentences, phrases, and words," he said. "Phonemes, too. Correlate with the associated biometrics, and then run a comparison." The process would take hours, he knew. "Port the results to my personal system when you've finished. Priority-level encryption."

ENOLA had taken Wendy's call at her vanity table. The wallpaper there was optimized with multiple camera pickups and lighting options, the better to test makeovers, but it could serve other purposes as well. The Project Halo head spoke to her from the work area's upper left corner.

"Was he rude or disrespectful in any way?" Wendy asked. Even in the relayed image, her eyes were bright and aware.

"Of course he was," Enola said. "Kowalski is always rude and disrespectful. To me, at least."

She worked as she spoke. She had a lot of work to do, all of it on herself, and she didn't particularly mind if Wendy Scheer saw. The two women had long since ceased even pretending that any real personal privacy existed between them. The Mesh connection that linked them was secure but unfiltered, with no miraging brainware active.

"He's rude to you because he'd like to be rude to me," Wendy said. She sounded slightly distracted, and she glanced intermittently in the direction of something off-screen. She was working, too, Enola realized, but presumably on something of a more administrative nature.

Enola dabbed the pad she held in cleansing cream. She ran the moistened puff of fabric across her face in smooth, easy strokes. With each, the pad came away darker, stained with cosmetics.

"He shouldn't," she said, with a hint of petulance. "I've never done anything bad to him. Neither of us has."

Wendy laughed. It was a sound like silver bells, and Enola felt all irritation fall away. She liked knowing that Wendy was happy.

"Of course we have, Enola," she said. "We proved that he can be wrong. Isn't that enough?"

Years before, when Enola had been falsely accused of terrorist activities, Hector Kowalski had uncovered the majority of evidence cited in her hearing. Wendy had worked with Erik and a very reluctant Kowalski to stage a demonstration of her innocence. The Over-Management security chief hadn't liked being proven wrong. He had liked Enola's appointment as Wendy's envoy even less but had been unable to prevent it.

"If Hector had his way, we'd both be on Earth now," Wendy said. "I would be in a relocation camp somewhere."

"That's silly," Enola said.

She passed the de-applicator wand along her cheekbones and nose, keeping the little instrument's tip several millimeters from her skin. One by one, the cosmetic appliances she wore fell away. They were consumer-quality gear, intended less to change her appearance than to refine it, but they were expensive enough that she was careful to stow them away properly. The wafer-thin devices were miniature wallpaper cells, configured to produce low-resolution images. She tucked them into their little cases.

"What did he want to talk about?" Wendy asked.

"Dailey Pym," Enola replied. Kowalski's inner sanctum was proof against the personal recorders she wore in her earrings. She couldn't have recorded the session without his permission, and she hadn't bothered to ask.

"Hmmm . . ." Wendy hummed. She didn't seem particularly surprised by the information. Even without focusing on the communications view, Enola could see her glance again at something offscreen. "Specifics?" she asked, in the same distracted tone.

"He wanted to know if I knew Dailey, and how well. He wanted to know if you knew him, too," Enola said. "He thinks our—your network is online still."

"What did you tell him?" Wendy asked.

Her hand drifted into view, as she raised it to inspect her fingernails. She had been coloring them, Enola realized. They had been done in a gradated spectrum of hues, like a prism's ray. It wasn't a style that Enola had ever liked, but she began to consider how it would look on her own nails.

Probably very nice, she decided.

"The truth, as I knew it," Enola said. The six words were something of a mantra in her work. Wendy authorized lies on her behalf only rarely, and only when absolutely necessary.

She tugged an applicator pad from the vanity caddy and opened the pouch. Fresh moisturizing cream scented her bedroom air. She went to work again, applying the stuff to her face and neck, her arms and shoulders and upper chest, anywhere likely to be on view.

When working for Duckworth, Enola had taken reasonable care of her personal appearance, but relied on health and good genetics to do most of the work. When she had attempted to transition to a role as Mesh spokesperson, an imaging specialist had provided her with a detailed analysis of her comeliness and guidance on how to enhance it. She used that knowledge in her current work.

All else being equal, men and women alike tended to prefer dealing with good-looking people. For Enola to do her job, people had to like her. They would never like her as much as they liked Wendy, but Enola did what she could.

"He's worried about something, I think," she continued. She dabbed more lotion. "That surprised me."

"Surprised?" Wendy asked. Her imaged eyes seemed to stare directly into Enola's.

"Concerned," Enola said, nodding as she selected the less emphatic word.

"What else did you tell him about Pym?" Wendy asked.

"That he likes Cajun food and jazz, and that his staff likes him," Enola said. "I told him he reminds me of you, in some ways."

Wendy laughed again. It was a beautiful sound. "He reminds you of me?" she asked.

Hoping that she'd said nothing wrong, Enola blushed and stammered slightly. "Yes," she said. "The way you both talk about space, and your work—"

"Oh, that's good," Wendy said, interrupting. She smiled broadly, so broadly that both sets of dimples appeared in her cheeks. Her eyes sparkled, delighting Enola. "Well done, Enola," Wendy said. "Very well done, indeed!"

CHAPTER 10

DINNER was perfection, familiar foods prepared with elegance and balance. The salad was fresh zucchini strips and cucumber slices, dressed in light vinaigrette. The cultured beef, programmed for porterhouse quality, had been crusted in black pepper, grilled, and served with braised asparagus. For dessert, Erik presented a selection of well-chosen cheeses, accompanied by a rich port wine.

"Oh," Sylva said, eyeing the empty plate before her and patting her still-trim stomach. "You still cook. I'd forgotten that. How did I ever let you get away?"

"We were on different paths," Erik said. He toyed with his wineglass. "We still are."

"I'm glad you realize that," Sylva said. "Arriving here, so suddenly, I didn't want you to think—"

He shook his head. "No," he said. "Don't say it. We said good-bye to that part of our relationship a long time ago." He smiled wryly. "We're on different paths, even if those paths lead to some of the same places, and even if they intersect now and then."

They were in his quarters. Erik had left his office early—again—and come home to prepare dinner and to supervise the hastily summoned cleaning service. By the time Sylva had arrived from her hotel, his residence's living area, at least, had been rendered immaculate. In the kitchen, the pseudosteaks were peppered and ready to sear, and the fresh salad produce lay in slices and shreds. Erik had done the work entirely by hand, and he felt better for having done so. A lifetime seemed to have passed since he'd done anything so satisfyingly productive.

"You're feeling better, I see," he said, changing the subject. "Adjusting well?"

Sylva nodded. He fair skin had regained its pinkish undertones, and her eyes were bright and clear. "I needed sleep," she said. "Sleep, and whatever it was the concierge gave me."

Erik smiled. "Zonix Hospitality people know their business," he said. "They deal with thousands of tourists a month."

"What about you, Erik?" his ex-wife asked him. "How long did it take you to adjust to life here?"

"Relocation is different," Erik said. His looked down at his plate. A shred of Stilton remained from the final course, and he toyed with it. "It's a matter of mind-set as much as anything else, I think."

"How long?" she repeated.

"A long time." His mind drifted back as he spoke. "I didn't want to come here, you know."

They had divorced several years before his transfer, but Sylva had always maintained a reasonable interest in his career, he knew. He had done the same for hers. It hadn't been difficult. She was a regional director for EnTek Custom Products, so their respective career paths were similar and their social circles overlapped to a remarkable degree, at least until his emigration.

"I know about Alaska," she said, referring to the behind-the-scenes scandal that had deeply offended EnTek upper management and led to his banishment.

What happened in Alaska had nearly ended his career. Rather than termination, he had been offered what technically was a promotion. One condition was that he had to accept a transfer to the Moon. Except in passing, he had not thought about the unpleasant sequence of events in years.

"I adjusted," Erik said. "It doesn't matter how long it took. I found a new place for myself, and I made things work. That's all anyone can do."

"You look the same, but you move differently," she said, surprising him with the observation. "You look *good*."

"I'm healthier, I think," he said. "Not as strong, physically, but that's the gravity. The body adjusts just as much as the mind does."

"I wish mine would," Sylva said tartly. She sipped wine. "I wish I could walk normally, at least."

"We can get you some smartshoes," he said. He ate the bit of cheese. "I wear them to exercise. They'll help."

She nodded. Her next words came very slowly. "You seem happier than I had expected," she said. When he flinched, she corrected herself. "No, you're not happier, but less sad."

He looked at her without speaking.

"I was so worried about you," she said. The words continued their snail's pace. "I was surprised how worried I was. When I contacted you with the news about the twins, you were so distraught . . ."

"It hurt, Sylva," he said gently, as her words trailed off into silence. "It hurts terribly."

"I know," she replied.

"But there are things that are supposed to hurt," he continued. His voice thickened. "It hurts that they're gone, and it hurts that we spent so much time apart. But there's nothing I can do about that."

Still, she studied him. "You're seeing someone, aren't you?" she asked.

"No. I spoke with a therapist, and I've started an interactive counseling program, but I'm not seeing anyone formally," Erik said carefully. Years in management had taught him that truth was a very technical quality, subject to nuance and tailoring.

"No," Sylva said. "I mean, you're seeing a woman, aren't you? I can tell."

"No," Erik said, shaking his head.

"I don't want to intrude," Sylva said. She surprised him by blushing, however faintly. He would never have imagined that she still felt any claim on him.

"I'm not in a relationship, Sylva," he said bluntly. "I have been, and I will be again, and I have a social life, but I'm not in a relationship at the moment."

She made a little moue of unhappiness, so faint that only long familiarity enabled him to see it. Whether it was because she didn't believe him or because she was disappointed at being wrong, he couldn't tell. It didn't matter.

"I'm sorry," she said, and he wasn't certain about the reason for that, either.

"It leaves me more time for you," he said. "In fact, I'd like you to attend a banquet with me."

"The exhibit dedication?" she asked.

"No, this is something different entirely. It's the last of a series," he said. In a few clipped sentences, he explained the candidate crew, the lottery system, and the reasoning behind the event. "I think you would enjoy it. The Horvaths intend to audit, so there will be some familiar faces."

"I would be delighted," she said. Her eyes widened slightly. "But, I'm not sure I brought anything appropriate to wear. Do they have shops here? Nice ones, I mean."

"I think you can find something to your liking in the Mall," Erik said dryly. The colony's commercial center included vendors targeting all income brackets and social backgrounds. "The concierge can offer suggestions."

TRINE Hartung was beginning to think that gravity had its uses, after all. Not Earth gravity, which she remembered as a crushing grip that had made her feel heavy and slow, or the ghost-gravity of Ship Site's spinning components, too negligible to matter in most circumstances.

Trine liked the Moon's pull, which she decided was an elegant compromise between the two extremes. It was strong enough that she could move with reasonable grace and control, but sufficiently gentle that she didn't feel like her feet had been welded to the floor. She could dance, if she wanted to, and if she did it slowly enough.

She was dancing now. She was on the main dance floor on the third level (of five) in the Party Sector, moving in time to the pumping beat of the Bazuki Brothers. The Bazukis were new to the Moon, but they had adapted quickly. The klezmer music they played pulsed with exacting specificity, precisely timed for the fastest dancing practical without artificial assistance. Trine rocked and swayed in time to the music, always aware that to step even a fraction more forcefully would send her careening into her partner.

He was a nice boy, perhaps six years younger than Trine and with the greenest eyes she had ever seen, so green that

Trine wondered if they were real. She'd met him somewhere on the Party Sector's first level. He'd bought her a drink and asked for a dance, but Trine knew that he wanted more.

"There's a jazz quartet on the fourth," he told her. His youthful tones sounded clearly in her ears, despite the throb of accordion and slide whistle. They each wore proximity phones, clipped to their ears like jewelry. "If you want something slower, I mean," he continued.

"No, no, I'm fine," she said. "This is fine. I like it loud and fast!" He was her third dance partner of the evening, and she'd already told him that he wouldn't be her last.

That wasn't all she liked. She liked the subtle interplay between the band and its audience, and the way one of the Bazukis smiled directly at her whenever she neared the tiny stage. She liked the way the green-eyed boy's body moved in perfect counterpoint to hers, and the human heat and scent that conditioned the air.

Nothing on Ship Site was like this. Nothing ever would be. Even the ship's largest hulls at maximum spin would simulate only half the pull of the Moon, and there would be no space for a construct like the Party Sector. The final crewmembers, once selected, would need to find another way to have fun. And they would. It was human nature.

The Party Sector opened onto the lowest level of the Mall and extended up and behind the colony's central well. The Sector's clubs and venues and drinkeries had been built inside disused access tunnels and leftover bits of excavation. There was an improvised, incomplete feel to the place that Trine found exhilarating.

The green-eyed boy's right hand lifted, taking Trine's left with it. His arm bent. Trine ducked beneath and spun. It was when she came out of the twirl and faced the boy again that she felt someone's finger tap her bare shoulder gently.

"May I?" Hector Kowalski said.

The boy's eyes flashed. They flashed literally, green light spilling from them, and Trine realized that the color was artificial, after all. She smiled at him, pressed her hand to one cheek, and gave the other a quick peck. "Maybe later," she told the boy in vague promise, and then she turned back to Kowalski.

"This is a surprise," she said. The lunch had been nice, but Trine had not particularly expected to ever see him again.

"I surprise people sometimes," Kowalski said.

"How did you find me?" she asked.

His only answer was another smile, cool and remote, and Trine realized how foolish the question had been. Part of Kowalski's job was finding people.

Nearly an hour later, after brief visits to the Sector's fifth and then second levels, he led her to a corner booth in a fourth-level drinkery. Shaped acoustics and suppressor fields gave them relative quiet, while he ordered drinks from the booth's dispenser system.

"Lethe water," he said, passing her beverage to her after it emerged from the dispenser niche. His own choice was fruit punch, and his nose wrinkled as he tasted it.

Trine sipped her Lethe water. It was a mild intoxicant, like alcohol scrubbed of both good qualities and bad. Trine liked it. Lethe would blur the world slightly, but it wouldn't make her drunk, no matter how much she consumed, and it wouldn't give her a hangover.

"Looking for perspective again?" she asked Kowalski, teasing. She wondered if he were looking for something else.

"In a sense," he said. "I had a bad day dealing with difficult people."

"I can be difficult," Trine said cheerfully.

Kowalski drank more fruit juice. For some reason, his face seemed to have more character than it had when she had last seen him. She wondered if he were wearing appliances or if simple familiarity on her part were a factor.

"But you're direct," Kowalski said. His bottle was empty. "I don't get to talk to very many people who are direct."

Trine wasn't sure what to say to that. Others had told her the same thing, but Kowalski seemed to mean it as a compliment.

"Erik Morrison seems straightforward," she said, thinking back to her chance encounter. She dragged her fingertips along the tabletop, enjoying the texture. It was nicked and scarred, either from heavy use or as a conscious design choice by management. Trine couldn't tell which.

Kowalski made a barely audible sound of acknowledgment but said nothing. He wasn't going to speak about his superior, Trine realized.

"But I understand what you say," Trine said. "I imagine people lie to you a lot."

"Lie," Kowalski said. "Mislead. Keep secrets. It's human nature."

Trine decided she didn't like hearing the powerful complain. Her childhood had taught her what real misfortune was. She changed the subject.

"I'm scheduled for the next banquet," she said. "Will I see you there?"

Kowalski made a great show of considering the question. He tilted his head back, stared into the distance, and half-closed one eye, as if reading a calendar. It was the most expressive that she had ever seen him. He could have been drinking alcohol rather than fruit juices.

"Yes," he said. He looked at her and smiled. "Yes, I think

you will. I'll see you, at least." Suddenly serious again, he asked, "Trine, what will you do if you don't make the final selection?"

The question sliced through the Lethe water blur and through the habitual, easy optimism that lay beneath. Trine stiffened slightly.

"I think my chances are good," she said. "Environmental systems engineer is a good billet. My scores are high, and so is my social interactivity rating."

"But if you don't?" he asked again, gently prodding.

Trine sipped more Lethe water. She toyed with the container that held it, passing the vessel from hand to hand. "If I can't do what I want to, I'll do something else," she said. The words were her father's. "I can still be part of the project. There will be plenty of follow-on work."

Planners projected that physical contact with the deep-space probe would be feasible for as much as three years, post-launch. Smaller craft could ferry needed supplies and other materials between it and Villanueva, if necessary, until progress along its trajectory made that impractical. Remote information exchange and personal communications would continue even longer, for the duration of the mission. Trained personnel would be needed to perform that work.

"But follow-on work isn't what you want," Kowalski said.

She shook her head.

He looked at her coolly, like a researcher running an experiment. "Pretend that's not an option, then. I've accessed your background files, and I know that you've worked most of your life for this," he said. "What if you can't be a member of the crew?"

The sense of easy companionship and camaraderie that Trine felt evaporated completely. "Why are you asking me this?" she asked, worried. "What do you know that I don't? They're not doing to down-select the entire—"

"No," Kowalski said emphatically. "Nothing like that. Don't even think that." He paused, then spoke more gently. "It's nothing about you, Trine. It's a hypothetical."

"I don't like it," Trine said resolutely.

"Please," Kowalski said. It was the first time she'd heard him use the word. "I need perspective. Tell me what you'd do."

She thought for a long moment. The response that came to mind was so obvious and self-evident that she felt obliged to find a different one. She couldn't.

"I'd work to find a way to be part of the project, in any way." Her strong fingers tightened around the bottle that held her Lethe water, and her knuckles whitened. "I'd work very hard," she said. "I'd do everything I could."

THE waiting area was little more than that. It was an austere box of a room, with doors at either end. The walls between were bare, bereft even of hardcopy images. A uniformed guard sat at small desk in one corner, but his presence seemed to be a required formality. He didn't look as if he could stop anyone from going through the second door, and he was obviously surprised to see a visitor enter his workspace.

"I'm here to see Wendy Scheer," Hector Kowalski said politely. "I'm here from Villanueva."

"Scheer is the project head," the guard said slowly, unsure what to do. If visitors to Armstrong were uncommon, visitors for the head of Project Halo were positively rare. "She's a busy woman."

"I think she'll want to see me," Hector said and told the seated man who he was.

The guard shrugged. He picked up a handheld and murmured something into it, not quite softly enough to prevent eavesdropping. His sloppiness was irritating; no one who worked for Hector would have been allowed to make such a call without suppressors.

"You can take a seat," the guard said, gesturing at the three hard-looking chairs that ran along one wall.

"I can stand," Kowalski said. "I don't think I'll be waiting long."

The guard shrugged, but fewer than ninety seconds later the door behind him whisked open and Wendy Scheer strode into the waiting area. She patted the guard on the shoulder as she passed him.

"Hector Kowalski!?" she said. Her surprise and disbelief seemed genuine. "It's been years!"

Before he could take evasive action, she had clapped one hand on his shoulder and extended the other in greeting. Not willing just yet to be rude, he hooked the offered thumb. Her skin felt warm and good against his.

She smiled. Like Enola Hasbro had done the previous day, she tilted her head and considered him. "Hard work must suit you," she said, studying him. "You look well."

She did, too. Hector had encountered Scheer only briefly and only on intermittent occasions, but he had reviewed her recorded image countless times. The two experiences were vastly different, more different than any other comparison in his experience.

Recorded, whether in Mesh feeds or still image, Wendy was trim and attractive, with strong, clearly drawn features and an intriguing smile. In person, she was something more. The objective details remained the same, but their cumulative effect differed radically. She projected personal charm that seemed wildly inappropriate to her role as an administrative manager.

Hector was acutely aware of her appeal as she escorted him to her office. The off-white corridors, as Spartan and undecorated as the waiting area, were punctuated with doors and cubical niches. As Wendy passed each, the voices of staff sang out.

"Hello, Wendy!'

"Scheer! You're back!"

"Visitors?"

"There are brownies in the kitchen, Wendy!"

Without breaking pace, she favored each of her staff with a smile or a nod. A chubby woman with one blue eye and one green approached them, beaming. Wendy gave her a smile and a wink and slid past her before any conversation could commence. The woman with mismatched eyes seemed scarcely to notice Hector when he moved past her, too.

Wendy gave him a sidelong glance and a shrug. Dimples appeared on her cheeks as she smiled wryly. "Sometimes it's a problem," she said.

"I can understand," Hector replied.

He could, too. Armstrong Base was not heavily funded, he knew. The facility's original function had been a Search for Extraterrestrial Intelligence (SETI) outpost, and many thought its job had been done and the place could be forgotten.

Hector thought that, too.

Despite the low budget, however, and despite minimal creature comforts, morale at Project Halo was almost unbelievably high, and staffers were dauntingly loyal. That was because people liked their boss.

Everyone liked Wendy Scheer. Even Hector liked her, even if he wished he didn't. Though he rarely thought about such things, more than once he had counted the world lucky that Wendy had not pursued a career as a religious figure.

"I imagine you've researched the installation rather thoroughly, but you've never been here, have you?" she asked, looking at him again. "Would you like a tour?"

"No," Hector said. "No, but thank you. Your office will be fine."

She nodded and led him down a side corridor and into something that even a midlevel manager at Villanueva would have considered a cubbyhole. A small desk rested between two support members, and the most notable decorative element was a daunting array of potted plants. None of them had blossoms, but the scent of greenery gave freshness to the air.

Two guest chairs nearly filled the open area before the desk. Wendy settled into one and gestured for him to take the other.

The chairs were less than two meters apart. Kowalski's preferred boundaries for such situations weren't particularly generous, but Wendy was well within his personal space.

"Hector," she said. "I can honestly say that I never expected to see you here. In fact, I never expected to speak to you in real time again, or see you in person."

He shrugged and smiled faintly. "I surprise people sometimes," he said.

"I assume you're recording?" Wendy asked.

"You can't honestly have expected I would come here without making a record," Kowalski said. He indicted the black metal clip that clung to his right ear.

"I told you, I didn't expect you ever to come here at all," Wendy said, but offered no objection. "Why *are* you here, Hector?"

Long years had passed since Hector had knowingly been in the presence of Wendy Scheer, but it felt like only moments. Already, he had fallen into an easy familiarity with her. To Hector, at least, the exchange seemed more like banter between friends than adversaries testing boundaries. He felt a twinge of mild guilt regarding his mission and opened his mouth to explain. Just in time, he pulled himself back from the conversational brink.

Almost.

"I'd like to talk about Dailey Pym," he said.

Saying the name made the world a more straightforward place, if one that blurred around the edges a bit. He could think more clearly, if not as quickly.

It seemed a small price to pay.

"Pym?" Wendy asked. She rested one elbow on her chair arm, then rested her chin on her open palm.

"The site manager at Heuristic. You must know who he is," Kowalski said. "The Proxy meets with him regularly."

"You're not being nice," Wendy said. "Enola doesn't like it when people call her that."

Kowalski pressed the issue. "An employment matter has arisen," he said. "How well do you know Pym?"

"I'm not at all sure we've ever met," Wendy said. "I know the name, and I know his work, but I don't think we've ever met."

She was lying. Kowalski was sure of it and pleased that he was sure. When dealing with Wendy Scheer, the human mind's default was to accept her word as the truth. Without conscious effort, he had doubted her, in her presence.

Hector grinned. "I don't think that's true," he said.

Wendy's eyes widened, and her easy smile seemed to become less easy. "Oh?" she asked, plainly puzzled.

Hector nodded. "Pym worked for Space," he said. "Not as part of the dedicated workforce, but on interagency loan for Census."

"That was on Earth?" Wendy asked.

"Yes," Hector said, still watching her closely.

"I don't recall meeting him under any circumstances," she said.

"During the period in which Pym worked for Space,

you visited Earth five times," Hector continued implacably.

"Earth is a big place, Hector," Wendy said. She chuckled indulgently. "A lot of people live there."

Hector didn't say anything.

"And when they call me home, it's for business," Wendy continued. "And when I'm there, I'm sick from travel and I weigh an ungodly amount. I don't do much socializing."

Her voice had a quality that he had never heard from her before, in person or via recordings. The ever-present warmth and playfulness had fled. In their place was something cooler and more analytical.

She knew, he realized. She didn't know why, but she knew that her gift was failing her.

"I can't verify it," Hector said. "But it seems likely you've met, and if you have, he's working for you."

"The people who work for me work here," Wendy said. "That's contractual."

"Enola Hasbro works for you," he continued. "Enola Hasbro lives in Villanueva."

"Enola is contractual also," Wendy said.

Her body language had changed, too. She sat erect in her seat, with her legs drawn together and her hands laced across her abdomen. She had assumed a classic defensive posture, perhaps without even realizing.

"That's true," Hector said. He was pleased, but careful not to let success make him overconfident. If Wendy wasn't at her best, neither was he; the protective measures he had taken carried their own price. His perceptions seemed faintly, almost infinitesimally blurred, and his thoughts were not entirely clear.

Despite that, he had the advantage.

"But Enola is a special case, and she's there with Over-Management authorization, he said. "Pym doesn't have that permission."

"Pym doesn't work for me," Wendy said flatly.

He pressed on. "You have the authority to file a complaint, if I apply pressure to have him removed from his contract," he said. "I'd like you to waive that authority."

"He'll be replaced," Wendy said lightly.

"That replacement will be fully vetted. He won't be anyone whose path has crossed yours," Hector said. "I can assure you of that."

"And if I *do* file a complaint?"

"Pym will be formally reinvestigated, and the inquiry will be more public than either you or he would like," Hector said. "Over-Management has excellent public information assets."

As if by force of will, her body relaxed. She leaned close to him, so close that he could feel the warmth of her breath. Again, she smiled, and again, she dimpled. "Really, Hector, is this necessary?" she asked.

"Of course it is," he said. "My office spent considerable person-hours and credit dismantling your old network. I'm not going to permit you to install a new one."

She pulled back, as if struck. "You have no proof that Pym works for me," she said.

"That's why he'll be allowed to keep his career," Kowalski said. He knew that Scheer worried about what had become of her former minions. In that, she was like Erik.

At last, grudgingly, she nodded. "I'll take it under advisement," she said. She paused again. "You know, Hector, I was surprised to be told that you had come calling. I'm even more surprised now."

Kowalski refrained from smiling, but only with effort.

CHAPTER 11

"WHAT the hell is this?" Erik said. He slid the hardcopy toward Kowalski, seated before him. He pushed the sheet polymer film too hard, so that it shot past the edge of his desk and drifted lazily in the cool office air.

The security specialist eyed it for a moment before plucking it from midair and midfall. His expression remained neutral as he quickly read the several lines of text.

"It's Dailey Pym's letter of resignation," he said. "It's not addressed to you, though."

Erik glared at him. "It was routed to me by Contracts," he said.

Kowalski returned his attention to the document. " 'With great regrets,' " he read from it. " 'Promising opportunity on Earth,' " He looked at Erik again. "This all seems in order," he said.

"I am not amused," Erik said. His voice softened and became more businesslike. "There will be repercussions from this, Hector. I should have had time to prepare."

"There's time," Kowalski said. He tapped the hardcopy with one finger, and the plastic sheet popped like a drumhead. "Pym will be here for some weeks, at least. If it's absolutely necessary, he can consult until he's been reconditioned for Earth."

Tourists and others staying short periods didn't require it, but immigrants from Earth underwent genetic therapy to ensure their health in the lunar environment. Long-term residents required additional treatment to readjust to terrestrial gravity. The human body was a flexible and forgiving instrument, but it had its limits.

"In that event, he'd require appropriate oversight, of course," Kowalski continued. He set the hardcopy resignation back on Erik's desk.

"You did this," Erik said. "You pressured him some way."

"No," Kowalski said.

Erik looked at him disbelievingly. Kowalski was an expert in creating untenable situations for staff who had outworn their welcome.

"I didn't," Kowalski said. "Scheer must have."

"You spoke with her," Erik said flatly.

Kowalski nodded, still completely at ease. If Erik's questions and accusations discomfited him, he kept it from his voice and expression. "She agreed to sign off on his removal," he said. "I didn't expect this, though."

The ALC and Villanueva's corporate culture had changed somewhat in recent years, but outright resignations remained rare. Most workers' career tracks consisted of promotions and reassignments, following lines of corporate authority and alliance.

"She must want to make a point," Kowalski continued. "She's a woman who likes to do things her own way."

"I thought we'd agreed that dealing with her directly was a bad idea," Erik said. Kowalski's actions made little sense to him. For years, the security chief had made a fetish of avoiding contact, even indirect contact, with Wendy Sheer. He had kept her at more than arm's length, working through Enola or other subordinates when coordination was absolutely necessary.

"When did this happen?" he asked.

"I visited Armstrong yesterday." Kowalski's cool words were a challenge now.

"You saw her in person!?" Erik asked. The news that his subordinate had delivered so casually stunned him.

Kowalski nodded.

"I thought we'd agreed—"

"You thought it was a bad idea," Kowalski said, still matter-of-factly. "I agreed to talk to Hasbro first, and I did. I never promised not to talk to Scheer at all."

"This isn't like you, Hector," Erik said. Slowly, reluctantly, he continued. "Do I need to question your—"

"My judgment?" Kowalski interrupted. "I don't think so, no." From a tunic pocket, he drew a flat plastic case. Mirroring Erik's earlier gesture, he slid it across the desktop.

Erik opened it. A black metal decorative clip lay inside, three bent prongs arising from a single base. It looked like a proximity phone or personal recorder. He eyed the thing skeptically.

"Very nice," he said. "But I rarely wear jewelry, decorative or otherwise."

"I'm not sure you should wear this, as a matter of fact," Kowalski said. "I'm not sure it will work for you, not anymore."

"What is it?" Erik finally asked. One of Kowalski's affectations was that he liked gadgets and toys. Another was that he didn't like to volunteer information.

"Have you ever used a sleep machine?" Kowalski asked. He seemed honestly curious. "I know that you had a hard

time adjusting to your relocation. Some doctors prescribe—"

Erik shook his head. He'd had difficulty with the transition, but in retrospect, he suspected that the primary
causative factor had not been his new environment but
stress and troubled memories. Many of those early nights
had been filled with bad dreams. They had been nearly hal-
lucinatory mélanges of the events that had led to his dis-
grace and new beginning.

"No," he said, making the word sound even shorter than
it was. "Meditation helped. Time helped more."

"Some doctors prescribe sleep machines," Kowalski
said again. "It's an old technology, but they work very well
for some people. The Russians developed them, back when
the Russians still developed anything. They use electrical
inductance to impose new rhythms on the brain. They're
good for producing REM sleep."

REM sleep, Rapid Eye Movement sleep, was the most
restful part of slumber, when the brain integrated the day's
experiences into long-term memory. There was more to it
than that, Erik knew, but those were the basics.

"I haven't slept poorly in years," Erik said. It was not
entirely true. Rod and Todd's deaths had given him some
troubled nights. "I don't need a sleep machine."

"No, keep it," Kowalski said, as Erik made to pass the
case back to him. "It's not a sleep machine; it's an adapta-
tion. I told you we'd been working on countermeasures."

Briefly, he explained, lapsing into jargon to discuss only
a few technical points. Although the precise nature of
Scheer's gift was unknown and likely to remain that way,
the years had yielded considerable empirical data regarding the effect she had on people. Erik himself had pointed
the way, monitoring his own metabolic readings during a
text-only discussion with Scheer. The diagnostic relay's

output had shown specific anomalies in his brainwave activity, weak at first but growing progressively stronger as he conversed with her.

Kowalski's people had taken those data and integrated them with more and then reverse-engineered the process. They had created a variation on sleep machine technology that used low-energy inductance to interfere with the ability of the brain to respond to whatever signal Scheer sent. The effect was itself an irritant, like a nearly subliminal buzzing and blurring. According to Kowalski, the benefit was worth it.

"I don't mind if the world's edge is blunted, as long as hers is, too," he said.

Erik took the black clip from its box. He hefted it. The bit of functional decoration weighed nearly nothing, but it seemed strangely heavy in his hand.

It was the thing's import that he felt, he knew.

"This is all we needed, all this time?" he asked. It was difficult to believe.

Kowalski's arms crossed before his chest. His shoulders went up and then came down again as he considered Erik and the question. "It's what *I* needed. I tried it," he said, then repeated himself. "I'm not sure it will work for you."

Erik dropped the clip back into its box. He knew how Kowalski's mind worked. "I'll ask," he said after a long moment, even though he already knew the answer. "Why not?"

"You like her too much," Kowalski said simply.

"Everyone likes Wendy Scheer," Erik said. The words were familiar. He wondered how many times he had spoken them.

"*I* don't," Kowalski said. "Not when I'm wearing one of those." He paused and pointed before continuing. "I don't much like her most of the time, anyway. I work very hard at that. I don't even like the Proxy."

"Enola is nothing like Wendy," Erik said.

Kowalski shook his head. "That's not true," he said. "You know it isn't, or you should. Maybe you're too close to the problem."

"Forests and trees," Erik said softly. Without warning and with sudden intensity, homesickness stabbed at him. There had been a time when he was counted as an outdoorsman.

"Hasbro worries me, too," Kowalski continued. "We don't have as much material on her as on Scheer, but what we have is sufficient. Working for Scheer has changed her."

"How?"

"There's her vocabulary, for one thing. Word usage pattern analysis performed on their historical material shows a seventy percent convergence," Kowalski said. His head tilted slightly as he considered Erik. "You meet with her more frequently than I do. You must have noticed it."

Erik sighed. He wondered when he had lost control of the conversation. "No," he said.

"You should have noticed," Kowalski said. He was plainly skeptical.

But Erik hadn't. More than once, he had seen a ghost or a shadow of Wendy Scheer in Enola's body language and facial mannerisms, but never in her speech. Now that Kowalski had pointed it out, though, there was no denying the echo. He thought back to their most recent dinner together and shook his head in self-disgust.

"What about Enola, then?" he asked.

Kowalski shrugged again. "She's contractual," he said. "Or her role is. Replacing her just starts the cycle over, and eliminating her billet will take time. I'm not sure what to do yet."

Another question hung in the air between them, even though neither man voiced it.

What about Erik?

Of anyone remaining within Villanueva, he had enjoyed the most, and most personal, contact with Scheer. He had dined with her and danced with her before discovering her gift. Even afterward, he had worked with her, albeit under tightly controlled circumstances.

Kowalski had once proposed the banishment of any Villanueva resident even slightly acquainted with Scheer. A handshake, a nod, a murmured greeting would have been justification enough for drastic action. In more recent years, he had softened that stance somewhat, targeting known associates who held project-sensitive roles.

People like Erik. He wondered if Kowalski could trust him. He wondered if he could trust himself.

"You're right," he said slowly. He took the ear clip from its case again and eyed it. "Thank you for this. I'll put some thought into the Enola situation."

"I don't think you should—"

Erik's hand came up in a gesture of dismissal, forestalling the comment. "Give me some time," he said. "Look into Pym first."

"HELLO again, Hector," Pym said warmly. He was seated at his desk in his office, a slightly bemused expression on his broad features. A technician had peeled back a section of one white wall and was busily extracting data conduits, modulators, and other Mesh connectivity components from the space behind it. She was young blonde, pretty in a pragmatic sort of way, and Pym kept an eye on her as he stood to greet Kowalski.

"Pym," the security chief said in acknowledgment. He didn't seem to notice Pym's proffered thumb as he dropped into the guest chair without invitation.

"I hope you'll pardon the disarray," Pym said. "Evidently, we're undergoing a technical audit." He grimaced. "It came as quite a surprise. It's the first since I've been here."

"They're periodic and random," Kowalski said. It was a lie, but not the kind of lie that anyone was expected to believe. The intent was not to deceive, but to avoid an unpleasant truth.

"Oh," Pym said. He nearly laughed. "I thought my resignation might have prompted some action on your office's part."

Kowalski ignored the question implicit in the manager's words. "I wanted to discuss that with you, as a matter of fact," he said.

The technician drew another two meters of conduit from within the wall. It was limp, like soy noodles. She fed one end of it into the ring-shaped terminus of a diagnostic wand and drew it completely through, in a series of smooth, steady motions. The wand chirped, and the technician glanced in Kowalski's direction. She shrugged. The reading had been indeterminate.

Kowalski pretended he hadn't noticed. "I understand you're leaving the Moon," he told Pym.

"Some opportunities are too good to forego," Pym said. He seemed less flustered than amused by his guest's comment. "I assume you're here for my exit interview?"

"Not at all," Kowalski said. "This is just a courtesy call. You've been local for three years?"

Pym nodded.

"You'll need reconditioning, then, before you go back to Earth. We'll have ample time."

Genetic retherapy and counseling were standard clauses in any Villanueva employment contract. Officially, they were intended to ensure the health and well-being of staff.

On a more practical basis, they offered management considerable room in which to maneuver during transition periods.

"Why are you here, then?" Pym asked. "It's the second time in only a few days." Real emotion showed in his voice as he grinned wryly. "Only the second time in three years, as well. I would hate to think—"

"It's a courtesy call," Kowalski said. He paused for effect. "I know that technical audits can be very disruptive to the workplace, sir. I want you to know that I appreciate your cooperation."

The blonde woman working on the wallpaper was only one of seven staff he had stationed on-site. In the production area, the others on Kowalski's team were busily dismantling and inspecting culture cabinets.

"I don't believe that I had any choice," Pym said.

Kowalski shook his head. "That's not what I mean," he said. "I spoke with my representative in the production room. He tells me you've been extremely accommodating."

"I just wanted to make things easier for whoever replaces me," Pym said.

The blonde technician had replaced the segment of data conduit with a new one. She took a modulator and jacked it into another diagnostic tool. It chirped, too.

"That's very considerate," Kowalski said. "I hope my personnel don't wear out their welcome during your transition period."

Pym's eyebrows lifted again. The smile he made this time was not wry, but sardonic. "A technical audit takes that long?" he asked.

"It can," Kowalski said.

"This one will," Pym said, in flat acknowledgment.

Kowalski nodded. They were still speaking in circles, carefully avoiding the true topic of conversation. By tendering his resignation, Pym had, to some degree, removed himself from certain aspects of the separation process. The security office could still bring considerable pressure to bear on him, but now a modicum of tact was appropriate.

Pym had a contractual right, even a responsibility, to ease the transition by readying his projects for his successor. Kowalski, for his part, insisted on some oversight during the process.

The true reason for his visit, and for the audit, was to let Pym know that they would be watching him.

"We have to verify the facility's physical and data management integrity," Kowalski said. "An audit Ship Site found anomalies in the coding clusters. We need to identify their cause."

"We had nothing to do with that," Pym said sharply. Now, at last, the geniality fell away. "My team does its job, sir. Our product has passed every functional audit. It performs to spec."

"It does," Kowalski said. "If it didn't, you wouldn't still be here. The issue is subtler than that." He paused. "Why did you resign, Dailey?"

Pym rubbed one of his temples and sighed. "An opportunity arose," he said. "I'd really rather not talk about it."

"When we spoke before, you said that this was the work you wanted to do," Kowalski said. He spoke more gently now. Even in his professional capacity, he was not entirely immune to compassion. "Do you really think your job is done?"

"My job *here*, at least," Pym replied.

SYLVA Taschen had highly refined tastes, and she'd been delighted by how well the Villanueva colony could indulge them. Zonix Hospitality maintained vast hotel spaces in and near the Mall, priced to meet all lines of credit. Sylva had commandeered the best suite available and had been pleased and surprised at how good it was.

The sitting room's physical configuration made it large and airy, and a variety of wallpaper options were available to make the space seem even larger than it was. Sylva had opted for a composite feed from the Greek islands, a view patched together from countless sources. Blue-green waters seemed to stretch endlessly in all directions as she and Erik sipped aperitifs on a simulated balcony overlooking the miraged Mediterranean.

"Did you enjoy the meal?" she asked.

He shrugged. "It was fine," he said. He held his wineglass in one hand, warming the beverage's deep ruby with his own body heat but not drinking. "More than fine, really. You've been considerate, Sylva."

She'd ordered a light dinner for both of them and taken pains to accommodate his remembered palate. A hotel chef had sautéed farm-raised calamari at their tableside, then served it with tomato and basil, both fresh from the hydroponics farms that Erik had explained lurked somewhere on the colony's lower levels. It was a meal that they'd eaten before, in happier times.

"Do you remember the first time we shared calamari?" she asked.

He surprised her by nodding. "Our honeymoon," he said. "In Tuscany. You'd never eaten squid before."

"And when was the last time?" she asked.

"At the divorce dinner," Erik said readily. "In the spirit of symmetry, you said."

Sylva smiled faintly in agreement. The last days of her marriage to Erik had been grim and contentious, but the end itself had gone remarkably well. They had worked together closely and with surprising accord. They had been united by a shared desire to become separate again.

How odd it was, then, to be here with him again, in surroundings that were at once familiar and new.

"Did you enjoy your day?" he asked.

"Oh, yes, much more than I'd anticipated," she said. "To be honest, I had never dreamed that there would be so many shops, or that they would be so nice."

"It's largely a consumer economy, Sylva," Erik said in mild reproof. He sipped some microscopic portion of his wine. "Even now, even with all the production work, people come here to spend credit."

"And believe me, I have," Sylva said. She smiled with easy self-satisfaction. "Did you know that Auguste Hartier is here?"

"Hartier?"

"That's just like you, Erik," she said. "You remember our honeymoon dinner but not the sculpture garden in our first home together."

"Oh. The cockroach gallery," Erik said. He flinched, clearly recalling the series of ornamental statuary that Sylva had loved so much. "I always hated that thing."

"It wasn't a cockroach," Sylva said. She rolled her eyes. "That was *Arthropod Variation Seven*."

Her handbag rested on a nearby sidebar. When she rose to retrieve it, her steps came easily and with more confidence than they had before.

"You're adapting faster than I did," Erik said, when she sat down again. "In a month, you'd be moving like a native."

"But I won't be here for a month," she said. From her handbag, she drew the cheap computer that she'd bought at a Mall kiosk. She thumbed it to life and opened the appropriate image. "Here," she said. "Look at this."

The thing in the picture was black and chitinous. It had claws and mandibles and wings, all in asymmetrical array, and all painstakingly shaped from lunar basalt. The dark stone had been polished and perma-glossed, and its contour lines were overlaid with silver traces. Sylva thought it was beautiful, in a dark and majestic way. It spoke to her of the exotic and the unknown.

Erik shuddered, too emphatically to be entirely sincere. "Another cockroach," he said, but he spoke in a light and bantering tone. If the comment was a joke, or even an attempt at one, it was the first she'd heard from him in a very long time.

"*Arthropod Variation Six-Three-Seven,*" Sylva corrected him. "Auguste has a gallery on the main concourse, and he remembered me," she said. "Isn't that nice? He's here because of his heart."

The Moon's lower gravity was kind to those with cardiovascular issues that couldn't be repaired otherwise. Relocation was radical therapy, though, and entailed a balancing act, weighing the hazards of travel with the benefits of arriving.

Erik examined the image more closely, accessing the callout that provided size and weight information. "Freight back to Earth won't be cheap," he said.

"I believe that I can afford it," she said, vaguely pleased by his observation. She realized that she'd missed his attention to the mundane.

"There's much I miss about life on Earth," he said. The computer rustled as he passed it back to her. "I miss hunting and fishing and nature. I don't miss cockroaches."

They spoke easily for a few minutes more. She told him of her other purchases, and he outlined some of the day's more interesting business.

Erik's role within Over-Management was largely one of

coordination. Five sister corporations made up the ALC superconglomerate, along with countless contractors and subcompanies. Erik's office worked to strike a balance between those many and diverse drivers and to coordinate contract activities between the ALC and its federal clients. He didn't provide many specifics, but the easy authority with which he spoke told her much. He wielded considerable power, she realized, at least on a practical, pragmatic level.

He had come far since being exiled from Earth.

The only member of his staff Erik mentioned specifically was a woman named Inex Santiago, and his tired eyes brightened when he did. His evident interest piqued Sylva's own.

"You said you weren't seeing anyone," she said, half teasing, half curious.

He shook his head but managed a smile. "It's more of a mentor/protégé situation," he said. "I'm an old man, Sylva."

She did something she hated. She giggled. "You're not old, Erik," she said. "You have a lot of years ahead of you. More than you would on Earth, and more than you would have in the last century."

"That's not always a blessing, Sylva," he said. He looked at her with infinite sadness. "It's a terrible thing, to outlive your children."

"I know," she said. She had loved Rod and Todd and perhaps had even known them better than he had, but they were his sons and not hers. The bonds of blood were very strong.

She sighed. "We should talk about them," she said. "We've delayed long enough, I think."

He nodded. His eyes brightened, and he looked old and tired, but his voice was clear when he spoke. "Tell me about them," he said. "Tell me when you saw them last."

She'd spent the previous Christmas with both twins and their wives, she told him, in a home they'd leased for the occasion. In Lima, Peru, in a penthouse apartment overlooking the Pacific Ocean, the Morrison sons had hosted a holiday gala, with her as the guest of honor.

"They loved you very much," Erik said. It was a simple statement of fact. He drank more of his wine. "I'm ashamed to say that I envied you that, sometimes."

"That's the past, Erik," she told him. "It's not what we need to talk about now."

"The ashes," he said curtly, with a sharp head nod.

"Veronica's only stipulation was that they not be interred," Sylva said. "She doesn't want them buried away somewhere, where they won't see the sun."

He almost laughed at that. "That's nonsense. They aren't going to see anything," he said.

This time, his hardheaded literalness annoyed rather than amused, but she made no complaint. "It should be somewhere appropriate," she said slowly. "I think that it should be somewhere unlikely to be disturbed."

"One of the preserves, then," Erik said. He gazed into the wallpaper, watching prerecorded gulls kite and wheel in the cloud-flecked pseudosky. His words seemed to come from a great distance.

"Preserves?" she asked.

"The Feds have retained control of several historical sites—where probes crashed and the early ships landed. They're landmarks, exempt from prospecting or industrial work," he explained. "It's not something we argue about."

"You can arrange something?" Sylva asked.

"I think so," he said. "God knows, Scheer's people owe me enough already."

"Scheer?" Sylva asked. The name was only vaguely familiar.

"Director of Project Halo," Erik responded. He scowled slightly. "I can send you a backgrounder. I don't feel like talking about her just now."

She had heard that tone in his voice before. This Scheer had hurt him in some way, hurt or betrayed him. Sylva wondered who she was and what had happened between them.

"If it raises contractual or jurisdictional issues—" she began.

He shook his head again. "It shouldn't be difficult," he said, dismissing her objections with a hand wave. "And Veronica is right. They shouldn't be buried away."

He was still gazing into the distance, as if looking at something she could not see. Sylva studied him carefully. His expression remained sad, but it was a gentler kind of sadness. His pain seemed to have lost some of its urgency. She wondered how long it would be before he was at peace again.

"Erik, you're dealing with this well," she said.

He turned and looked at her quizzically. "It doesn't feel that way," he said.

"No, you are," she continued without challenge. "When I spoke to you from Earth, I was *so* worried. But now that I'm here—"

"Your being here helps," he said. "It means more than you can know."

"No," she said. "It's more than that. I don't know what steps you've taken, but they're helping."

He looked at her for a long moment, in complete silence.

CHAPTER 12

"ERIK," Sander Adkins said. He blinked in mild surprise. "You're early."

"I hope you don't mind," Erik said, entering. "My schedule is in flux at the moment. I have a lot on my plate, and I'm constantly trying to rearrange it."

Adkins's current office was new to Erik's experience. He liked it. If simple economics said that the paneling and shelves had to be plastic, at least they looked like aged oak. They were real, too, physical structures rather than trompe l'oeil wallpaper images. The barrister-style bookcases were crammed with old-style hardcopy books and antique bound volumes of professional journals. Along their tops and on the walls were numerous trophies and plaques that Erik assumed were awards. The decor gave the place a sense of solidity that Erik found reassuring.

"The decor is something of an affectation, I know," Sanders said, noticing his interest. "The books alone have taken me years to accumulate, but it's a one-time expense.

I'm in Villanueva to stay; I won't be paying freight for a return trip to Earth."

"Do you have family on Earth, Sander?" Erik asked. The personal question surprised him even as he spoke it. "Do you miss them?"

"A former wife, a son, a daughter-in-law," Adkins said easily. "I suppose I do. But I speak with them regularly, and I have new family here." His lips twitched. "That's the kind of question that I should ask you, you know," he said.

Erik settled into a guest chair styled to match the shelves. If the seat held diagnostic equipment, it was well concealed. "Three former wives," he said. "One of them is here, now. Two sons, both deceased. I miss them terribly."

"Ah. Of course you do," Adkins said. He turned in his seat so that he faced Erik squarely. "I'm sorry. I should have been more sensitive."

"I miss them, even though years had passed since we spent much time together," Erik continued. Part of him thought the words should have hurt more than they did. "That was my fault, I suppose."

"*Fault* isn't a very good word in this kind of situation," Adkins said. His right index finger traced a geometric pattern on his desktop. More gently, he continued. "Are you here to see me in a professional capacity, Erik? It would be a good idea, but there are procedures—"

Erik shook his head. "Not professional, but business, at least," he said. "But first, I want you to know that I've made some progress. A beginning, I think."

"Are you seeing anyone?" Adkins asked.

He shook his head, then changed it to a nod and grinned, however faintly. "Well, I'm seeing my ex-wife," he said.

"That's not what I meant," Adkins said.

"I know," Erik said. "But she's here, and it helps. She wasn't the boys' mother, but . . ."

His voice caught and thickened. He felt his eyes sting. By the time that Adkins offered him a tissue, however, he had reasserted control and felt safe waving it away. "They were very close," he continued. "Seeing Sylva helps."

"Why *are* you here, then?" Adkins asked.

"I wanted to know who spoke to you about me," Erik asked. "About me, about Rod and Todd, about the entire situation."

"I was concerned," Adkins said. "Media Relations alerted me to the deaths—"

"It was more than that," Erik said. "Someone asked you."

He was sure of that now. For the past few days, his thoughts had come more easily, and he had devoted more than a few of them to Adkins. The counselor's office call had been no mere professional nicety. He had thought that from the first, and he thought it more strongly now. Someone had set Adkins on him deliberately, choosing him because of their past sessions.

"You're an EnTek man, Erik, and a highly placed one. Or you will be, when you come back from Over-Management," Adkins said. "The company takes a proprietary interest."

"Who was it?" Erik asked again. His voice hardened a bit. "Kowalski? Inex?"

Adkins shook his head. Whether it was to reject the names or to deny that he would answer at all, Erik could not tell.

"You have a history," Adkins said slowly.

He meant the drinking, Erik realized.

"You tend to retreat," Adkins continued. "People notice that, especially in a manager, and especially in a senior manager."

"I'm working full days again," Erik said. Today was the first, but he saw no need to provide that detail.

"You tend to retreat from personal pain." Adkins was choosing his words carefully. "When you were injured—"

"That was a special case," Erik interrupted. "Those were unique circumstances."

"During our sessions after your injury, that became evident," Adkins continued. "We talked about your initial relocation to the Moon, remember?"

Erik snorted. "We didn't talk very much about that," he said.

Adkins made another faint grin. "We spoke enough," he said. "I know that you pulled back from dealing with that, too."

"There wasn't much to pull back from. It was a figurehead position," Erik said. He had succeeded, almost by misadventure, in finding and seizing more meaningful responsibilities. Chance had given him the *Voyager* find and, they told him, a place in history. Even so, his original billet had been little more than a sinecure.

"You drank," Sanders said.

"You didn't know me then," Erik said. Once again, as it had with Kowalski, control of the conversation was slipping away from him. For the moment, it didn't matter, he supposed. He was learning at least some of what he wanted to know.

"No, but I spoke with people who did," Adkins said.

"And you've been speaking with them again?" Erik prodded.

Adkins didn't answer the question. "The morning I visited you at your office, you'd been drinking heavily the night before," he said, instead. He raised both hands and wiggled his fingers, making it obvious that they were bare, but also reminding Erik of the rings he had worn. "I was wearing diagnostic gear. I knew."

"Not to excess," Erik said.

"You have a history of drinking to excess," Adkins continued. "At least under stressful circumstances."

"No," Erik said.

"You're not unique," Adkins said. He seemed to think they were words of consolation. "Alcohol is the oldest drug, and the potential for alcoholism lives deep in the human genome. You might say that it's human nature."

"I don't drink too much," Erik said doggedly.

"I don't think you're the best judge of that, frankly," Adkins said. He looked serious. "You were showing all the signs of clinical depression. It's only reasonable that the people who know you best took notice."

"Who sent you to me?" he asked yet again.

"I can't tell you that," Adkins said. "But it was out of concern."

Erik snorted again. "And what did your report say?"

"Report?" Adkins looked at him blankly for a long moment before comprehension dawned and lit his face. "There was no report for me to make, Erik," he said. "I'm a medical professional. We have a doctor/client relationship, even now, and I'm in no position to judge your fitness for duty in any official capacity. I came to see you because someone was concerned about you, worried for your sake. I wasn't commissioned to write a report on you."

Erik felt no reassurance. Adkins's professed stance didn't track well with what he understood of the way the world worked. He pushed the thought around in his mind, pulling it this way and that, trying to find a weakness. He couldn't.

"You don't trust very easily, do you?" Adkins asked. He looked at his computer and grimaced. "You arrived early," he said. "But so did my next appointment. Do we need to talk about anything more?"

"One thing more," Erik said. Something occurred to him. "A moment ago, you said I was showing signs of clinical depression."

Adkins nodded.

"Was," Erik said again, emphasizing the word.

Adkins nodded again.

"What about now?" Erik prodded.

Adkins drummed his fingers, a thoughtful expression on his face. "I can't offer a formal diagnosis," he said. "If you want one—"

"Just tell me," Erik interrupted. "You've been studying me enough, from the sound of things."

"You're still grieving, but something has changed, I think," Adkins said. He looked at a discreetly placed computer display. "The chair says you haven't been drinking as much. You seem to be engaging directly with issues. From what you've said, you're reaching out to family and friends." He paused, thinking. "You've made progress," he continued. "More than I would have thought likely in such a brief period, especially without help." He paused again. "Have you had help, Erik?"

AT this time of the standard day, Ship Site's orbit put it low on the horizon, as far as it could be from Villanueva Base without being blocked completely by the Moon's mass. On Earth, the equivalent circuit would have posed no problem or even inconvenience, and communications would have been transparently easy. But Earth was surrounded by a dense halo of artificial satellites, built up by more than a hundred years of development.

The Moon was different. Trine's academy instructors had more than once made the point that Luna was not so much a satellite as a partner in a twin-planet system. It was a world itself, even if a small one, and vastly less occupied with only a relatively rudimentary orbital infrastructure. Inter-Mesh communications between Ship Site and Villanueva was extremely data-intensive and tightly prioritized. From the construction site's current attitude, discretionary throughput was weak and spotty.

That was why Michelle Esposito's image flickered in and out of focus as she spoke to Trine. That, and the hostel's cheap Mesh assets.

"Hello, Trine!" Michelle said. "Do you still have your feet? Or are your ankles bloody nubs now?"

"It's not that bad, once you get used to it," Trine said, and laughed. She was perched on the edge of her rented bed, stubby legs folded neatly. The smartbucket was in its storage niche. "You'd be surprised," Trine continued. "Gravity can be nice."

Michelle rolled her eyes in mock disgust. She was Trine's cabinmate in the Ship Site dormitory, and they had much in common, but Michelle had never been a fan of life on the Moon's surface. As soon as she had qualified for the candidate crew, she had relocated to Ship Site and never looked back.

"Tell that to my mother," Michelle said, composing her pretty features neatly again. More than once, she had told Trine of her mother's medical problems and how they had led her to live on the Moon. "She would have loved Ship Site."

They had de-spun the residential module for some reason, Trine realized. Michelle's low-resolution image drifted lazily in the visual pickup's field of view. Even the miniscule pseudogravity of their home had been canceled. Michelle must have been in heaven.

"Why are you calling, Michelle?" Trine asked. Receiving the link cost her nothing, but she didn't like to see credit wasted. A feed this poor wasn't worth any price, no matter how low.

"I wanted to know when you're coming back, silly," Michelle said. White teeth flashed in a grin. "You keep filing for extensions."

"I still have downtime left," Trine said.

"Are you going groundhog, Trine?" Michelle asked.

"No, no, don't be silly," Trine said. She crossed her arms and pretended to shudder at the very idea. She had worked long and hard to join and stay with the Ship Site candidate crew. The idea that she had doubts now was mildly offensive, even offered in jest and even offered by a friend. "But I've been so busy, and I've been having so much fun—"

Michelle's grin widened. "Have you met someone, Trine?" she asked.

"You're still being silly," Trine said. "But there's the Party Sector and the shops and the Mall, and I knew that I would need to come back here for my banquet—"

"Your banquet," Michelle said. Even with poor audio quality, the disdain in her voice was clear. Contrary to almost everyone's advice, Michelle had declined her invitation to the congratulatory banquets. She had opted to audit hers from orbit rather than venture into the Moon's shallow gravity well, without a more compelling reason.

Trine wondered sometimes what Michelle would do if down-selected for the final crew assignments. She was likely to find adapting to ground-bound life difficult.

"—and I was invited to the museum exhibit dedication, too," Trine said. "By Erik Morrison himself."

Michelle's eyes widened in question. Trine answered them in short, fast sentences. She told Michelle about her chance encounter with the powerful man, and about his causally tendered invitation.

"That explains it," Michelle said suddenly, marginally more businesslike. "That explains why they keep clearing your extensions. You have friends in high places."

She spoke with unconscious irony. At the moment, she was higher than anyone in Villanueva, at least physically.

"What do you mean?" Trine asked. "I have plenty of downtime left. It's use-or-lose."

Somewhere offscreen, Michelle's fingers released whatever handhold they had gripped. The other girl's image began to rotate slowly on the screen. "We're working double shifts here, Trine. Even a work addict like you would feel the heat," she said. "The only new leave requests they're clearing are for the banquets."

"Why? What's happening?" Trine asked, worried now. Being absent in crush time, even if unknowingly, could be bad for her career.

"They're flushing the Gummis completely! All of them!"

Trine felt her eyes widen. "What!?" she demanded.

Michelle nodded emphatically. Combined with her leisurely spin and the import of her words, the new movement was enough to make Trine faintly queasy. "We're going to have to recalibrate *everything*," she said.

"Why would they do that?" Trine asked. The news of the mass dump was difficult to grasp, and the ramifications were enormous. "Those were only a few months old!" she said. She paused as a new thought struck her, recalling the recent audits. "Michelle, should we be talking about this?" she asked.

"I don't see why not," Michelle said. She bent her legs at the knees and drew them up tight against her body. One had pushed against something, and she rolled lazily around a second axis. Combining somersaults and cartwheels was a specialty of Michelle's. She had remarkable body control and could keep herself on-camera with no apparent effort.

"Stop that," Trine said sharply. "Be nice and look at me when we speak."

Michelle ignored the demand. "They *say* it's a routine upgrade," she continued. She shrugged, adding another element of diversity to her gyrations. "They *say* it's nothing to worry about."

"Do you believe that?" Trine asked. She didn't. The series of reviews had been nearly without precedent in their comprehensiveness.

"I think so," Michelle said. "They haven't told us *not* to talk about it, and I haven't heard any screams from the questioning rooms. Besides, I interned on the original calibration sequence for this series, and I haven't seen anything go wrong since then."

"And you're an expert?" Trine asked, but relief mingled with skepticism in her voice. Michelle *was* something of an expert. If she thought the situation was an operational problem and not a security drive—

Security. The word seemed to ring in Trine's ears, and she abruptly realized why her downtime hadn't been canceled or interrupted.

It had to be Kowalski.

"We miss you, Trine," Michelle continued. She was still spinning. "I need someone to yell at."

"It hasn't even been three weeks," Trine said. She had planned to stay for a far shorter span, but the visit's duration had crept upward in one- and two-day increments. The expense was minimal, if she planned carefully enough, and she hadn't been eager to shuttle between Ship Site and the surface without pressing need.

"We could use you here," Michelle continued. "They

flushed the third dormitory module yesterday, and all the environmental systems are out of whack. Luther is going crazy."

Luther Guinn was Trine's crew chief. He should have been the one telling Trine that they could use her back on Ship Site. "Luther doesn't need me," Trine said.

"Oh, yes, he does," Michelle said knowingly. She leered, and her fingers wiggled.

"Stop that! He's older than time!" Trine said again, but this time she giggled. The only use Luther Guinn had for her was to calibrate system interfaces. "Michelle, tell Luther I'll be back soon," she said. She paused, recalling the terminus date of her most recent approved extension. "I'll be back after the dedication ceremony, I think."

"Why do you want to attend that?" Michelle asked. "Isn't the banquet enough? Are you a fuss-hog?"

"I want to go," Trine said obstinately. "And I think someone wants me to be there."

"TRINE Hartung messaged you," Inex said, concluding her report. "She's messaged you four times, as a matter of fact. The answerer flagged her message and responded, but she keeps calling."

Erik nodded. The name was familiar, but only vaguely. After a moment's thought, he remembered a short and dynamic girl in her stocking-clad feet, beaming at him. Hartung was the crew candidate he'd met in the Mall. He wondered what she wanted.

"I don't know," Inex said when he asked. She shrugged. "I don't even know who she is."

"She works on Ship Site," Erik said, mildly surprised that she'd thought the messages significant enough to forward but not to research.

"I know that," Inex said. "Environmental systems engineer and Biome company bones, even though most of her duties involve Duckworth-cognizant systems."

Erik looked at her quizzically.

"I know who she is," Inex said sweetly. "I don't know who she is to you."

"Just an acquaintance," Erik said stiffly. This was an aspect of herself that Inex only rarely put on display. He didn't like it, but he took the bad with the good.

"An acquaintance that you fast-tracked onto the VIP list for the exhibit dedication," Inex said.

Erik wondered why he'd done that. It had been an impulsive gesture and one that cost him nothing, but a pretty smile on a bad day really didn't justify violating protocol. He sighed. What was done was done.

"Have someone respond personally," he said. "Tell her she's still welcome but that we can't accommodate guests, if that's what she wants."

The most minor item on his agenda resolved, he returned his attention to affairs of greater import. One by one, he and Inex worked their way back up the list of items she had presented. More than a few, he delegated to her and granted permission for her to delegate them in turn.

There was a lot to do, and the resources at his beck and call were stretched thin. Most of the work was logistical in nature, simple but time consuming. With Erik's authorization, Kowalski had set into motion a wide array of systems security measures, many of them presented as simple administrative drills.

Kowalski personally was conducting a functional audit of the Heuristic site and had assigned much of his available workforce to the job.

Over-Management Personnel had been tasked to initiate a candidate search, to identify potential replacements for

Dailey Pym. The search criteria included preliminary background questions that, again, were of Kowalski's personal creation.

Ship Site personnel were in the midst of an abruptly scheduled dump-and-replace cycle, removing Gummis and installing new ones that had been force-grown by Heuristic personnel under Kowalski's close supervision.

The net result was that processes had been disrupted, personnel had been reassigned, and Erik had been deprived of the services of one of his closest subordinates.

He did what he could, feeding Inex data and insights gleaned from his own experience and authorizing new budget items and charge numbers.

"How is morale?" he asked, during a lull.

"Your staff is fine," Inex told him. "They're very happy with you. All of them."

That wasn't why he'd asked, but the data point pleased him. "What about you, Inex?" he asked.

"I'm happy with you, too," she said, and favored him with a patrician smile. "Dawg isn't, but that will pass."

"Dawg?" Erik asked.

"From Accounting," she reminded him. "I've been working evenings and have had less time for him."

A few weeks before, he would have been surprised to hear her tender personal information so casually. Things had changed, however. His off-loading of responsibilities onto her trim shoulders shorted the line of authority between them. She was still very much his subordinate, but a subordinate with new authorities of her own, and those duties put their dealings in a slightly different context.

"Make time for him," Erik said. "Or if not for him, make time for someone." He said it lightly, not wanting to give her a wrong impression. It was one thing to have a passing interest in her personal life; it would have been quite another to be interested in her personally.

But he didn't want her to make the mistakes he had made.

TRINE didn't like spending, but she liked shopping. She liked what her mother called "shopping with the eyes," moving from display to display and examining the offered wares and services. To buy would be to spoil the fun, so she bought as rarely as possible, and even then with great reluctance.

The Mall offered ample opportunity for her favored pastime. Dress shops offered scandalously expensive outfits that would flatter even Trine's stocky build, but who would she wear them for, once assigned her final billet? Michelle?

Personal accessory shops offered wafer-thin persona proximity phones and cosmetic appliances that would respond to pheromone cues, but Trine thought they were silly. Enhancement was one thing, but wholesale deception was quite another. Sooner or later, everyone got naked, and Trine wouldn't like being asked to explain why she looked so different.

Galleries offered art and artifacts, but Trine's quarters Ship Site were small and shared. She had no space for any but the most minimal decorations, and few of those. Trine lived a life defined by pragmatism and functionality.

One piece caught her eye, however. It was on a stand before a tiny gallery off the main concourse, overseen by a malign-looking little man with suspicious eyes who watched her carefully. The sculpture was black basalt traced with silver, and it looked like an insect with serious genetic disorders. Feelers, legs, and a mandible sprouted from the thing at intervals that looked random, but the end result had rhythm and style.

"Arthropod Variation Eight-Nine-Twelve," the man said. He tapped the pedestal that held the thing. "A limited-edition casting, of course."

"Of course," Trine said. She had no idea what he meant, but manners cost nothing. "It looks like a palmetto bug."

The man laughed, but with warmth and honesty that Trine found surprising. "It's nonrepresentational," he said. "It's an allegory of the human soul and the endless struggle of the downtrodden against the forces of geometric imperialism."

"It looks like a palmetto bug," Trine said again, leaning close to it. "We had palmettos in Hawaii. I grew up there. Did the artist?"

"No, I am from France," the little man said. He laughed again. He clicked his heels together smartly and made a little bow. "Auguste Hartier, at your service."

"Oh!" Trine said. She blushed, genuinely embarrassed. "I didn't mean to insult your work."

"You didn't," Hartier said, still smiling. "I would much rather one of the Variations be likened to a palmetto bug than to a cockroach." He winked. "But truly, the work is symbolic."

Trine remembered his words as she glided back into the Mall and wandered the concourse, one patron among countless others. She thought about them some more as she settled onto a bench and watched the world go by again.

It really had looked like a mutant insect, she decided, whether palmetto bug or roach. She hadn't seen an actual insect since leaving Earth. Local plant life had been gene-tailored to pollinate quite nicely on its own, thank you, and the recycling species did their work under very carefully controlled circumstances. Bugs had no place here.

They had been omnipresent in her childhood, flying and crawling and eating their way through a world they surely could not understand. They had their roles, but did their lives have any meaning beyond brute function? Trine wondered.

She felt a vague sympathy. There was much about her present circumstance that she didn't and couldn't understand. Mere weeks before, she had been doing work she loved and was well on her way to achieving a goal she had set when little more than a child.

Now, things were different. She had in some way come to the attention of at least two very powerful men. If Michelle was correct—and she probably was; she usually was—at least one of those men had taken an interest in her life.

After her conversation with Michelle, Trine had messaged Luther Guinn. Upon careful prompting, he had confirmed that a flag had been placed on her file and that she was free to stay on the surface. It wasn't an order, but Guinn gently encouraged her to stay where she was, if only to curry favor with his own supervisors. Four hasty calls by Trine to Erik Morrison's office had gone unanswered.

Worrying didn't come easily, but she was beginning to develop the knack. She remembered her conversation in the Party Sector, when Hector Kowalski had asked her what she would do if the future she wanted so badly were taken away from her.

"Popcorn?" he asked her now, and waved a sack of popped kernels beneath her nose.

She nearly leaped from the bench. Hector Kowalski was seated beside her. He had settled into place so smoothly and quietly that he might have materialized.

"Where did—what!?" Trine asked.

"Popcorn," he said. "It's fresh."

"How did you find me!?" she asked sharply.

Kowalski merely smiled. He didn't withdraw the bag until Trine had accepted his offer and scooped up a handful of kernels. They were tender and fresh and bathed in mint-butter. She realized suddenly that she had forgone lunch.

"Thank you," she said. "It's good." She paused. "Hector, am I in some kind of trouble? Would you tell me if I were?"

He looked at her. The neutral expression on his face could have come from lack of knowledge or an excess of discretion. "Do you think you are?" he asked, and filled his mouth with popcorn. "Have you done anything wrong?"

"No," Trine said. She shook her head. "I don't think I have, but people like you don't talk so much with people like me unless there's a reason."

Kowalski didn't answer, not directly. Instead, he gestured to his left and said, "Look. Over there."

Trine looked. At odd angles from them, an attractive Asian woman was walking briskly along the opposing concourse, laden with purchases. She was taller than Trine and leaner, with hair that had been styled short and tight, so that it looked like a black metal skullcap. She wore a designer outfit, a white tunic with a moiré pattern, black toreador slacks, and a red half-cape. Trine had seen one like it in a shop window only moments before. The other woman had delicate features and large, luminous eyes, and even at a distance Trine could hear her heels click as they struck the floor.

The woman seemed oblivious to or at least unmindful of her surroundings. She didn't seem to notice the women and men in her path, many of whom (men and women alike) turned to eye her in the wake of her passage. The Asian woman seemed to have eyes only for her destination, whatever it was.

"What do you see?" Kowalski asked.

"Someone with a lot of credit and good genes," Trine

said. Michelle would have said the same thing, but in a nastier voice. "I wonder where she bought them?"

"More than that," Kowalski said, taking some more popcorn. He *was* an eater.

"She's lived here a long time and knows how to walk," Trine said. "Whatever she does, she's paid well for it; those are designer bags. She knows how to dress well and likes trendy things; that's a new outfit. She knows she's pretty, and I think she uses cosmetic appliances to stay that way, but I don't think she's on the hunt."

Kowalski nodded. "Not on the hunt," he said. "That's good. Why not?"

"She doesn't look at anyone."

"What else?"

"She's not famous, but she acts like she is," Trine concluded. "What do *you* see, Hector?"

"I hardly see her at all anymore," Kowalski said. He amended his statement. "I hardly notice her, I mean. That's the Proxy."

He told her what Trine suspected was a very abbreviated account of the life and times of one Enola Hasbro, who had been a design modeler and a Mesh personality and who worked now as a representative of the federal government. By the time he concluded, the Proxy was lost to Trine's sight.

"I deal with Hasbro so often that she's almost invisible to me in most circumstances, like a maintenance crewman or casino waitstaff," Kowalski said.

"Is she nice?" Trine asked, unsure again. She didn't like the conversation's new direction. "Do you—*like* her?"

Kowalski shook his head. "I don't like her at all," he said. "That's problematic, too, because I can't be neutral when I review evidence. The Old Man likes her. I'm not sure how much."

The nickname made Trine pause. "She's too young for Erik," she said. The first name came easily.

"Maybe," Kowalski said. He upended the bag and ate the last of his popcorn. Hard kernels cracked as he chewed. "But the real problem is, she's *wrong* for him."

He didn't sound as casual now. Undercutting his usual faint humor was an edge of steel. It was the sound of authority, and it set Trine's teeth on edge.

He really didn't like the Proxy, she realized.

"Hector," she said. "Why don't you want me to go back to Ship Site?"

"You're free to go," Kowalski said. It wasn't quite an answer.

"But I haven't been called back, and my crew chief says that my file has been flagged," Trine pressed on. "Why?"

"I like talking to you," Kowalski said. "You see things well, but you look at them differently than I do. I like your perspective."

"Oh," Trine said, relieved and disappointed at the same time. She realized suddenly that she had half expected something else, something more.

He stood. The plastic bag, completely empty now, crackled as he shoved it into a disposal slot. "I have to get back to work," he said. "I'm running a functional audit, and I don't want the targets to get overconfident."

Trine nodded. She should get back to work, too, she thought. She wondered if returning to Ship Site would be a good idea, no matter what he said.

He seemed to read her mind. "Don't worry about your crew, Trine, or your downtime," he said. "You're not in trouble, and you have nothing to worry about from me." He flashed one of his wider smiles. "You're an honored guest, and not just the Old Man's."

CHAPTER 13

SLEEP came poorly and with bad dreams. They fled when Erik awoke, bathed in sweat and tangled in his sheets. His heart was racing, and his voice came in short, sharp gasps.

"Light," he said in his command voice, and gentle illumination slowly filled the room, brightening as his eyes adjusted.

The final moments of the nightmare retreated, conquered by reality. As always, he tried to remember the content of the dream. As always, his success was only partial and fleeting. In seconds his subconscious had reclaimed its own.

He twisted and turned to sit on the edge of his bed. He took up a drinking glass from his nightstand dispenser and drank greedily. The cool water tasted good, but it felt better going down. He glanced at the clock and grunted. The time was halfway between standard midnight and dawn.

It was a bad time to be awake, a lonely time. Modern man, at least, was a diurnal beast. It shouldn't have mattered in the sunless colony city, but circadian rhythms had proven surprisingly persistent, at least for him. Erik knew that he'd get no more sleep that night, at least not without help.

Usually, Erik didn't particularly mind being alone, but now, for some reason, the emptiness of his home oppressed. He wanted to talk to someone, but he didn't know who.

The housekeeper was in nighttime mode. It stayed there as it tended to his needs. The system stayed silent, and the wallpaper displays remained blank, but the illumination seemed to follow him as he shuffled out into the apartment's main living area. The self-heating carpet felt good beneath his bare feet.

At first, he headed for the refreshment nook and the various bottles there. A drink would help him sleep. Mere steps away, he drew up short as he reconsidered.

A drink wasn't what he wanted.

"Give me the metronome," Erik commanded.

Obediently, the housekeeper generated a gentle tock-tock-tock noise. Erik listened as he opened the appropriate storage niche. A padded mat lay inside. He unrolled it on the floor and nodded. Years had passed since he had last used the thing, but the artificial fibers still smelled fresh and sweet.

Some things, the body seemed always to remember. He realized that yet again, as his legs folded beneath him and he assumed the lotus position without conscious thought. The mind might conceal or confuse, but the body never forgot.

Erik's eyes closed. His breathing slowed, and his heartbeat gentled, matching pace with the metronome. The world seemed to go away as he retreated into him himself. His last thought before entering trance state was to realize that this had been the true reason for leaving his bedroom.

He had learned this technique many years earlier, when

his journey to the new world had also proven to be one to nightmares as well. The shock of relocation, the new environment, the genetic therapy, and so many other factors had rendered him almost incapable of sleep. By learning meditation, he had learned to impose order on at least certain kinds of chaos. He could guide the body into a rest state and make the mind follow.

The body remembered the way. The body always remembered.

HE heard music. In a seamless, transparent transition, the metronome beats had resolved themselves into something more complex. Strings, woodwinds, brass, and piano mingled in three-quarter time.

It was a waltz. He was dancing to Strauss.

He was dancing with a woman, her left hand in his, her right hand resting lightly on his shoulder. She was looking up at him, gazing into his eyes. For some reason, even so close, her face was a soft-focus blur, but he scarcely noticed. He could see the sparkle in her eyes and the flash of flawless teeth, and that was enough.

Surrounding them both was the scent of old-growth forest. Rich and dense and organic, it was at once ancient and fresh. Underbrush crackled under their feet; impossibly, it both shifted and offered secure footing as they danced in the woods.

Déjà vu whispered a reminder in Erik's ear. He had been here before. He had been here, with this woman. The sense of familiarity was strong but not overwhelming.

"Are you happy?" she asked. The beauty of her voice made the orchestral music sound like industrial noise.

"No," he said. He could not lie.

"You should be happy," she told him.

A terrible sorrow swept through him, tidal in its force and overwhelming in its intensity. Tears stung the corners of his eyes, and he looked away so that she would not see. "No," he said. "I can't be. Not now."

"You can," she insisted.

Their bodies continued to move in time with the music, but her hand left his shoulder and found the line of his jaw. Gently, she guided him to face her again.

"I can't," was all he could think to say. "I'm broken inside."

"You can be happy," she told him. "You can heal."

"I can't," he said.

"You can," she said. Her tone was gentle, but the words were a command. "You can be well, Erik. You can heal. Do it for me."

The blur of her face resolved itself, but as it resolved, it changed. The framing halo of auburn became a tight shell of black. The lines of her jaw and chin shifted subtly. The eyes, colorless a moment ago, became dark and welcoming.

"I want you to be happy," his dance partner said, speaking in Enola Hasbro's voice. She rested her head against his chest, as if to listen to the beating of his heart.

The music played on.

ERIK'S eyes opened lazily, and his breathing became faster. Without conscious thought, as if running a brainware routine, he went about the business of rejoining the world. His cheeks were wet, so he dried them. He rolled the mat back into a tight cylinder and returned it to its lair. By the time he had accessed another glass of water, this one from the refreshment nook, his thoughts had coalesced sufficiently that he could consider what had happened during the trance.

It hadn't been a dream. He knew that. Dreams were the brain's way of filing information. They were chaotic jumbles of data, mixing old and new. Their content could be significant in a blunt, hammering way, but they were unreliable. This had been something entirely different.

Dreams were hard to recall. This event's specifics lingered in his mind, as clear and precise as a high-resolution Mesh production.

Those specifics were familiar. Now that he was awake and aware, he recognized the setting of the psychodrama. He had been dancing in the Grotto, an exclusive meeting place and social club that catered to the discreet and powerful. The Grotto had once been a fixture in the Mall, but its doors had closed years before.

Erik had gone to the Grotto with Wendy Scheer, soon after meeting her. He had danced with her, and they had spoken, though with less emotion and of other things. He had even encountered Enola Hasbro there, while Wendy saw to their reservations.

He had not thought about his visit to the Grotto in years. Why had he recalled it now? What was his mind trying to tell him? Why was it using old memories to tell a new experience?

The answer came to him abruptly, with the power of truth, obvious and undeniable. It made him pause in midsip, even in midbreath. The new knowledge filled his world so thoroughly that a moment passed before he could act on it.

"I need a file review," Erik said in his command voice. "Access all communications logs for the last month." He paused. "Detail any Mesh communications links between any of my accounts and Wendy Scheer."

"Scheer representatives?" the housekeeper asked. He had configured it well.

"No," Erik said. He shook his head. "Scheer-specific."

The query should have found no match, but the Gummi confirmed his worst fears. It offered up a time and date and duration data.

He had spoken with Wendy Scheer. He was one of the few with the authority to do that, but it was the kind of power that no one was ever supposed to use.

He had spoken with Wendy Scheer, and he couldn't remember what they had talked about.

"Was I drunk?" he asked.

The housekeeper's response was a blood alcohol estimate, based on breakdown products found in his exhalations. The number was impressively high.

Erik drained the last of his water. He licked his lips nervously and eyed the array of bottles in the refreshment nook. The fluid levels in too many of them were distressingly low.

"Play the conversation back," he commanded.

"That file has been deleted," the housekeeper answered. Placeholder music played as it searched its archives. *"All backup matrials have been deleted."*

"On whose order?" Erik asked.

"Yours."

•

CHAPTER 14

HOTEL Zonix offered guests service staff in matched sets. Sylva's selection for the day was a trio of Samoans. They were three men with postgraduate degrees in physical therapy, shiatsu, and Rolfing. They were huge men, big with both muscle and fat, and precisely similar to one another in form, feature, and attire. Sylva had to wonder if they were triplets or clones or both.

Their skills defied questioning, however. Sylva, sprawled facedown on the massage table, sighed in relief as ten strong fingers dug into the muscles of her shoulders and lower back, driving the tension from them. Another twenty fingers moved in eerie synchronization as they worked her calves and thighs.

As the three men worked, Sylva opened a Mesh link to Erik. "Good morning," she said, when his image appeared in the table's little dedicated viewer.

"Good morning, Sylva," he said. Erik had neglected to put mirage filters in place, she decided. He looked vastly

better than when she had spoken to him from Earth, but his eyes were bloodshot and hooded with fatigue. He looked tired and worried.

"Did you sleep well?" Sylva asked.

"I slept," he responded. He spoke in the pleasant but noncommittal tone she remembered well from their life together on Earth.

He was hiding something, she decided, and then decided that it didn't matter. She pressed on. "Are you free for lunch?" she asked. "Auguste is hosting a buffet at his gallery. I thought you might like to see him again."

"No, I'm sorry," he said, even though she suspected that he wasn't. He offered a courtesy smile. *"Extend my regards, though. For him and for his art."*

Sylva rolled her eyes. "It's not a cockroach, Erik," she said, with emphatic patience.

"I really am sorry, Sylva, but I'm not free for lunch," he told her again.

She continued. "Erik, I'm enjoying my stay—"

"I'm glad," he said, interrupting but with absolute sincerity. *"I'm very happy that you're here, Sylva. I only wish the circumstances were better."*

"I know," she said. She took a deep breath. "But I can't stay forever. I have business of my own back home. There are things that can't be managed at a distance."

He nodded. *"I'd hoped you'd at least stay until the dedication,"* he said.

"Of course I will," she replied. "But we both know that's not why I'm here." She paused, uneager to continue. "Have you been able to make the arrangements for Rod and Todd?" she asked.

"I'm speaking with someone later today," Erik said. He looked abruptly older and more worn. *"It shouldn't be difficult."*

"Good," she said. She paused. "I'm sorry we can't lunch today, Erik," she said. She meant it. Her time with him had been surprisingly pleasurable, especially given the circumstance.

"We'll see each other this evening," he reminded her. *"At the candidate crew banquet."*

TRINE woke late to find her living area nearly doubled. The hostel room, which had been scarcely larger than a monk's cell, had grown while she slept. One of the configurable walls had receded into its slot, joining her room with the one next to it. Together, their sum total was something that would have been modest by most standards, but bordered on sumptuous according to Trine's.

The cheap Mesh terminal was live, and it chimed as she stirred to life. A message in cursive script stretched across the low-resolution screen. *"Compliments of the management,"* it read.

Over-Management's compliments were more likely, Trine realized. Kowalski must have issued one of his directives.

The gift was unnerving but welcome. The annex included a small worktable and chair, so that Trine no longer had to breakfast in bed. She opened one of several prefab meals she had bought the day before, far cheaper than anything the hostel offered, and seated herself. As she ate the soy-elves, the course of the day took shape in her mind.

Tonight was her designated banquet session. Famous people would be there, ostensibly to honor her and her coworkers, but more likely to see and be seen. Even so, she was sure to draw attention. Two high-ranking members of Over-Management had taken interest in her. And it seemed that, for at least one of the two, that attention was more than casual.

She couldn't count on being simply one anonymous attendee among many. Prominent people were likely to speak with her, and that meant she would be there to be seen, too.

Trine nibbled her lower lip. Hector seemed very nice, in his own strange way, but she wondered if she might not have been wiser to stay with the green-eyed boy. Certainly, he'd have been less complicated.

Her best dress hung in the original room's armoire. It was a red shift with black offset, a garment of classic lines and reasonably high quality, but nothing terribly expensive or special. As recently as two days before, it had seemed entirely adequate for the official function. Now, it cried out for accessorizing.

On the hanger next to the dress was a logoed bathrobe that Trine had commandeered during a previous vacation. She shrugged into it, gathered up her personal toiletries, and headed down the corridor to the hostel's public 'fresher nook.

She sighed. She liked shopping, but she didn't like spending, and she knew that she had to do both.

"WHAT are you *doing*!?" The worker's question was midway between yelp of protest and angry demand. "That's four months work!"

Hector ignored him. Instead, he watched his assistant watch the growth cabinet's digital display as it presented sharply declining values tied to multiple metrics. The assistant seemed pleased with what he saw, so Hector was happy, too. Only the lab worker seemed perturbed.

"We're flushing the breeders, sir," the security assistant said. He wore white lab gear like the worker's, but with the ALC five rings rather than the Heuristic logo. "We encountered corruption in the coding strands, and we're starting over. The next batch has to be clear, and I need to make sure it is."

"I reviewed that report! Those were segregated alleles," the Heuristic staffer said. His outrage seemed sincere. "They weren't hurting anything!"

Something within the growth cabinet made a liquid gurgle that was barely audible over the apparatus's constant hum. In moments, the culturing medium drained away completely.

"Four months," the Heuristic worker said softly. He looked like he was on the verge of tears.

"We need to remove this," was the only reply that Hector's assistant offered. He tugged at the cabinet's cover and nodded as the Heuristic employee helped him remove the light shell of reinforced plastic.

"Erik Morrison," Hector's personal phone whispered in his ear.

Hector turned away from the two men as he knelt beside the tank and accepted the call.

"I'm meeting with Enola Hasbro," Erik's familiar voice said without preamble. *"I thought you should know."*

"When? Where?"

"Following lunch," Erik said. *"In my office. Are you going to join us?"*

The words could have been an invitation or a command. As Hector tried to decide which, he cast his gaze about the low-ceilinged production space. Unhappy-looking Heuristic staff stood at equipment banks, watching as Hector's team undid months and even years of hard work. Their displeasure and anger was a deliberate part of the functional audit process; Hector wanted to see how suspect personnel behaved in times of stress.

"I'd rather not," he said. "We're very busy here."

"How busy?" Erik asked.

Dailey Pym stood in the doorway to his office. The

dark-haired black man looked in Hector's direction. Their eyes locked briefly before Pym looked away again. He looked disgusted by the situation but not worried.

Hector wanted him worried.

"I think I'd better stay here," Kowalski continued. He saw no point in mentioning the previous day's brief run to the Mall, to reassure Trine Hartung. "Do you need me?"

Morrison's words came after a pause that seemed much longer than it actually was. *"No,"* he said. *"It's a scheduled session, routine business for the most part, but considering the Scheer situation—"*

"Scheer is why I should stay here," Hector reminded him. Something in Morrison's voice concerned him. "I can audit easily enough, though."

"I don't think that will be necessary," Morrison said, after another pause. *"But we should speak after, though."*

INEX'S assistant was Moon-born. A gangly young man with delicate-looking wrists and hands, he had slender legs that had never known the Earth's pull. As Inex's duties and development tasks consumed more of her time, she had off-loaded many administrative tasks to him. That was her decision, but Erik wasn't sure he agreed with it.

He doubted her decision even more as he watched the Moon-boy usher Enola Hasbro into the small interview room just off Erik's office. "Would you like something to drink?" the young man asked obsequiously. Erik half-expected him to bow and scrape. "A light refreshment?"

"We're fine," Erik told him, once Enola had shaken her head. He seated himself at the table and gestured for Enola to do the same.

His words went unheeded. The assistant continued,

clearly enthralled by Enola. Directing his words to her, he said, "We have real coffee and—"

"We're fine," Erik said firmly. He waved in dismissal.

"He seems sweet," Enola said, as the young man exited.

"He needs to remember who he works for," Erik said. The words came out more harshly than he intended.

Enola smiled, utterly at ease. She was accustomed to being the center of attention, for a wide variety of reasons, and she enjoyed it. Perhaps that was why she worked so well with Scheer. Enola had been recruited once to serve as a Mesh spokes-personality, and Erik was certain that she would have prospered in the role.

"You're a bit of a celebrity," Erik said. "And he's new at this."

"He'll learn," Enola said. She considered him. "That's something we—I've noticed over the years, Erik," she continued. "You have good staff, and they nearly always go on to better things."

Erik grunted, made uncomfortable by the compliment. "I've been fortunate," he said.

She shook her head. "I think your subordinates have," she said. "When I was with Duckworth—"

Once again, Erik gestured in dismissal. "That's not why we're here," he said. Talking about others' management styles without reason was something he found offensive. "And it was a long time ago."

He considered her carefully, trying neither to hide nor advertise his interest. He had known Enola longer than he had almost anyone else on the Moon, certainly longer than any other non-coworker. Even with that familiarity, it was sometimes difficult to draw a line from the flirtatious young woman he had met at Duckworth to the assured co-ordinator seated across from him.

"We all grow," Enola said.

She proved it as they conferred over production schedules, budget line items, and policy revisions. The ALC fully intended to profit directly from deep-space exploration, but that was a long-range goal. In the short range, federal funding was vital to the collaborative effort, and accepting that funding meant coordinating with Project Halo. Coordinating with Halo meant dealing with Enola.

At first, years before, Erik had thought that Enola had merely parroted information and insights provided by Halo when they worked together. Countless sessions had convinced him otherwise. For whatever reason, by whatever process, years as Wendy Scheer's representative had awakened unexpected aptitudes in Enola.

It was thirty minutes into this meeting that Enola raised the issue that had been on both their minds, the events at the Heuristic Genetech facility.

"We're concerned about the functional audit Kowalski is conducting," Enola said. "It seems unusually thorough."

"Hector doesn't like half-measures, Enola," Erik said. "You know that."

"Retroactive rejection of the most recent Gummi generation seems an excessive measure," Enola continued.

"It had to be done," Erik said. "There were quality concerns. The outfitting crew is bringing the previous generation back online until—"

"At considerable expense and delay," Enola said, interrupting. She looked at him seriously. "The systems that you're so busily scrapping had capabilities that the backups don't. You're sacrificing throughput, data processing capacity, and increased regenerative abilities."

"It's a quality-control issue," he asserted again. "We're working to resolve it."

"The delays are having a ripple effect on Halo's schedules," Enola continued. The scientific staff at Armstrong Base had responsibility for installing and configuring numerous analytical arrays on the deep-space probe.

"It's not my decision," Erik said.

"You could make it your decision," Enola said. Now she sounded like Wendy again, at least in word choice.

"I'm only a coordinator," Erik said.

"Nothing important happens unless you sign off on it," Enola said. "Officially or unofficially, you're the man who makes things happen."

"That's not true," he said stiffly.

"It's true enough," Enola said, pressing the issue. She leaned forward, her hands pressed flat against the tabletop. "I know how you work. I know that people listen to you."

"Hector ran an audit Ship Site and made the assessment. He reported his reasoning directly to Wendy," Erik said. "I'm sure you know that."

" 'Directly to Wendy,' " Enola said, quoting him. "Onsite, at Armstrong."

Erik shrugged again, but said nothing. Ordinarily, the game of feint-and-parry engaged or at least amused him, but not now. He felt old.

"Doesn't that strike you as unusual, Erik?" she said, dark eyes watching him. "Did you send him?"

"It's within his purview," Erik said. Kowalski had helped shape the containment policy regarding Scheer and was one of the few permitted at-will access to her.

Hector had never undertaken such a visit on his own volition before, however. Always, he'd conferred with Scheer only at Erik's behest.

"It's not like him to come calling, though," she said, echoing his thoughts. "Wendy was curious about that."

Erik allowed himself a smile, however slight. "Hector

told me about their meeting," he said, recalling Kowalski's careful account. "He seems to think it went very well."

A look of disgust flowed across Enola's features, so fleetingly that it registered fully only once it vanished. She said nothing.

"What's the matter, Enola?" Erik asked. He was all too aware that Enola still harbored a grudge against the security chief. "Are you concerned about keeping your job?"

Enola liked that. She leaned back in her chair and laced her fingers together over the smooth curve of her stomach. Still gazing at him, she laughed, hard enough to dispel the hint of tension that had built slowly between them.

Erik had heard that laugh before, but from someone else. It sounded like silver bells ringing.

"Oh, Erik," she said, still amused and still showing it. "I have no need to worry. Wendy likes me too much."

"Does she like you, or do you *think* she likes you?" Erik asked. The question was an honest one, and one he had wanted forever to ask.

"She likes me," Enola said. She said it with conviction, the absolute assurance of someone who spoke an undeniable truth. "I know that."

"How can you?" Erik asked.

"I *know,*" Enola said.

Erik wondered. That was the most confounding aspect of Scheer's gift; it was subtle and pervasive and extended even to the most fundamental of human interactions. Dealing with her directly on issues of business or policy was possible; cold reason could override Sheer's allure, even if only briefly and with great effort.

Personal dealings were different, however. People liked Wendy, and that made them want to believe that she liked them. No one could be truly objective about such things.

Enola took his silence as another question, one that he

would never have asked. She answered it gently. "She likes you, too, Erik," she said. "She doesn't care for Hector at all, but she likes you very much."

He flinched.

"She thinks you're important," she said. The words seemed to flow from her.

"That's to the good, I suppose," he said slowly. He was unsure how to respond.

"She knows about your sons," Enola said. Her tone was very gentle. "She's sorry. She's sorry about them, and she's sorry that you're so sad."

Her posture had shifted, moving from something languid and casual to a more formal, even authoritarian kind of poise. The lids that hooded her dark eyes lowered into a half-squint that he found tantalizingly familiar, and she held her head differently. The words she spoke seemed to echo faintly, like a stereo feed with the channels out of phase with one another.

"You're strong," she continued. "You'll heal. You have to."

He had heard words like that before, too.

"Who am I speaking with now?" Erik asked. The question surprised him as he spoke it. It seemed to arise of its own accord, from somewhere in the depths of his very being. Even as he spoke, he was aware that he had not addressed the seated woman by name.

Her response was in kind. She smiled and said, "To me, of course." The echo effect persisted.

Erik felt the hairs on the back of his neck struggle to stand on end.

"Thank you," he said slowly. He felt as if were not speaking to Enola now, but past her or through her. He felt as if he were speaking to someone not in the room with him. The effect was unsettling. He wished Kowalski had been there to experience it.

In his childhood, Erik had been an avid viewer of Mesh productions that dealt with the occult. He had spent many hours viewing programs about vampires and werewolves, about ghosts and demonic possession. He felt now as he'd felt then, swept up in something that defied normal experience, but this time, the experience was real.

"If there's anything—"

"There is," Erik said. He pressed fingertips to his temple and rubbed nervously, moving slowly to avoid breaking the spell.

Her eyes met his. Impossibly, they had become lighter in color, verging on a familiar hazel, and the effect did not seem to derive from cosmetic lenses. She waited.

"It's not a policy issue," he said, still speaking slowly. "Or not a major one. It's a personal favor. My sons' ashes—"

It happened then, or un-happened. Enola changed. Something seemed to flow out of her, and she settled back into her chair, a portrait in elegant repose. Her eyes widened and darkened again, and the cadence of her breathing shifted.

"You should ask her directly, then," the Proxy said. She smiled. Her face and her voice were her own again. "I can make the arrangements."

She spoke as if nothing had happened. Perhaps she didn't even realize that it had. He had seen Enola manifest Wendy's mannerisms before, but not like this. The effect had been stronger than ever before, yet even less clearly defined. Enola's transition from her personality to Wendy's had been seamless, without a clear-cut beginning or end. It seemed to have affected her more deeply, as well.

"That's not a very likely option," he said.

"Wendy often says she'd like to see you again," Enola said. "Coventry can be monotonous." Lips the color of pomegranates arched into a perfect smile. "And Hector is hardly her idea of a welcome visitor."

"It's about my sons," Erik said. He kept his words calm, but only with an effort. Emotions, turbulent and confusing, swept through him. Sorrow, attraction, confusion, and irritation all contended for expression. He gestured helplessly, feeling vulnerable and knowing how awkward he must sound. He said, "My former wife—"

Enola's cool hands, small and delicate but very strong, caught one of his. She held it for a long moment, gazing at him steadily. At her touch, he felt his mind clear, however minimally.

He had known Enola for a very long time. Her touch was welcome.

"Talk to her, Erik," she said. "Talk to Wendy."

"This can't be a quid pro quo," he said.

"You need to speak with her personally," Enola said. "You've done it before."

He knew that she was right.

SYLVA'S day was a good one, far better than she could have expected. For the first time since coming to this strange place, she felt in her own element. The gravity was wrong, and the air tasted different, but she had found much that was familiar.

The open house at Hartier's gallery was a delight. She sampled tapas and sipped an entirely credible Riesling while exchanging niceties with the sardonic little sculptor. Remarkably, as she mingled with other patrons, three more familiar faces presented themselves. A friend from her days in France had relocated to Villanueva, both husbands in tow.

"It just proves that the world is a small place," Sylva said.

"Worlds," the other woman said, correcting her. *"Are."*

After the exhibit, Sylva prowled the Mall for a bit. She gambled at the Zonix casino, opting for the high-stakes blackjack tables, the ones with human dealers. Hers smiled at her as she won and lost and then won again. She gave him her modest winnings as a gratuity and moved on. She spent money at designer shops and arranged for her purchases to be shipped home. She eyed absurdly priced jewelry at three vendors before making a small purchase, two bracelets. Of classic design, simple and elegant, they were crafted of lunar silver, mined somewhere near Chrisium. After a moment's thought, she bought a third band, this one stolid and gray. The jeweler told her that it was of meteoric iron. She thought Erik might like it.

They met late in the afternoon and had an early dinner at a bistro he suggested. The meal was salmon fresh from the hatcheries, poached in a local wine and served with lemon and cilantro. Over desert, she presented him with the iron bracelet and was pleased that he wore it when they made the trip back to his quarters.

Sylva surprised herself by staying the night.

It was completely unplanned and spontaneous, but more than welcome, and she felt as if the moment had been coming since her advent on the Moon. It was graceful and awkward, work and fun, familiar and new. When they were done, they lay as they had so many times before, her head on Erik's chest, his hand on her shoulder.

"Some things *are* different here," she said.

Erik laughed. It was the most relaxed, natural sound he'd made since the beginning of her visit. "Not very different," he said.

"More work," she replied. She felt his heartbeat more than she heard it.

"We're older," he said, still amused.

"Not *that* old," she said sharply.

"And the gravity," he continued.

She knew what he meant. Something as basic as walking demanded thought. Sex was even more basic. There was a lot to relearn.

Erik seemed to have managed, though.

"I spoke with a Zonix hotel director about it once," Erik said, as if he knew what she was thinking. "He told me that the concierges have to process some pretty silly questions from first-timers."

Sylva sighed. "I can imagine," she said.

They lay in silence for a long time after that, completely at ease with each other. Sylva was reluctant to break the mood. She couldn't believe that a moment like this would ever come again.

Of course, she hadn't thought so earlier, either. Life still had its surprises.

Finally, she said, "We need to talk, Erik."

"About the boys," he said. He spoke only inches from her ear, but his voice was distant. "Yes."

"Have you made the arrangements?" she asked.

"Not entirely," he said, following her lead and talking around what was on both of their minds. "There's a site in Tranquility," he said. "Where the first *Apollo* made landfall."

"Tranquility," Sylva murmured. She liked the way the word felt in her mouth.

"It's under federal cognizance," he continued. "I have to arrange it with Scheer."

He'd mentioned Scheer before. She was the head of Project Halo, the federal SETI project housed at Armstrong Base. The backgrounder he'd sent on her had been surprisingly sparse, listing only academic qualifications and a few career accomplishments.

"If you can't make it happen—"

"I can," Erik said. His easy confidence reminded her of the considerable power he wielded. "The only question is when." He sighed. "It's like everything else, Sylva. Getting things done isn't very hard. Deadlines are."

"I can stay for a bit if—"

"No," Erik said. "You're welcome to be here as long as you want, of course, but this needs to be resolved." He sighed again. "I need closure. We both do."

CHAPTER 15

LUNAR residents didn't spent much time on the surface, unless their work took them there. Tourists visited the airless desolation only in guided groups, and not often even then. They stayed beneath the world, inside the commercial colony, where creature comforts abounded. The surface remained available via countless Mesh links. The images impressed, but the reality had a quality that they could never match.

Erik thought about that as he stood by himself in the pressurized maintenance station. The place was little more than a high-tech storage cubicle, a piece of space defined by sealant-lined walls and ceiling, home to scattered racks of equipment and supplies.

Windows ran along all four walls. They were little more than horizontal slits, positioned at eye level and heavily insulated. Their only smart-options were default filters, configured to protect the human eye. Erik stood before one of them now, looking at the vista beyond.

It impressed. The Moon's surface was a study in monochrome, simultaneously stark and subtle. At first glance, everything seemed to be one of two shades, the deep black of absolute shadow or the off-white of bleached bone. Gradually, however, more detail became evident. Subtle hints of gray defined irregularities and softened the shadows, however slightly. Beyond the level surroundings, past the up-thrust peaks and ancient craters, was the horizon. Even after many years, it looked too close and too sharply curved.

The Moon was in Earth's shadow now. The sky was black, and the stars were plentiful and unblinking.

Erik liked what he saw. On Earth, he had been an outdoorsman. He had spent countless nights beneath the open sky, surrounded by the rich ferment of life in what remained of Earth's wild. The Moon was a dead world; life was an intrusion here. Yet, strangely, he felt at home.

Behind him, the airlock chimed. His guest had arrived. Hidden pumps and motors whirred, and with a squeal that testified to long disuse, the metal panel slid back. A spacesuit-clad figure stepped though and raised one gloved hand to him in greeting.

"Hello, Wendy," Erik said as the spacesuit opened, separating into its vertical sections like a banana peel. Gloved hands came up, lifted the visored helmet.

"Hello, Erik," Wendy Scheer said. She smiled, and the cool air of the maintenance station seemed to warm several degrees. She looked at her surroundings, quickly taking in the raw, industrial look the maintenance station. "You always did have a flair for the dramatic," she continued.

He saw her only rarely, but each time it was with the sense of discovering something new. She had a pragmatic, natural beauty, nothing that was soft or pretty in the traditional sense, but it compelled, and she had more than that.

Someone like Auguste Hartier might spend days or years trying to record Wendy with his art, but he would surely fail.

"I wanted privacy," Erik said. His voice echoed on the hard surfaces of cast-stone walls, hardware racks, and crated supplies. They sounded hollow.

"Why, Mr. Morrison, I'm surprised," she said. When he didn't laugh, she continued. "Does Hector know you're here?"

He snorted. "What do you think?" he asked.

Wendy knelt gracefully and gathered up her disassembled spacesuit. Before he could move to help her, she'd risen again. She hung the gear on a convenient rack beside the airlock door and hummed softly as she connected the suit's systems to jacks and conduits that would replenish them. "Better safe," she said, glancing back at him.

Erik hadn't bothered with environmental wear. He hadn't needed it. The maintenance station was one of fifty-seven that dotted the surface above and near the colony, accessible from below. Some early design team had thought they might serve double-duty as supply caches and as emergency exits from Villanueva proper. In retrospect, the secondary function seemed absurd—where would the evacuees go?—but the access tunnels had been bored and remained. Erik knew where they were and knew the codes that would unseal them. He was one of the few who did.

"We could have met in my office. I know I'm not welcome in Villanueva, but Project Armstrong is always happy to receive visitors," Wendy said. She spoke lightly, but the words stung. "I'm sure Hector told you that we treated him well."

"Hector was doing his job," Erik said.

"Hector is *always* doing his job," Wendy said. "But so was Pym."

She placed the heels of her hands on a workbench's edge and pushed. In a single fluid motion, she perched on the dusty surface, her legs folded beneath her as she eyed him. Clad in a jumpsuit uniform and with auburn hair arranged in a neat, practical coif, Wendy looked utterly at ease. Erik had seen jungle cats that looked less assured.

"It's been a long time, Erik," she said. When he nodded in acknowledgment, she continued. "You look good. Is the earring new? I don't recall you wearing much personal jewelry."

"This?" Erik asked, and indicated the black clip that clung to his right ear. "It was a gift."

"From Hector, I assume," Wendy said. She tilted her head. "He was wearing one like it. I think it looked better on him than on you."

She knew, he realized. He had half-expected that. Wendy was an intelligent and observant woman, and the unprecedented visit from Kowalski was certain to have put her on her guard. At the very least, she'd deduced the existence of Kowalski's countermeasure, if not its nature.

"He thought I needed it more, though," he said.

"Does it work?" she asked.

"I don't know," he said, before he could stop himself. He laughed wryly. "I honestly don't know for sure, Wendy."

The clip had come to life upon Wendy's entry. He could feel a slight loss of mental focus and almost subliminal sense of distraction as the world receded a bit. Kowalski had warned him of that. Beyond that, the device's effect was less certain.

"Well, we've known each other a long time," Wendy said. She looked sad. "We're old friends, at least at a distance. Erik, do you really think you need a defense against me?"

"I don't know," he said again. "But it seemed like a good idea."

The words hurt. They hurt him to say, and he could tell that they hurt her to hear. Erik realized with dulled surprise that Enola had been right, and that she had been utterly sincere. Wendy truly liked him.

"Enola said you wanted a favor," Wendy said. She brought her hands together and made a steeple of her fingers. "Let's talk about Pym first."

"This can't be a quid pro quo," Erik said. His sense of duty remained strong, even in this situation. There were prices he wouldn't pay.

"We'll talk about Pym first," she said sharply. It may have been the first time that such a tone in her voice had actually registered on him.

"He knew you," Erik said. He managed to sound confident, even though Kowalski had not been able to verify that particular aspect of Pym's background.

Wendy nodded. "We've met, even though he doesn't know it," she said. "Like *our* first encounter."

The first time Erik had met Wendy, he hadn't realized who she was. Part of running the now-dismantled Scheer Network within Villanueva had been using numerous cover identities, fabricated or borrowed. Facial appliances had made the strategy practical. Wendy's gift made it easy.

Who would ever question a person they liked with unconscious, intuitive ease?

"It's not a crime," she said. She didn't meet his gaze directly but looked at him slightly off-center.

She was eyeing the clip, he realized.

"He's not being treated as a criminal," Erik said, careful to speak in a reasonable tone.

It was strange, arguing with her. He'd never really done that before. His rare conversations with Wendy were almost always exercises in assertion and agreement, pleasant exchanges about issues that concerned them both. That was why Enola served as an intermediary, and why he had so little experience challenging her.

It felt good; strange but good.

"And it *was* a violation of our agreement, Wendy," he said, concentrating. The clip was helping. "Your network—"

"My 'network' never did you or yours any harm at all, Erik," she said. "My people gathered information. That was all. I never tried to influence policy."

"Maybe not directly. Maybe not then," Erik said. He had his doubts, but conceding the point was a courtesy that cost him nothing. "But Kowalski thinks Pym has done something to undermine Gummi production."

"Hector is wrong. Think about it," Wendy said. "Why in the worlds would anyone connected with me want to do anything to hurt the Ad Astra project? Erik, this project is my life!"

He groped for an answer but could find none. She was right. Sabotage simply wasn't in Halo's self-interest, despite Kowalski's assertions and the empirical evidence that supported them.

"And when your network was up and running, you tried very hard to track down the *Voyager* find before I did," he continued. "How would things have played out then, Wendy?"

"No one would be dedicating a museum to you, for one thing," Wendy said. "And you'd have been forced into retirement, I think."

He flinched. Exile to the Moon had been intended as punishment, but he had managed to turn it into an opportunity. No one within EnTek, Over-Management, or the entire ALC would have dared remind him of that. Only Wendy.

"Besides, the old NASA built and launched *Voyager*," Wendy said mildly. "It's federal property."

"The laws of salvage say otherwise," Erik said. "The

courts agree." He paused. "Your goals aren't always ours, Wendy."

"How are they different?" Wendy asked. "We move in the same direction. Outward."

What she said was literally true, but the situation was more complex. Erik paced slowly across the dusty tiled floor, considering his words carefully. After a moment, he asked, "Why do *you* think we're here, Wendy?"

"Here? On the Moon?"

He nodded.

"It's just a stepping-stone," Wendy said.

"Maybe in a sense, but—"

"A stepping-stone," she said more firmly. "We're here because we *need* to be here, so that we can take the next step." She spoke with a fervor he had never heard from her before.

"We're here so that we can move on?" Erik asked. The answer was elegant and self-contained. He rejected it immediately but could offer no effective response.

She nodded. "The *Voyager* find, the ALC's profit projection, none of that matters. They're just excuses, pretexts," she said. "Exploration is a fundamental human drive. So is scientific inquiry. I've told you that before."

He remembered her words of some twenty years previous. He nodded, then caught himself and shook his head. "No," he said. "That's nonsense. Hominids in their caves didn't try to build microscopes."

She laughed, but now it was a harsh sound. "You're arguing semantics," she said. "They certainly labored very hard, trying to learn how their world worked." She paused. "That's what *made* them men, Erik—men, and women. That's what made them human."

"That's an interesting worldview," Erik said slowly. He had a far more pragmatic view of human nature, and thus of human history. He would have argued that his ancestors' drive for knowledge had been a drive for survival and prosperity and that modern business was another expression of those same drives.

Wendy's worldview must have had considerable impact on her career track. An old metaphor came to him, half-remembered from his readings. She was putting the cart before the horse. He said nothing.

Wendy bit her lower lip and ran the fingers of one hand across her face. She was nervous, he realized, and he felt suddenly sorry for her. A lifetime of cheerful compliance from almost everyone must have left her ill-prepared for any kind of argument, especially with someone she saw as a friend.

"We didn't come here to talk about such things," he said. "At least, I didn't."

"You want a favor," Wendy said. The fingers of her hands curled and laced together. "I want one, too."

"I can't promise—"

"I want to attend tonight's candidate banquet," Wendy said. She made the words sound like a command. It was the same request she'd made earlier, via Enola, and the same request that he'd rejected out of hand.

"You can't, Wendy," Erik said. "You know that. I can't allow you to attend."

"Won't," she said

"Can't," he repeated.

"I deserve to be there, Erik," she said. There was a coaxing quality in her voice now, one that it would be easy to respond to. "I've worked long and hard to help make the project a success. You *know* that."

It was true, and her argument was one that he could well understand: self-interest.

"I know," he said. "And I'm sorry. It just isn't possible. You know that, and you know why."

She looked uncomfortable. In their relatively few in-person discussions, they almost never spoke specifically about her gift. They usually spoke around it, acknowledging it only indirectly and only when absolutely necessary.

That had been Wendy's choice, he realized. It always had been. As with most topics, he had followed her lead, at least until now. But the choice was no longer hers to make.

He pressed the issue. Even with the clip's help, it took effort, but each word came more easily than the one before. "One-fifth of the crew candidate pool will be in attendance, the best and the brightest of our recruits," he said. "Upper-level representatives from all five ALC sisters will attend, too, and many will be there in person." He thought about Sylva. "I can't allow you to become part of their lives."

Tears formed in Wendy's eyes. Erik felt as if he had been stabbed as he she blotted them with the back of her hand. He had never seen her like this before.

"I don't *want* to become part of their lives," she said. Her words came in a plaintive rush. "I want to be there, with you and the others, to celebrate the hard work we've done together. I want to have dinner, and I want to dance with a stranger, and I want to meet new people. I'm tired of living in Coventry."

She was sincere. He had no doubt that other, ulterior motives applied, but the core of her argument was distressingly simple and all too human.

Wendy really was lonely, pure and simple.

"I'm sorry." The words were hopelessly inadequate, but they were all that he could think to offer.

"There's a way," she said softly. In a single liquid movement, she flowed from her workbench perch and stood before it.

"There isn't," he said. The air between them seemed thick with attention. He wanted to give her a hug, or offer his shoulder, or do anything to express the sympathy sweeping over him now. He wanted to be at her side but forced himself to remain distant as she spoke again.

"That clip you wear. The others could wear them, too." She approached him. "You could hand them out as party favors."

His mind raced. He wasn't certain precisely how complex the little devices were, but it wasn't inconceivable that a large number could be fabricated and distributed. If he explained to the attendees—

Hector had been right, he realized. The suppressor clip wasn't consistently effective. It worked for Hector better than it worked for him. How well would it work for anyone else? There was no way to know.

He shook his head. "You don't want that, Wendy," he said. "If I did that, I'd have to explain. You and your gift would become common knowledge. No one wants that."

"It wouldn't make any difference now," she said. "Thanks to Hector."

Wendy's hand came up. Before he could pull back, her fingertips grazed his cheekbone, his hair, his ear. Erik felt something like an electric shock as she moved toward the clip he wore. Just in time, his own hand came up and sheltered it.

"No," he said sharply.

Wendy took a step back.

More gently, he continued. "Do you really want to spend the rest of your life being analyzed and monitored and interviewed?" he asked.

"You'd be surprised how much of that's already happened," Wendy said coldly. "You'd be surprised at how much work I've had done."

"By people who work for you, and under your direction," he said. "Did you share the results?"

She shook her head.

Wendy's abilities were a given in his life, but not many knew of or truly believed in them. "I'm certain that the ALC would take a more intrusive approach, now that Hector has made it possible. Would that really be better than exile?"

Wendy's shoulders dropped, and she slumped slightly. Her face went dead. She looked utterly defeated, and the sight tore at his heart. "No," she said softly. "No, I suppose not."

Neither spoke as she retrieved her spacesuit from its rack and arrayed it on the floor. She positioned herself carefully and the suit came to life, sections slithering up along the contours of her body and joining together. In seconds, all that remained was to replace her helmet. Before she lifted it into place, she looked at him again.

"You wanted a favor," she said. Her voice was dull. "It's about your sons, isn't it?"

He nodded, wanting to know how she knew but not wanting to ask. "I want to arrange their inurnment," he said.

"Of course you do," she said. Her eyes brightened as comprehension dawned. "That's why your wife is here. She must have brought the ashes."

"Former wife," Erik said. For some reason, the correction seemed important. Asking how she knew about Sylva didn't.

She continued. "You want them in the columbarium at Tranquility, don't you? Strictly speaking, that's not for civilian contractors, but I can authorize an exception. I'll make the arrangements."

"Thank you." The words were inadequate. Following their tense exchange, the original purpose of the meeting felt like a half-forgotten afterthought. Even so, he was surprised at how casual she was as she reminded him of it, and how gracious in her response. Perhaps they really were friends.

"Wendy," he said slowly. "I have to ask you something more."

She waited, helmet gripped in gloved hands.

"I called you recently, didn't I?"

Wendy nodded.

"What did I say?" he asked. "What did we talk about?"

"Nothing you need to worry about," she said after another moment had passed. "You needed someone to talk to. I was just surprised that it was me." She paused again. "Surprised, and pleased."

That must have been one reason she had thought he might grant her the permission she wanted so badly. Erik felt even worse.

"Was I—had I been drinking?"

She nodded. Now, at last, the familiar knowing smile formed again on her features. "You were drunk," she said. "You were *very* drunk, Erik."

"I'm sorry," he said, embarrassed.

She shrugged, noticeable even in the bulky surface gear. It was the only response she made.

"What did we talk about, Wendy?" he asked.

"You don't remember?"

He shook his head. "No," he said. "For some reason, neither does my housekeeper. I hope I didn't say anything—"

"Hush," she said. "Don't apologize. You did nothing wrong."

"What did we talk about, Wendy? What did you say to me?"

Her response was to raise the helmet above her head

and thumb its systems to life. As she lowered it, she said, "I'm sorry for your loss, Erik. I didn't know him very well, but I liked Rod. He reminded me of his father."

She spoke lightly, but her words hit like a hammer. Stunned, he stared at her. Before he could shape any response, she had set her helmet back in place and locked it down. The visor filters activated themselves, obscuring her features. He could no longer see her eyes.

Erik's heart raced. He gestured, demanding her attention again. She ignored him. He paged her on his personal phone, but she ignored that, too, as she turned and reentered the airlock.

A digital display next to the egress frame presented the hatch mechanism's progress through its cycle. Erik could do nothing but watch as the inner door's seals activated, hidden pumps sucked air and created vacuum, and the outer hatch opened. Wendy stepped back out into the lunar night and to a waiting surface vehicle that would return her to Armstrong Base.

Erik watched and kept watching long after mechanisms had fallen silent.

CHAPTER 16

THE auditorium shook with applause as Erik stepped onto the dais. Even with the room's acoustical suppressors on-line and live, the cascade of clapping hit him like something physical. He could feel it inside himself, in his bones and muscles, and it only became more emphatic as he stood next to Inex.

She waved one final time to the assembled multitudes and then smiled at him, ceding the podium to him with a graceful two-handed gesture. He mouthed a silent "thank you" to her and waited for the crowd to quiet as she left the stage.

"Good evening," he said, when he could hear his own thoughts clearly again. "Before I continue, I'd like to thank Inex for a job remarkably well done. This gathering is the fifth of five, and it's Inex who has made the series a success. I just hope you'll forgive me for reclaiming the host duties."

As the new wave of applause built and crested, Erik

looked out over the crowd. The auditorium's basic foot-print was a rough quarter-circle, with the dais at what would have been the circle's center. Tables and terraces were arrayed in long curves that ran from wall to wall. The podium offered an enhanced view, presented on a curved screen of one-way wallpaper-type display that only the speaker could see.

He ignored it. Instead, he looked over and beyond the arched screen. He looked for familiar faces and tried to make eye contact with them, however briefly.

He saw Sylva, beautiful in a designer gown, sitting at a table reserved for VIPs. Inex was beside her, along with a stocky Hispanic, probably her friend Dawg. He saw Enola, also at a VIP table, but she sat alone.

Theirs weren't the only familiar faces, but they were the ones he knew best. Everyone else fell somewhere on a scale that stretched between "casual friend" to "total stranger," a scale that Erik had never calibrated with partic-ular closeness.

Even so, he felt as if he knew most of them. They were familiar as exemplars of a type, if not as specific individu-als. Some two hundred were in attendance; perhaps half that number were members of the candidate crew. Those were the people who mattered this evening, not their es-corts for the evening, or the management grandstanders, or even himself. That thought remained foremost in his mind as the applause faded and he began to speak again.

"As I said, this is the fifth of five," Erik said. He smiled. "But it's going to be a bit different from the others—and not just because I'm not as pretty as Inex." He paused for laughter and got it. "I'm going to do the most dangerous thing a man in my position can do. I'm going to dispense with my prepared remarks and try something new."

The podium screen offered him a high-resolution view

of Inex. She looked mildly aghast and bent to whisper something into a personal phone.

"First, an apology," Erik said. "I'm sorry to say that this is the first time that many of us have met, and that the roles we play mean that it may be the only time. I hope that later in the evening, each of the crew candidates will do me the great honor of hooking thumbs or sharing a word or two. You've all worked long and hard on the project, and there's more hard work to come. Hard work, and, I know, disappointment. You deserve my thanks."

More applause thundered, and Erik found himself warming more and more to his own words. Originally, the series of banquets had been intended at least partially as an exercise in media relations. It had long since become something more. As so often happened, function had followed form.

A flagon of water and a glass were perched on the podium. Erik took a drink and waited for the applause to fade. When it didn't, he raised his hands for quiet.

"You're all so young," he said.

THERE were no truly bad seats on any of the auditorium's terraced levels. Architects had worked very hard to ensure all attendees of unimpeded views of the dais and of the screens behind it. Even by that standard, however, Trine had been singularly fortunate in her designated table.

Comfortably ensconced near the front of the second level, Trine could see Erik clearly without reference to any of the place's many wallpaper displays. Her table was only half-occupied, and she had not bothered to bring an escort, so empty chairs stood to either side of her. She didn't mind. The nature of her work Ship Site had long ago taught her the simple comforts of being alone.

Besides, she half-suspected that at least one of the empty

seats would be occupied before long. Based on recent experience, it seemed likely.

Morrison looked well, she decided. It was difficult to believe that this was the same man she had encountered in the Mall so recently. He could have been ten years younger; he stood straighter, and his voice was clear. His eyes seemed to be, too. Either he'd been ill before, or imaging specialists had worked wonders with him. Trine wasn't sure which.

She sipped wine and eyed her surroundings, trying to be casual about it. Apparently, Michelle Esposito hadn't been the only one to opt out of attending in person. As many as a quarter of the tables reserved for crew candidates had two or more empty chairs. Perhaps the workload Ship Site was even greater than her friend had said.

Trine felt mildly scandalized by the overall opulence. She had never before attended any function so lavishly appointed. Her order for rosé wine had been taken and filled by a live steward with a wheeled cart, rather than by brainware and a table dispenser. The unused decorative place settings were being reclaimed by human waitstaff, as well. The uniforms they wore looked at least as expensive as Trine's finest evening attire.

She could think of a dozen better uses for the credits. More occurred to her as she sipped wine and listened to Morrison's remarks. She said nothing, neither to the facility personnel nor to the strangers who were her tablemates. There seemed to be no point.

"You're all so young," Morrison said. *"Looking out at you now brings that home."* He smiled wryly. *"There's a world of difference between reviewing demographic crew backgrounders and seeing you all seated here together. You make me feel old."*

Trine shook her head silently. There was nothing old

about Morrison. There was maturity and wisdom, but nothing of age. Tonight, at least, he had the vitality of a much younger man.

She wasn't the only one who disagreed with his self-assessment. Whispered comments flitted through the audience, enough in number to make a susurrus that seeped through the sonic suppressors. Trine could see other heads shake, too.

Morrison laughed. *"Old in a good way,"* he said. *"I don't mind being old if it means seeing twenty years of our hard work come to fruition."*

Trine decided that she like being part of the "our."

He gestured at something that Trine could not see. It was a small VIP table on the auditorium's bottom level, blocked from her line of sight by the lowest seating terrace. Now, at last, Trine resorted to her table's screen, and she blinked in surprise at who she saw, seated together.

"And not just our work," Erik said.

HECTOR slid into the waiting chair moments before Morrison's speech began. He moved almost silently, but it was his grace that counted for more. He had learned that years before, during his earliest stealth training, and had applied the lesson with increasing skill ever since.

You could dress poorly. You could make a significant amount of noise, as long as it was consistent with your surroundings. It didn't matter. As long as you took reasonable precautions about how you smelled and kept careful control of your body language, it was surprisingly easy to approach even the wariest quarry without warning.

It worked this time. She didn't seem to notice his arrival, but kept her attention focused on the dais and the man who stood on it. Only when he tapped one bare shoulder gently did she turn to look at him.

"Hello, Enola," Hector said, seating himself. "Sorry to leave you unattended for so long, but I had to greet someone."

She flinched. She seemed poised to leave her seat and find a new one. Instead, she merely favored him with a poisonous glance. "Hello, Hector," she said, with frozen politeness. "It's so nice of you to favor me with your presence."

Even on the VIP level, where people sat less to see than to be seen, Hasbro demanded attention. She was resplendent in a black and ivory ensemble that played well against her natural colors. She wore sliver jewelry, simple, elegant geometric forms that doubtless hid personal Gummi systems.

They wouldn't work here. Hector had seen to that.

"Once Erik confirmed your invitation, I asked for your table," Hector said. He spoke softly, careful not to draw undue attention. Erik's speech had begun, and he had no desire to disrupt it.

Hasbro looked disappointed, but she recovered quickly.

"Or did you expect him to join you after the speech?" Hector asked. He pointed at another table on their level. A woman shared it with Erik's assistant and her guest. Next to the woman was an empty chair. "Sylva Taschen," Hector told Hasbro. "She's Erik's former wife. He'll be sitting with her, I think."

Now, Hasbro glared at him. He didn't mind.

"Why are you here, Hector?" the Proxy asked. The words were little more than a snarl.

"Strange," Hector said. "I asked Erik the same thing, about you." Earlier in the day, when he'd finally found time to review the banquet guest list, he'd been annoyed to find

Hasbro's name there. Several calls from the Heuristic spaces had yielded no answers that he found satisfactory.

"That isn't an answer," Hasbro said. She spoke sharply and loudly enough that the table's suppressors came to life, and her words took on a clipped quality as brainware nibbled at the syllables.

A wine caddy rested on the tabletop between them. It had come with a pair of glasses, and one sat half-filled before Hasbro. Without asking permission, Hector took the second and half-filled it.

"Why sit with me?" Hasbro demanded.

"Because I don't trust you," Hector said. "Because I wanted to let you know that, as far as I'm concerned, you're not welcome at—"

Morrison had been speaking continuously during the tense exchange, but Hector had hardly taken notice. The familiar niceties and platitudes registered as little more than background noise. That changed now, with a suddenness that took him completely by surprise. Hector's fingers tensed, and he set down his wine glass hastily, for fear of shattering its fragile stem.

"I don't mind being old if it means seeing twenty years of our hard work come to fruition," Erik said. *"And not just our work, but the work of our partners on this watershed project, the staff of Project Halo."*

Hector stared at the dais, aghast. Nothing like this had been in any of the drafts that Inex Santiago had forwarded him for review. This was entirely new.

Hasbro grinned at him and extended her pink tongue in derision. "Not welcome, Hector?" she purred.

"I call them partners, *but that might not be the best word,"* Erik continued. He looked utterly at ease. *"Perhaps* collaborators *would be better."*

"Customers," Hector half-muttered, half-growled, with

an intensity that surprised him. The federal government and the enclave at Armstrong Base provided funding and information, but the deep-space project was the ALC's. The profits would be, too.

Many in the audience seemed to feel the same. Hector was acutely aware of murmured comments that could be heard, just barely, from the other tables.

"No one who has seen my résumé or is familiar with my work can doubt how strongly I believe in the power of human industry," Erik continued. *"But there's another perspective—"*

SYLVA'S gown was little more than a wrap of white chiffon, accented and given shape by metal clips that were both decorative and functional. The fabric ran along her body in a lazy spiral that covered what needed to be covered, but also drew attention to what it concealed. The ultimate result was a kind of elegant simplicity.

"You must tell me where you shop," Inex Santiago said softly, between sips of white wine.

Sylva looked away from the dais and her former husband. There would be time enough for Erik later. "Guillermo's," she told the attractive young woman. "On the fourth Mall level, I think."

"Ah," Inex responded. "I thought so." She turned to say something to her escort for the evening, whom she had introduced to Sylva as "Dawg." Whatever she said, it made the toothy man smile and nod in a agreement.

Erik continued his remarks. She only half-listened. There was no denying that he was a skilled speaker, but very little of what he had to say thus far tonight held any interest for her. The Moon seemed like a nice enough place, and she was glad she had come, even given the circumstances, but local business dealings lay far outside her area.

"But there's another perspective," Erik said. *"And it's one I'd like you to consider, especially those who, when the time comes, take the long voyage out."*

Inex blinked and gave a soft gasp. She came to attention in her chair, a sudden motion that Sylva felt as much as saw. Earlier, Inex had expressed mild reproof at Erik's departure from the cleared text, but this reaction was far more emphatic.

Whatever Erik was about to say, it was something she hadn't anticipated.

"I met with an old friend earlier today," Erik continued. His voice became softer, warmer, and Sylva wondered just what kind of friend he referred to. *"She's a member of senior management at Armstrong Base. She said something to me that I'd like to share with you:*

"'Exploration is a fundamental human drive. So is scientific inquiry.' She said that it's what makes us human.

"Now, I'll grant, that's not a particularly original observation. She'd said it to me before, for that matter, years ago. But today, it was as if I'd never heard it before. Tonight, I find myself thinking about it as I see you all, younger than my own children, readying yourself for an adventure that will come to fruition only long after I'm gone and forgotten.

"I'd like you to think about what she said, as you go about your work. For those fortunate enough to join the final crew, I hope you'll take her thoughts with you, as you take the long journey. You're doing work that's intrinsic to the species. If there's a nobility in the human spirit, you're doing noble work."

Erik's comments might have been extemporaneous, but they were well chosen and resonated with their target audience. Sylva realized that as the rolling thunder of applause began anew.

This time, incredibly, it was even louder than it had been before. This time, the young men and women of the candidate crew rose en masse, to deliver their applause standing.

After a long moment, Sylva joined them.

AFTER Erik's speech, other ALC figures took the podium, one after another. Little said by any of them held much interest for Trine, or for the rest of the audience. Whether because of Erik's prominence in the community, or because of the unexpected vigor of his opening remarks, all that followed seemed tired and old. Trine had heard much of it before.   •

She was alone at her table by the time the last of the speakers took the dais. He was a Duckworth man, with a clumsy-sounding title that involved titanium castings, and he spoke with halting ponderousness. No one paid much attention to him or what he had to say, certainly not Trine.

Her tablemates had abandoned their meals in midcourse to meet Morrison, who had remained on the VIP level and was now surrounded by well-wishers. Trine, no more eager to waste food than money, was left by herself to enjoy the last of a truly remarkable mushroom torte. There would be time enough later to renew her acquaintance, minimal as it was, with Morrison.

"What did you think?"

This time, Kowalski's question didn't surprise her, nor did his sudden arrival in the chair next to her. She had become nearly accustomed to his appearances. Trine speared the final bit of pastry-and-fungus and eyed it before answering.

"I think maybe Michelle was right," she said.

"Michelle?" Kowalski asked.

Trine told him about her crewmate and the other girl's plan to audit the reception via Mesh. "I think I would have enjoyed the Party Sector more," Trine said, then popped the final morsel into her mouth. Morrison's speech had been engaging, perhaps even inspiring, but everything else had been anticlimax. She wondered when the dance floor would clear.

"What did you think of Erik's speech?" Kowalski asked. He had found the bread basket. He broke a crusty rye roll, spread it with something soft and cheesy-smelling, and began to eat. Flakes rained onto the tabletop.

"He was talking to himself," Trine said.

Kowalski paused in midbite and looked at her quizzically.

"He was talking to us, but he was talking to himself, too," she amended. She had heard men speak like that before, mouthing ideas that were still new and fresh to them. Novelty begat enthusiasm. Luther Guinn, her crew chief, had sounded like that after finding religion. "He liked what his friend had to say."

"Why?" Kowalski asked. The rye roll was gone and he had attacked a baguette.

Trine shrugged. She set aside the fork she'd been toying with, empty now. "I don't know," she said, and looked at Kowalski. "Why ask me?"

Music had begun to play, something that was nice but prerecorded. Trine glanced at a nearby screen and saw work crews collapse VIP tables and stack them on wheeled carts. They were clearing the dance floor, she realized.

Kowalski tucked the last fragment of French bread into his mouth, chewed, and swallowed. He stood and offered her his hand.

"We should leave," he said, surprising her. "I'd like to talk to you, somewhere private."

"But Erik asked everyone to—"

Kowalski grinned. "You've met him before," he reminded her. "Believe me, the second time is just more of the same."

"SOMEWHERE private" proved to be something Kowalski called a safe house, a nice appointed residential suite that he told her was reserved for official use.

"Do you bring many girls here, Hector?" Trine asked as he opened the kitchen refrigerator and began poking around inside.

"No," he said, and shook his head. "It's not for that kind of official use." He gave her another grin, and Trine realized that they seemed to come with increasing ease. "That wouldn't be official, anyway."

"Oh," Trine said.

"Would you like something to drink?" he asked.

"Lethe would be nice," she said from the conversation pit.

"Just one," Kowalski said. "I brought you here to talk."

He lobbed a plastic bottle in her direction. It came slow and low, and Trine caught it easily. The bottle hissed as she opened it. Hector emerged from the kitchen carrying his own selection, a container of fruit punch, like the one he'd ordered at the Party Sector. He gestured for her to sit, and when she complied, he did the same.

"I need to trust you on this," he said. "It's about Enola Hasbro and Wendy Scheer."

Trine looked at him and blinked. It hadn't been a question. She could think of no other response.

For a man who seemed to enjoy being cryptic and remote, Kowalski could download information in a remarkably straightforward manner when he chose to. Slumped in an easy chair, he told her about Wendy Scheer, the head of

Project Halo, and about her gift. In broad strokes, he outlined the intelligence network that her gift had enabled. He told her about Enola Hasbro and about how Scheer had helped clear her of murder and terror charges, and how the two had begun to work together at Erik's behest.

"That's why you call her the Proxy," Trine said.

Kowalski nodded. He sipped his fruit drink.

"And the Scheer Network? That's gone?"

Kowalski shrugged. "I used to think so," he said. "But now, I'm not sure."

He summarized the Dailey Pym situation for her. More than two weeks of effort and detailed audit had revealed no information that was of any use. The junk genes were clearly some manner of deliberate media corruption, but to what end? They'd had no operational impact that Kowalski or his people could identify.

"But Pym works for Scheer," Trine said.

"I think so," Kowalski replied. "And to be honest, I can't imagine why Scheer would want to undermine the project."

Trine had sense of déjà vu. She remembered viewing Auguste Hartier's statue and feeling sympathy for the insect it represented. Again, she felt a kinship with the bug. She felt like an insect moving along complex machineries, blind to their intricacies but vulnerable to them.

She didn't like feeling this way.

"Why are you telling me this?" Trine asked. She had expected something else entirely from him, something that she had half-decided she wanted. She hadn't thought she'd be going back to the hostel tonight.

Kowalski's drink was empty. He set it aside. "Think about it, Trine," he said. "You're a hard worker, and I like the way you think. I've told you I trust you."

She thought. When the answer came, it wasn't what she'd expected at all.

"Oh," she said. "You want me to work for you," Trine said. "You want me to do the kinds of things you do. I'm not trained for—"

"I can teach you what you need to know," Hector said. "But you already have the right kind of mind."

"No," Trine said. The enormity of what he suggested made her feel cold. "I'm sorry, but no. I worked very hard to qualify for the candidate crew, and I—"

"I want you to work for me as a member of the crew," Kowalski said. "It's going to be a long journey. Order and discipline will be important. I'll need a liaison onboard."

"I don't even know if I'll qualify," Trine said.

"I can promise you a billet," Hector said, cool and matter-of-fact.

"You can't *do* that!" Trine said sharply. The system was supposed to be inviolate. It balanced randomized selection from a qualified pool against genetic and psychological factors. Candidates could improve their chances of being selected only by working hard and well. Instructors had told her again and again that the lottery was tamper-proof. She said, "No one can make that kind of promise!"

"*I* can," Hector said. He was watching her carefully as she considered what he had said.

Michelle and the others had worked very hard to qualify for candidate status. Trine had, too. It was one thing to hope and struggle for a lottery win; it was quite another to sidestep the system. It seemed like cheating.

Trine didn't like cheaters.

With conscious effort, she kept the emotion from her face and voice as she continued. "I wouldn't want it that way," she said.

It was the right answer, she realized, as Hector nodded and smiled. The offer had been a test, and she had passed it.

"That's fair," he said. "Work for me now, then. If you're down-selected, I'll make a place for you here. If you're not—"

Trine nodded.

"Good," he said. "Now, based on what I've told you before, tell me what you think about Dailey Pym."

The answer came without conscious thought, like a reflex. "He certainly seems to be keeping you busy," Trine said.

Hector stared at her. He had the look of a man who had just been shown a great truth.

CHAPTER 17

ON Earth, the Janos Horvath Memorial Colony Cultural Life Museum would have been a stand-alone facility, prominently positioned amid neatly tended landscape and affiliated with an institution of higher learning. On the Moon, in Villanueva, it was an adjunct of the Mall, tucked away on the fifth concourse, where it could be accessed easily but didn't distract from more immediately profitable endeavors.

Tourists and locals alike visited the place but didn't spend much credit there. They might buy ALC jerseys and EnTek new-coffee mugs and holo-portraits of Janos Horvath, but they did the majority of their spending elsewhere.

Erik had always thought the place a bit of an indulgence and an exercise in corporate vanity. The addition of an exhibit bearing his name had only reinforced that opinion. The sheer amount of space the place occupied was enough to embarrass.

"I'm impressed," Sylva said. She smiled up at him and

sipped Lethe water from a stemmed and footed cocktail glass. "You've learned to appreciate yourself."

Erik grunted. He sipped his own drink, mineral water with a citrus infusion. "You have no idea how hard I fought this line item," he said.

Sylva cocked an eyebrow at him. She had revised her hairstyle and cosmetics for the event and looked vastly younger, but Erik wasn't sure he liked the effect. "It wasn't your choice?" she asked.

"No, of course not," he replied, irritated. She knew him better than this.

"Then why—?"

"Colony planners," he said shortly. "Quality of life engineers and media specialists." He paused, then quoted from memory. " 'Studies show that a general awareness of cultural history promotes social stability among the residential populace.' I didn't believe them. I still don't, but it wasn't my decision."

"You make it sound like you were actively opposed," Sylva said.

Erik shrugged. "They told me the people wanted a hero," he said. "That isn't me."

"You sell yourself short sometimes," Sylva said in mild reproof.

He shrugged, unable to think of anything to say. It didn't matter, anyway. The exhibit was a fait accompli, over his objections, and Sylva would return to Earth in a matter of days, effectively out of his life once more. How he felt about Life Accomplishments of Erik Morrison, Father of the Ad Astra Project, was a moot point. So was the question of whether or not Sylva was of the same mind.

Museum management had dedicated an impressive amount of space to his life and work, however. The exhibit area was a near-sphere, flattened at the bottom. Above them, the domed ceiling was lined with wallpaper displays set to planetarium views. Hanging from the ceiling was a model of the Ad Astra ship, nine modules that could dock and inter- lock to reflect mission needs. On the floor below was a long, low case that held the exhibit's centerpiece, the *Voyager* find, along with other smaller exhibits. Erik and Sylva were on the broad mezzanine, home to still other displays, both real and wallpaper.

Just now, that mezzanine was also host to refreshment stations, where uniformed attendants dispensed drinks and light snacks to the attendees. Dozens of other ALC execu- tives and management members drifted along the concourse, nibbling and sipping and chatting quietly among themselves while they feigned interest in the track of Erik's career.

He found it all a bit embarrassing.

"You're Morrison, right?"

The words came in a booming baritone, even as a mas- sive hand clamped down on Erik's shoulder. With conscious effort, he managed to avoid flinching as he turned to greet and hook thumbs with the burly man who had suddenly ap- peared behind him.

"Hamner Kaine," the man said. Erik was a big man, but Kaine was a bigger one, tall enough that he had to look down to meet Erik's eyes. "Duckworth, Alloy Develop- ment Division."

Erik started to introduce himself, then realized that there was no need and introduced Sylva instead. Kaine murmured a nicety, kissed her hand, and returned his atten- tion to Erik.

"I wanted to thank you personally," he said.

Erik managed a smile. "Thank my staff, Hamner," he said. "They made the arrangements."

Kaine waved one massive hand at his surroundings. He had long hair and a bushy beard, both the color of old rust, and blue eyes that flashed electrically as he snorted. "For the party, you mean?" he asked.

"The opening," Erik corrected him, acutely aware that Sylva was watching the exchange with some amusement.

"Hah," Kaine said, dismissively. "I didn't mean the food and drink. I meant that." He waved his hand again, pointing this time.

He meant Ad Astra, Erik realized.

"For the last seven years, my team's had at least sixty percent revenue growth," Kaine said. "Ship Site contracts made up most of that. You've kept a lot of people working, and working productively, Morrison."

"That wasn't only me—"

Kaine snorted again. He had a bigger-than-life quality that would have been more appropriate to a Mesh performer than to an engineering manager. "You found *Voyager*," Kaine said. "You got the whole project rolling, and you kept it going. Everyone knows that!"

Sylva was almost laughing, Erik realized. "You're too generous," he said. "Really—"

"Hah!" Kaine said. He shook his head and grinned. "I just wanted to thank you personally," he said, then half-bowed in Sylva's direction. "Sorry to interrupt your conversation. I hope we can talk again sometime, in more detail."

Erik watched as Kaine ambled away. In moments, the big man had cornered Enola Hasbro, another guest at the gathering, and the two were deep in conversation.

"People like having a hero," Sylva said, smiling openly now.

"Don't be silly."

"A leadership figure, then," she said. "A pioneer or figurehead."

Erik surprised himself by blushing. "A glad-hander," he said.

"That's your friend, isn't it?" Sylva asked. Her glass was empty. She tapped it with one enameled nail, making a ringing sound, and led him toward a refreshment station.

"Enola?" Erik said. He nodded. "Halo asked that she be put on the guest list."

"You were going to introduce me," Sylva said. Her glass was full again, but she held it without drinking.

"A bit later," Erik said.

Sylva cocked an eyebrow at him again. They had fallen again into the easy rapport of their best years, communicating nonverbally nearly as often as with words. He knew the expression.

"Once she's finished with Kaine," he amended. "Once Kaine is on the other side of the hall, I think. Or gone."

Sylva laughed again, a sound perilously close to a giggle. He nearly blushed.

"Let's take the tour," he said, and led her along the mezzanine floor, away from Kaine and Hasbro.

Progress was slowed by well-wishers and the exhibit itself. Archivists and researchers had done an excellent job in making the slightly messy progress of his career seem like an inexorable march to greatness. Endless loop recordings played in twenty dedicated display units, each presenting a different major project that had succeeded at least in part because of Erik's participation.

There was the Australia Pylon, a communications tower serving half the Pacific Rim. Erik had coordinated the growth and installation of Gummi processors that drove the unit.

There was New Sacramento, the replacement city that had been built in record time. Personnel under Erik's direction had configured the Mesh infrastructure, discovering new approaches that remained in use even today.

There was the Quebec Repository, the vast data repository

dug deep beneath the city. Engineers selected by Erik had hardened the facility against nuclear attack.

"Revisiting past triumphs, eh?" asked a short man with a blonde Mohawk hairstyle. He extended one hand, thumb cocked.

"Rex Blaisdell, Zonix Dramatics," the man said. "I'd like to talk about you about Mesh rights for your story, if you've got a moment."

Erik forced himself to sound apologetic. "Not today, Rex," he said. "Not here. You can contact my office, but this isn't the time or the place."

"Heroes," Sylva reminded him, as Blaisdell moved away. This time, Erik wasn't amused.

He made a mental note to meet with Inex or her assistant to discuss screening criteria for callers during the days and weeks to come. In less than an hour (so far) he'd met at least forty people. Most had expressed the desire to meet with him again, under more private circumstances, to pursue business or investment or even social opportunities. A high percentage of his new acquaintances were counted as important in their own circles, and avoiding them would demand some finesse.

"Erik," Sylva said. "Over here." Her eyes were bright, and she sounded almost giddy in her excitement. They were on the exhibit hall's floor now, and she had made her way to the long, low plastic shell that shielded the exhibit's centerpiece. Her nails clicked as she drummed her fingers on the diamond-hard casing.

"You never told me that it was so beautiful," Sylva said, gazing at the case's contents.

"I never really thought it was," Erik said.

Unlike many of the other displays, what this one held was not recorded imagery but something solid and real. That specific something was cumbersome and ugly, at least a dozen generations more primitive than any equivalent apparatus in current use. The design principles and technological strategies it embodied were hopelessly obsolete, so much so that a modern eye had difficulty discerning their function.

It was mystery, given form. Erik could not look at it without seeing the shape and structure of his life laid bare.

The *Voyager* probe had been launched from Earth in 1972 and thought to have exited the solar system some eleven years later. Erik had found the man who had found it and brought the discovery to the attention of the ALC, setting in motion forces that promised to shape history for centuries to come. ALC technicians had labored over it like paleontologists with a dinosaur's bones, reassembling what they could and replacing what they could not.

Erik supposed that some might think it beautiful.

Someone ran fingertips along his forearm, demanding attention. With an apologetic glance at Sylva, he turned in response. Beside him was a young woman dressed in black and red, the top of her head barely reaching the level of his shoulder. She beamed up at him, an incandescent smile that prompted memory of her name.

"Hello, Erik," Trine Hartung said. "I am *so* pleased you invited me."

"And I'm pleased you came," he said, with more warmth than he had been able to muster for almost any other guest. It might have been her youth, or her status as a member of the candidate crew, but he liked something about the Hartung woman.

Trine's knuckles rapped the display case. "I've seen images," she said. "But the genuine article is so beautiful." Her words echoed Sylva's. "You must have been thrilled when you found it."

Erik had no answer. Instead, he turned to face his former

wife. "Sylva," he said. "I'd like you to meet one of the young people who are getting the job done." He gestured. "Trine Hartung, Sylva Taschen."

"You were at the banquet," Trine said. "I saw you there! You had the wonderful white gown."

Erik's estimation of Trine slid upward another notch. His former wife wasn't particularly vain, but she appreciated compliments. Intuitively, Trine had said precisely the kind of thing that Sylva loved to hear. In seconds, the two women where immersed in conversation.

The encounter could almost have been a planned diversion. Even as the two women engaged with one another, Hector Kowalski appeared at Erik's side. The security chief's habitually neutral features were tense, and he looked concerned.

"I didn't think you were attending," Erik said, surprised.

"We need to talk," Kowalski said.

"Now?" Erik asked.

"Now," Hector confirmed. He eyed his surroundings, taking in the management figures and other VIPs thronging the newly dedicated exhibit. With a shrug of irritation, he tugged Erik into an alcove that was lined with wallpaper images of a childhood spent on Earth.

"Scheer is up to something," he said. His words were clipped and hissy, since he had set his privacy unit to maximum effect.

Erik looked at him with genuine irritation. After the surface visit with Wendy, he was no longer particularly disposed to share Kowalski's suspicions. He especially resented being interrupted at the dedication ceremony.

"Is this about Pym?" he finally asked.

Kowalski shook his head. "Nothing Pym has done is any kind of threat," he said. "As far as I can tell, he hasn't compromised Ad Astra's infrastructural integrity."

"And how much credit have we spent to come to that conclusion?" Erik asked. He looked past Kowalski's shoulder. Trine and Sylva were still deep in conference. Beyond them, on the other side of the *Voyager* display, Enola Hasbro was chatting with Rex Blaisdell. The Proxy was being especially social today, for some reason.

Erik's entire world seemed to be coming together within the space of a few square meters.

"It was just a matter of asking the right person the right question," Kowalski said. He leaned against a nearby wall. "I have a new member on my staff. She saw something I missed."

Erik didn't say anything.

"Pym is just a diversion," Kowalski said. "The junk genes were to draw our attention." He paused, looking unsettled. "*My* attention," he corrected himself. "I'm the one who failed."

"We can worry about that later," Erik said, with patience he didn't feel. "You said that no damage has been done?"

Kowalski nodded. "I just spent a few hours reviewing the data," he said. "I don't know what to look for now, but I know that what we were looking for wasn't there." For the first time in Erik's memory, Kowalski looked chagrined. "We were outflanked, pure and simple," he said. "The functional audit drew most of my attention, and in the wrong direction."

Erik's opinion of Wendy Scheer, already high, rose a bit. It wasn't easy to fool Kowalski, and it had become harder in the years since the Enola incident. If he was correct now, however, Scheer had managed to do just that, by exploiting his suspicious nature and attention to detail. She had used the security officer's own strengths against him.

"She wanted to attend the final banquet," Erik said, in a

voice of dumb wonder. "She asked repeatedly, and all the time she was playing games with you."

"You spoke with her?" Kowalski asked sharply. Now, his air of concern changed into something stronger. "You didn't authorize anything, did you?" he demanded.

"No, of course not," Erik said, stung. The question bordered on accusation.

Kowalski drew a deep breath. "I'm prepared to resign," he said.

"Why?" Erik asked.

"It happened on my watch," Kowalski said.

"And on mine," Erik said sourly.

Neither man said anything for a moment. The silence stretched out long enough that Erik became acutely aware that he had abandoned his guests. He could almost feel Sylva's gaze on him.

"We can worry about that later," he said again. "If I leave now, people will notice. Go back to your office and prepare a report. I'll need to know everything before I speak to her."

"You're going to talk with her?" Kowalksi asked sharply.

Erik nodded. "I have another ceremony to attend tomorrow," he said. "It's under her jurisdiction. I was planning on a courtesy call afterward."

"I don't think that's wise," Kowalski said. He seemed to be studying Erik carefully.

"I really don't think we have anything to lose at this point," Erik said. Before Kowalski could object, he turned to exit the alcove.

One long step took him beyond Kowalski's privacy field's effective range. A second took him back out to the hall's main exhibit area. With his third, he nearly collided with Enola Hasbro.

"There you are, Erik!" she said brightly. "I wanted to say good-bye."

"You're leaving?" Erik asked in mild surprise, his mind still preoccupied with Kowalski's news. "Already?"

"Busy, busy, busy," Enola said. "I'm sorry we didn't get a chance to talk." She gestured. "Is that your wife?" she asked.

Erik looked where she had pointed. Sylva was still chatting with Trine between sips of Lethe water. As he watched, Kowalski approached the two women and leaned to whisper something in Trine's ear.

Kowalski and Trine? Erik blinked, suddenly realizing the likely identity of Kowalski's new security recruit. He watched in mild disbelief as the two left together. Kowalski had run a diversionary exercise of his own, he realized.

Sylva saw him looking in her direction. She raised a perfectly manicured hand and waved. He waved back, then returned his attention to Enola.

"My former wife," he said. "The third of three."

"She watches you, you know," Enola said.

Erik hadn't, but he could think of nothing to say.

"I'm sorry I didn't get a chance to meet her," Enola said.

"There's still time," Erik said, but Enola shook her head in instant response before he could say more.

"No, I think I should leave," she said. "It's time for me to go."

She sounded odd. Her words had an echoing, out-of-phase quality, reminiscent of the one he had heard before, but different and fainter. They were colored with emotion. Erik wondered what was wrong.

Before he could ask, she surprised him by placing her hands on his shoulders. With unexpected strength, she pulled him close to her, then kissed him once on the lips, hard.

"Good-bye, Erik," she said. "I'll miss you."

Before he could react or reply, she released him and stepped back. In seconds, she had melted into the throng of visitors. The last he saw of her, she passed through the same exit recently used by Kowalski and Trine.

CHAPTER 18

"WE'RE here," the driver said. The surface transport shuddered to a halt, and its motors shifted to idle mode, making a dull hum that could be felt more than heard. She glanced at the control panel clock. "We're on schedule, too. We'd better suit up."

She didn't mean it literally. Like Erik and Sylva, she already wore a pressure suit, but unsealed and open. Moving nearly as one, all three raised their helmets then lowered them into place.

Suit Gummis took over from there. Obeying brainware prompting, the seams of the suits tightened and then checked themselves for integrity. Helmet seals hissed and clicked, and the surface gear's internal environment systems came fully on line.

As the suits pressurized, the transport's cabin did the reverse. Air drained into holding tanks. Seconds later, the cabin's plastic dome retracted, releasing the last wisps of internal atmosphere into the eternal lunar vacuum.

"Let's go," Erik said, taking Sylva's gloved hand in his. Together, they clambered out of the transport and dropped onto the arid surface.

"Someone will meet you," their driver said. *"Your suits know the way. I'll stay here and run a maintenance check."*

It was Sylva's first time in a spacesuit, but she already moved with greater grace than Erik could muster. She seemed utterly at home in the Ultima as she shuffled along the dusty floor of the Sea of Tranquility. Even with the added mass of the carryall she had looped over one shoulder, she progressed with complete self-assurance. Erik felt a twinge of envy for her adaptability.

For most, it was a rare thing to set foot on the Moon's surface. Engineers and surveyors traveled from point to point as quickly as possible. Those tourists not satisfied with live Mesh feeds made the trip in guided groups, riding opulent tour buses in pressurized comfort, sharing drinks and meals and sparing a moment now and then to peer though centimeters-thick plastic ports. Prospectors and researchers might disembark and explore on foot, but normal people didn't.

The driver had been correct; their suits knew the way. Responding to beacons planted in their bone-colored surroundings, the Ultima's Gummis whispered guidance. Erik was thoroughly sick of the synthesized voice by the time their goal came into view.

Flanked by a guard hutch and maintenance shed of vastly more recent vintage, the ancient craft squatted on the gray, dust-strewn stone floor of *Mare Tranquilitatis*. It was a blocky, squared-off thing, with spindly jointed legs and the old flag of the United States emblazoned on one side. Another, matching flag flew nearby, braced with wires to simulate the effects of winds that had never blown here. Erik had seen the tableau countless times in history feeds and as the logo of an entertainment provider, but the reality was infinitely more impressive. He paused in mid-stride.

"Welcome to Edwin E. 'Buzz' Aldrin, Jr., Memorial Preserve," his suit said. *"This facility is under federal jurisdiction. Trespassers are cautioned—"*

"Shut up," Erik said, speaking in his command voice, and the suit Gummi went silent.

Sylva's helmet swiveled so that its visor faced in his direction. It paused, turned a short distance, then repeated the action in reverse.

She had heard him over the open inter-suit link, he realized. She was shaking her head at him, presumably in reproof.

"Sorry," he said. It was better not to explain.

"Mr. Morrison? Ms. Taschen?" a third voice sounded in his helmet. *"I have you on my screen. If you'll wait a moment . . ."*

They waited. The hatch of the guard hutch opened, and a figure emerged. The spacesuit he wore was government issue, starkly utilitarian in comparison to Erik and Sylva's Ultimas. The blunt lines of the less-sophisticated environmental wear made the attendant look oddly like a child's toy as he approached.

"Walter Davis," he said. *"Director Scheer asked me to extend every courtesy."*

"Thank you," Erik said.

Davis's helmet was immobile, but hints of his features were visible through the thick filtered visor as he glanced from side to side. Seeing that Erik and Sylva were unaccompanied, he asked, "Will there be clergy?"

"No," Sylva said. She sounded remarkably calm, given

the circumstances. *"There was a ceremony on Earth. We're here to install the cremains in the columbarium."*

"Of course," Davis said. *"If you'll pardon me for a moment . . ."*

Erik's helmet phones fell silent as Davis accessed another frequency. He could see Davis's lips moving behind his mask. Presumably, the attendant was checking in with a coworker, or with the driver who had brought them there.

Sylva was staring at the aged lunar craft that was the preserve's centerpiece. "How did they ever make the journey in that?" she asked, in a wondering tone.

"They didn't," Erik said. "That's just part of the ship, what they left behind. Its base became a launching pad."

"That's right, sir," Davis said, startling them both as he rejoined the conversation. *"They left the passenger module behind, too. Jettisoned it in orbit, and it crashed to the surface a considerable distance from here. Made quite a mess."*

Erik was familiar with how a spacecraft looked when it fell to ground, but refrained from saying so.

"If you'll follow me," Davis said.

They followed. On the opposite side of the site, beyond the landing module base and guard hut, stretched a long, low structure constructed of native lunar rock. No taller than Erik's eye, the columbarium ran some twenty meters in length. Marking its vertical face were scores of plaques, each one a panel of matte-finished steel. More than half bore names and dates, and the remainder were blank. One of the panels had been removed, revealing the niche that it had covered.

"Erik?" Sylva said softly.

He turned as he heard his name and saw that she had opened her carryall. One by one, she passed him the black plastic cylinders she had brought from Earth. Once before, he had refused to take the containers that held his sons' remains, but this time, he accepted them.

They seemed cold in his hands, despite his suit's environmental systems, and he knew that the sensation had to be psychosomatic. Even more impossibly, they felt heavy, as if freighted with the weight of the world.

With an effort, he raised them to the open mouth of the niche. With even more of an effort, he slid them inside, into the shadowed darkness. For as hard as they had been to hold, they were far more difficult to release. After he had let go of them, even after he had stepped back from the columbarium's austere lines, he wanted desperately to scoop them up again.

"I'm sorry, boys," he said softly. "Good-bye."

Strangely, he felt no need to cry.

Davis had been watching from a respectful distance. Now, he approached. With practiced ease, he set the niche's metal faceplate into position. Its surface bore the twins' names and their birth and death dates and the same quaint Gemini symbol that had marked the urns. The plaque sealed itself into place with an electric flash. As quickly as that, it was over.

Davis turned to face them. *"I'm sorry for your loss,"* he said. *"Director Scheer couldn't be here, but she asked me to extend her personal sympathy."*

"Thank her for us," Sylva said. *"Tell me, Walter—is this a duty you're called upon often to perform?"*

"Often? No," Davis said. *"This facility hasn't seen much use in recent years, really. It's intended as a place of honor for local federal employees who've made the ultimate sacrifice in the line of duty."* He paused. *"I believe that the misters Morrison are the first private-sector staff ever to be inurned here, and the first from off-world."*

Erik thought about that for a moment. Wendy had told him the columbarium was reserved for federal personnel, but he hadn't realized that it was so exclusive. He supposed he should feel flattered.

"Thank her for us," Sylva said. *"We're in her debt."*

"I'D like to have dinner tonight," Sylva said. "I leave for Earth the day after tomorrow, and I need to get ready. This might be the last night I have any kind of appetite."

They were halfway back to Villanueva, suits open again. Beyond the transport's dome cowling, the Moon rolled slowly past. Erik watched it idly. He felt utterly drained.

"I wish you didn't have to leave," he said. His own words surprised him.

"So do I," Sylva said. "I've loved seeing you again, even under the circumstances, but we both know that I have to go."

Erik nodded in resigned acceptance. He said, "We raise exceptional shellfish here, and I know a Chinese specialist who can do amazing things with squid. I can have it served at home, if you'd like." He didn't feel like being out in public.

Sylva nodded. "That sounds very nice," she said.

"I'll make the arrangements when I get back from Halo," Erik said.

She cocked an eyebrow. "Halo?" she asked.

"Project Halo. I have to go to Armstrong Base," he explained. "I need to make a courtesy call."

"Will you meet with Scheer?" Sylva asked. "Could I accompany you?"

"I don't think that would be a very good idea," Erik said. "It's only partly a courtesy call. Kowalski has raised some issues that I need to address."

THE man was lean and of Asian descent, well into the depths of middle age. He had neatly styled black hair and dark eyes that grew expressive wrinkles when he showed his perfect white teeth in a warm smile. He was dressed in work clothes, dark slacks and a jersey imprinted with the Project Halo logo.

"Mr. Morrison!" he said, as he came out from behind his massive, cluttered desk. "Come in! Please, forgive the clutter!"

He extended his hand. Somewhat nonplussed, Erik did the same. Rather than hook thumbs or even shake the old-fashioned way, Tanaka clasped Erik's hand in both of his and pumped it. He smiled warmly. "It's so very good to see you, sir, especially after all these years! I am Ralph Tanaka!"

"Have we met, Ralph?" Erik asked warily as he re-claimed his hand. The name was tantalizingly familiar, but he was too preoccupied with his surroundings to search his memory.

Something had happened here, or was in the process of happening. The space he had known as Wendy Scheer's of-fice was a study in chaos. Stacks of storage cartons and pack-ing crates vied for space on the cluttered floor. The walls' display panels had been peeled free and new ones lay rolled up along the baseboards, presumably awaiting installation. The massive slab of a desktop was littered with hardcopy files, and the air was grimed with freshly disturbed dust.

"No, sir, we have not," Tanaka said. He gestured toward the only guest chair not burdened with office bric-a-brac. When Erik sat, Tanaka perched on the leading edge of his desk and smiled even more widely. "But not for lack of try-ing," he continued. "I was project director when you relo-cated to Villanueva."

"Ah," Erik said, embarrassed as the memories came. Re-peatedly in those days, Tanaka had extended invitations to visit Armstrong Base. Repeatedly, Erik had declined them.

It was only when Scheer had ascended to the directorate that he had actually made his first visit.

"This was my office then," Tanaka said. He gestured at their surroundings. "Please excuse the disarray. Wendy never really liked it. Too large, too impersonal, she said, but of course it was much too prominent for anyone of lesser rank. She used it for storage. Now that she's gone, and I'm back—"

"Wendy's gone?" Erik asked sharply, interrupting.

Tanaka nodded. "She accepted a new assignment," he said. "On Earth. I'm her replacement, even as she was mine." He leaned forward attentively and peered at Erik. "Is something wrong?" he asked.

It was as if the world had gone into soft focus and slow motion. Erik was abruptly aware of the sounds of his own lungs and heart, and his hands clenched reflexively. His surroundings no longer mattered; memory commanded his complete attention.

"I can't do my work from Earth," Wendy had told him during their meeting on the surface. *"Not without assets that I don't have now."*

"Good-bye, Erik. I'll miss you," Enola Hasbro had told him at the museum opening, after introducing herself to scores of key management figures.

Except it hadn't been Enola who had spoken to him then, he realized sickly. The motive behind the elaborate Heuristic diversion was obvious now.

Tanaka persisted. "Are you unwell?" he asked. "We have physicians on call—"

Erik shook his head, partly to clear it. "No," he said. "That won't be necessary. I'm fine." He paused and took a deep breath. "Ralph, I wonder if it would be possible to speak to Wendy? She did me a great favor recently, and I'd like to thank her personally."

"She's already en route and unavailable," he said. "But she told me you'd ask." From the litter of documents on his workstation, he plucked an envelope and handed it to Erik. "She asked me to give this to you."

She'd remembered that he liked old things. The envelope was of paper, actual and antique, and so was the letter inside. It rustled softly as he unfolded it and began to read the neatly handwritten words.

Dear Erik:

I hope that this finds you well. I believe that it will. You're a strong man, stronger than you think, but I'm sorry for the trouble I've no doubt caused you.

You've probably realized by now that I managed to attend the dedication ceremony, after all. It wasn't very difficult to pretend to be my own Proxy. Enola and I have worked together closely for a very long time, after all.

It's strange. In all the time that she was coming to resemble me, no one seemed to notice that I was becoming like her, as well. By now, we're both on our way to Earth, beyond your reach or Hector's. What I need to do now, I can do from there.

Hector may have told you about Pym's belief in the Gaia Hypothesis. If he hasn't, I encourage you to research the subject. It was a great comfort during my years in Coventry.

I think we both of us serve a purpose. I don't know precisely what that purpose is, or what our roles are. I don't think we can know, but I rather like Dailey's fantasy of a plant sprouting to issue seeds. If that's an accurate metaphor, we've been part of that process, you no less than me.

I want you to know that I never lied to you, never asked you to do anything that was contrary to your own nature. That would have been a betrayal. I don't betray the people who work with me, even if they work unaware.

Remember now what I said to you, the night you called.
All love,
Wendy

Even at remote remove, the closing instruction had its power. The words drifted up from his subconscious, freed at last. They seemed to sound in his ears with perfect clarity, as if he were hearing them for the first time.

"You can be well," Wendy had told him. *"You're a strong man and you can heal. If not for yourself, then for the people who depend on you. If not for yourself, then for the memories of your sons."*

It had been the following day that he'd effectively quit drinking, he realized. It was only a short time later that he'd had his session with Adkins, for that matter.

He'd obeyed her. Perhaps because they'd known each other so long, he'd obeyed her better than he would have imagined possible, and then he'd forgotten the command.

Until now.

Tanaka had watched him read and was watching him still. Erik's hands felt numb and clumsy, but he forced himself to seem composed as he returned the letter to its envelope and tucked both into a pocket. "Thank you," he said.

His host still seemed worried. "Would you like some refreshment?" he asked. "If the dust here bothers you, we can adjourn to a conference room."

"No, I'm fine," Erik said. He stood and offered his hand again. "I just recalled that I have a dinner engagement. I hope we can meet again, at another time."

Tanaka looked perplexed rather than offended. "You only just arrived," he said in mild objection.

"I know," Erik said. "And I'm sorry. But I really must go."

EPILOGUE

TRINE had arranged to be outside when the exit burn came. Now she trudged along the familiar contours of the third habitat module, waving her wand from side to side, verifying systems integrity yet again. Her new responsibilities as security officer gave her considerable input into staff scheduling, but her certifications as environmental systems engineer still came in handy. They made extravehicular activity easier to justify. Officially, she was here primarily to perform a final checkout and to lockdown external ports and hatches.

That was only a reason of convenience, of course. She was where she was because that was where she wanted to be.

Other crew prowled the hulls with her, widely separated and joined via inter-suit links supported by the Ship Mesh. Trine audited their dialogue with her left ear, half-listening to the uneasy mix of technical talk and good-natured griping that was endemic in this type of work. Trine was very happy to be where she was, but the others would much rather have been inside the *Ad Astra*. They would have preferred the ship's modest creature comforts and to be able to view the launch ceremony via ubiquitous Mesh displays.

Trine thought that was silly. Why come so far and work so hard to sit on lounges and watch wallpaper? Why rely on artificial eyes to view what lay mere meters away? It made a joke of winning the lottery.

Even so, she had set her right earphone to primary Mesh audio and half-listened to the launch ceremonies and speeches as she worked. They were remarkably boring. Everyone who had done anything, however slight, to contribute to the mission seemed to have found a way to commandeer Mesh time. Only Erik Morrison was missing from the list. With a modesty that Trine had come to know fairly well, he had ceded Mesh time to someone else. According to the program guide, more than a hundred VIPs had delivered solemn comments and pronouncements. Unfortunately, those one hundred seemed to have only ten or so observations between them.

"*—the legacy of a long tradition of innovation and exploration in pursuit of economic growth,*" a relayed voice said as Trine checked another reading. "*The same ideals that led my father-in-law's skilled stewardship of the Ad Astra program in its earliest days. If Janos were still with us, I'm certain his heart would swell with pride to see his dream made real.*"

That was Enoch Matthews speaking, according to Trine's program guide. He was a withered prune of a man and, all things considered, Trine was pleased that she couldn't see him. Matthews was related by marriage to the Horvath family, and Janos Horvath had been Erik's advocate in the early days. From what Trine had been able to determine through desultory research, the elder Horvath had possessed no heart at all, at least not in the figurative sense.

Trine's gait as she moved along the curved hull was half-step and half-shuffle, only partly by conscious choice. The major ship modules had been locked the previous week and spin applied. The technical justification for spin at this point was to ensure stability for the burn, but it had other effects, as well. Inside, ghost-gravity ruled, and crew could sip drinks from bottles instead of pouches, if they chose. Outside, centripetal force could be felt with a strength just sufficient to make the human nervous system wary.

Trine knew she was safe, and so did her smartboots, but the spin's Coriolis effect made her inner ears think differently. They worried that she was about to be tossed into the void, and they were making their concerns known.

The suit Gummi interrupted her thoughts. *"Twenty minutes to exit burn,"* it announced in stereo, overriding both ambient feeds. *"All personnel are cautioned. Secure stations."*

Cautioned. Trine snorted dismissively. She had run the exit burn countless times in simulators, and she knew what to expect. In twenty minutes—nineteen and a fraction, really—the main engines would engage and flare to life to push the *Ad Astra* from orbit. Ship Site would at last become ship, and the long journey would have its official beginning.

But the push would be a nudge, really. The journey was long, and acceleration would be slow. People watching on the Moon and Earth might gape in wonder when thrust commenced, but surely no crewmember would. Onboard, the exit burn would feel like a gentle shove, less disruptive than the already completed process of aligning and integrating the major hull segments.

Even so, there were preparations to be made. Trine took a last environmental reading. She collapsed her wand and stowed it in its belt caddy. In her command voice, she said, "Open a secure link to base."

"*Password,*" the suit brainware prompted.

"There is no password," Trine said. Passwords were silly. If the suit couldn't tell it was her via internal sensors, she wasn't going to be able to convince it with nonsense words.

"*Accepted,*" the suit said.

The chatter in her ears fell silent, and then something else replaced it. "*Hello, Trine,*" a familiar voice said. It was hissy and clipped and overlaid by static from the ship's primed engines, but easily recognizable.

"Hello, Hector," Trine said, flashing a smile that she knew that he could not see. "We're nearly ready to go."

"*I know,*" Hector said. "*I think everyone knows. Everyone, everywhere.*" More static sounded as he paused. "*I wish you'd reconsider the password issue, Trine.*"

She stuck out her tongue and rolled her eyes, secure in the knowledge that the expression would go as unseen as her smile. Rather than respond directly, she said, "I have some data summaries for you."

Inside her helmet, just below the visor's bottommost edge, was a miniature display screen. A graphic status bar ran along it. The suit had initiated data transfer immediately upon connection. Trine watched as it passed personnel summaries, informal psych profiles, and other useful information to her superior. "These will be the last for a while," she told him as the process ran.

"*How long is the exit burn currently scheduled for?*" Hector asked patiently. As long as the primary engines were engaged and actively firing, communications would be difficult. The sheer amount of local background noise tended to overwhelm information exchange.

"Current projection is twenty-three days," Trine said. The display screen flashed. The last of the files, compressed and encrypted, had been spat into the void.

"*I'll count them,*" Hector said. Even distorted by transmission, his voice held a kind of warmth that was unusual for him. *"Good voyage, Trine. I've enjoyed this last year."*

"Don't talk to me like that," Trine said, chiding him. "We'll see each other again. You promised, remember!"

He had, too. For a period of approximately three years, transports between Villanueva and the *Ad Astra* would be possible, if increasingly difficult and expensive. Hector had assured her that he would make use of that window of opportunity.

"One minute to exit burn," her suit announced.

"I have to go, Hector," Trine said.

He tried to respond, but all that Trine could hear were stray syllables, random and intermittent. The long-range communications blackout had begun.

Trine's trek had taken her nearly three-quarters of the ship's length from its engines array. She turned to face aft and locked her boots in place, just to be on the safe side. Her visor darkened automatically to its maximum setting. The hull plates shuddered beneath her feet.

She was facing the engines from the ship's fore, but from their rear. Their energy and reaction mass spat away from her, not toward, and she watched through a brainware lens that was effectively opaque. Even so, the glare was enough to make her eyes sting and water. The suit's brainware issued admonitions, but Trine ignored them. She knew her own limits, and she knew that she wanted so see.

The engines' backwash glare seemed to burn brighter than the Sun.

THE trio of groundskeepers were spiderlike, each the approximate size of a human hand. They were top-of-the-line and no doubt absurdly expensive; their programmers had made the greatest possible use of their Gummis' brainware capacity. Self-directed and self-taught, the little things scuttled a meter or so ahead of Erik, inspecting and cleaning each black slate stepping-stone in advance of his approaching footfalls. Brushes whisked particles of sand aside, and tiny scoops removed more obstinate debris as he descended the stairway.

His feet hurt. His legs and back hurt, too, but his feet hurt the most, despite the constant ministrations of the smartboots he wore. The doctors had warned him that not even six months of continuous therapy and aggressive exercise would prepare him completely for the return to Earth, and they had been correct.

"Do you need help?" Sylva asked. She was at his side, matching him step for step, even as she watched him carefully. "I arranged for an assist-chair."

Erik shook his head. With his chin, he pointed in the general direction of the forearm crutches he wore. "No," he said. "These are humiliating enough."

He moved forward, ignoring his former wife's sigh of exasperation. His feet hurt, but that was a small price. The afternoon sun's rays were warm and gentle, and the spray-scented sea air seemed to fill a void within him, an empty space that he had not been aware of.

His crutches confused the little robots, he realized. One unit kept its primary optics trained in his direction. No doubt its mechanical partners were receiving a continuous feed of information, the better to model this strange, four-legged man's progress. If he made the trip enough times, they would be able to anticipate his moves. By then, he'd probably not need the aids any longer, of course.

Two robots were in the lead, followed by a third, and then by Erik and Sylva. They made an odd procession as they made their way down the cliff and to the beach.

The stairway became a path, and the path became a broad furnished patio looking out onto the sea. Erik lowered himself into a waiting lounge. Sylva did the same, but not before opening a small refreshment counter and inspecting its contents.

"Wine?" she asked, presenting what Erik knew was a perfectly respectable Shiraz.

He shook his head. "Water will be fine," he said. The habit of alcohol seemed to have fallen away from him.

She poured herself a small glass of the red and passed him a bottle of spring water. He popped it open and drank eagerly, without even waiting for it to chill.

The view was spectacular, even more remarkable than he remembered. The sky was a perfect blue, flecked with fleecy clouds, and the wrinkled sea was a darker, more textured azure that complemented it perfectly. The Sun had dipped low enough to become very slightly reddish, but the air was still warm and invigorating. Beyond the patio's perimeter, waves pounded the pale sand that had cost so much to install and refresh.

"It was here?" Erik asked, more to start the conversation than to gain new knowledge. He recognized the vista from years past and from repeated audits of more recent feeds.

"Here," Sylva said. She nodded, then sipped, still watching him. "The ceremony itself was here, I mean. We held the wake up at the house."

He watched the sea, instead. The waters seemed to stretch on forever, always different, always the same. The ashes of his sons were out there somewhere, he knew, inextricably mingled with the blood of the world.

"I wanted to see if it looked different," he said.

"The world goes on, Erik," Sylva said gently.

There was no denying the truth of her words. Things

changed, and things stayed the same. It was hard to believe that twenty years had passed since he had visited this beach, and more than a year had gone by since he had last seen Sylva. He felt as if he had stepped into yesterday.

"How long will you be here, Erik?" she asked. "When do you go back?"

"I'm not going back," Erik said.

Sylva's fingers opened. Her wineglass fell with a speed that was now alien to Erik's eye, long accustomed to the Moon's slower descents. Crystal shattered, and wine splashed in all directions. He had surprised her at least as much as she had surprised him with her arrival on the Moon, a year before.

"What?" she said.

He had to laugh at her reaction, but he made the chuckle soft and indulgent. "I wondered how you'd react," he said, still smiling.

"What do you *mean,* you're not going back?"

"I can stay on Earth now," he said. "I had more time to prepare, there are new procedures—"

Sylva's eyes narrowed into a glare. She was in no mood to play conversational games.

"Media Relations is still processing the formal announcement," Erik said, changing tack. "I've stepped down as site coordinator."

"You can't be serious," Sylva said. She was perched on the edge of her lounge now, leaning close. The groundskeepers were careful to avoid her slipper-clad feet as they went about their work.

"Of course I am," Erik said. "I wanted to step down earlier, but it didn't seem politic. I'd become too strongly identified with the effort."

"You're retiring!?" Sylva sounded baffled, as if her world had taken complete leave of its senses. He could have grown a second head and gotten scarcely less vehement a reaction.

"No," Erik said. "I've taken a consultancy. I'll be advising EnTek management in negotiations with the federal government, along with various ancillary responsibilities."

He paused and smiled again. "That's from the draft announcement," he said.

"What happened?" Sylva asked.

He shrugged. "My work there was done," he said. "The *Ad Astra* edged out of lunar orbit last week."

She shook her head. "What happened, *really*?" she asked. "This isn't the kind of move you'd make without a very good reason."

"It isn't, is it?" he said, and took a deep breath. "There was a situation, not something that many people know about, but I was one who did. I could have dealt with it better."

He told her about Wendy Scheer, about the other woman's gift and how she had used it. Sylva interrupted several times with questions that were perfectly reasonable, but nearly impossible to answer. That had always been the most confounding aspect of the Scheer situation. The woman's presence had an effect that was nearly impossible to quantify or even fully describe. Sylva seemed to accept what he said and understand the ramifications, though.

"Did *I* ever meet her?" Sylva asked. A worried expression settled on her refined features. "Would I know if I had?"

"Is that your wife?" Enola had asked Erik at the exhibit opening. *"I'm sorry I didn't get a chance to meet her."* But she hadn't been Enola, and he had to wonder if her words had carried a hidden meaning.

Had Wendy's comment been an expression of regret

about a missed opportunity? Or had it been a parting gift, a reassurance that part of his life, at least, was free from her influence?

He didn't know. He couldn't.

"No," he said. "You haven't met."

Sylva had a new glass of wine now. She looked noticeably relieved as she sipped it. Erik could understand. Wendy's gift had long been an accepted factor in his life, but even after many years, the knowledge of her influence made him uneasy.

"But too many others did. She was at the exhibit ceremony, and she managed to introduce herself to at least a hundred key management figures before returning to Earth," Erik said. "I need to be here, to help deal with the situation."

"And she's why you're relocating?" Sylva asked. She sounded slightly annoyed.

Erik smiled gently. "There are other reasons," he said. He looked at her but said nothing more.

She reached out her hand to him. He took it, and they sat quietly together, listening to the sound of the sea, watching the sun set.

In time, a full moon rose, huge, bright—and now for him, forever distant.

Don't miss the first book in the
Inconstant Moon trilogy

HUMAN RESOURCE

by
Pierce Askegren

All Erik Morrison wants is to earn enough as
EnTek's new Site Coordinator so that he can
return to Earth as soon as possible. But he's about
to uncover a shocking revelation on the moon's
colony that some want exposed—and that some
will do anything to keep secret.

0-441-01079-2

**Available wherever books are sold or at
penguin.com**

A322

Book Two in the
Inconstant Moon trilogy

FALL GIRL
by

Pierce Askegren

On Earth's moon, a starship is being built to explore an alien artifact. But one newswoman has become a pawn in a conspiracy that could end the project—as well as her own life.

0-441-01297-3

Available wherever books are sold or at penguin.com

New from Ace

Mystic and Rider
by Sharon Shinn
0-441-01303-1
Award-winning author Sharon Shinn weaves a new world wrought
with magic and mayhem, in which the fate of
a troubled land may rest in the hands of those few
who would remain loyal to their king—and each other.

Myth Directions
by Robert Asprin
0-441-01384-8
The beautiful Tanda wants the Trophy. The problem is, getting it
for her will take all Skeeve's unproven magical talents and a
charming demon not above a little interdimensional thievery.

Sharper Than a Serpent's Tooth
by Simon R. Green
0-441-01388-0
Private Eye John Taylor is the only thing standing between his
not-quite-human mother and the destruction of the
magical realm within London known as the Nightside.

Wizard
by John Varley
0-441-90067-4
Second in the *Gaean Trilogy*.

Available wherever books are sold or at penguin.com

THE ULTIMATE IN
SCIENCE FICTION AND FANTASY!

From magical tales of distant worlds to stories of
technological advances beyond the grasp of man, Penguin has
everything you need to stretch your imagination to its limits.
Sign up for a monthly in-box delivery of
one of three newsletters at

penguin.com

ACE
Get the latest information on favorites like
William Gibson, T.A. Barron, Brian Jacques,
Ursula Le Guin, Sharon Shinn, and Charlaine Harris,
as well as updates on the best new authors.

ROC
Escape with Harry Turtledove, Anne Bishop,
S.M. Stirling, Simon Green, Chris Bunch, and many
others—plus news on the latest and hottest in
science fiction and fantasy.

DAW
Mercedes Lackey, Kristen Britain, Tanya Huff,
Tad Williams, C.J. Cherryh, and many more—
DAW has something to satisfy the cravings of any
science fiction and fantasy lover.
Also visit dawbooks.com.

*Sign up, and have the best of science fiction
and fantasy at your fingertips!*